THE
BOOK
CLUB
& OTHER STORIES

Natalie Conyer

Clan Destine
P R E S S

First published by Clan Destine Press in 2024

PO Box 121,
Bittern Victoria 3918
Australia

National Library of Australia Cataloguing-In-Publication data:

THE BOOKCLUB AND OTHER STORIES

ISBNs: 9781922904867 (paperback)
         9781922904874 (eBook)

Cover design by Willsin Rowe

Design & Typesetting by Clan Destine Press

Clan Destine
P R E S S

www.clandestinepress.net

For Sisters in Crime Australia

CONTENTS

THE BOOK CLUB

WHEN YOU SAY BODY *IN* THE LIBRARY, WELL, ALLOW ME TO CORRECT you. Body *all over* the library would be more accurate. A leg, hairy, wedged between books. It was so unexpected it took time to decipher. Then on another shelf, what turned out to be a torso. Male, barrel chest. The head was further on, fiftyish, shaven, looking startled. No sign of a struggle; not much mess. It wasn't until I saw the arm, hand clutching a whip, that my blood ran cold. The dead man (I thought there was probably only one) was telling us something.

Librarians by day, dominatrixes by night. Or should that be dominatrices? In any case, we had excellent work-life balance. Sleep was a problem sometimes, getting enough of it, but we installed a camp bed and worked out a roster.

By *we*, I mean Lynette, Daisy, Wayne and myself: Eleanor, Chief Librarian. We'd worked together for years. We mastered technology, ran story sessions for the young, helped the elderly find large-print. Shelved and shelved and shelved. And one year, over Christmas lunch at the RSL, we found ourselves bemoaning our narrow lives, not for the first time. None of us was married. Lynette was divorced, Daisy not interested, Wayne not legally able and I – well, my romantic dreams were just dying embers.

It was Daisy's idea. Christmas hat on her curls, she proposed turning our basement archive – empty because we'd made everything virtual – into some sort of club. *An establishment*, she said proudly. *What this suburb needs is an establishment.*

We warmed to the idea. We'd be equal partners. We couldn't advertise, of course. We had to remain anonymous. *What we need is masks*, joked Wayne. Daisy's face lit up. She raised her hand and said, in her light voice, *think about Fifty Shades of Grey. What about, oh, I don't know, an S&M establishment?* We researched it. We had to overcome some preconceptions but we each invested and then we were up and running. We called our venture the Book Club.

Word got around faster than I could have imagined. Most of our clients had jobs so we didn't see them in the day, but occasionally one would come in with a wife or child, looking lost, not comfortable in a library. *Let me serve that one*, Wayne would say, meaningfully.

For a while all went well. We found ourselves fitter and somehow more confident. We recouped our investments and more, so that Christmas lunches became increasingly luxurious. We stopped complaining. And then Jacqueline arrived.

One morning the mayor, bluff and wide, came thrusting through the glass doors. Behind him trailed a small young woman, the palest I have ever seen. Jacqueline. Big black-rimmed glasses, tights, T-shirt. Hair scraped into a bun. The mayor explained that Jacqueline had dropped out of a third secretarial course; a most expensive one. He was, he said, *at the end of his tether* and he would like Jacqueline to join the library as an intern. *Suitable work for a woman*, he said. Jacqueline kept her eyes on her Doc Martens. I protested, to no avail. Jacqueline would start on Monday.

We held an emergency meeting on Sunday at the Book Club. It looked strange with the lights on, black walls and the dungeon and the ornamental axes. But we were oblivious. What to do? In the end we didn't have much choice. We would just have to hold our tongues. And, suggested Lynette, we would have to dissuade Jacqueline from becoming a librarian, at least with us. *I look to you, Eleanor*, she said, *to take the lead.*

Jacqueline arrived. It pains me to say this but we were not welcoming. To her fell all the jobs we hated, shelving in particular. Daisy, to whom shelving is like breathing, taught her. She picked it up very quickly. But Jacqueline was hard to make out. She arrived early, she left late. She was quiet to the point of self-effacement. At break-times she sat by herself, huddled over a computer or reading. Once I found her with Voltaire.

Another time with the *Wall Street Journal*. Jacqueline was clearly not stupid. Why was she here? What was going on in that pale skull of hers?

And then, walking to my car in the early hours, I was approached by two large and unattractive men. One tapped me on the shoulder, the other blocked my path. They told me a "Mr Bishop" knew about the Book Club, that it intruded on his "patch", and that unless I closed it down within a fortnight they would have to, and here I quote, 'Give the papers something to print'.

I needed a strategy. I had read of Mr Bishop, a so-called *colourful identity* who continually evaded the law. I certainly didn't want to antagonise someone like that. On the other hand, I was doing extremely well out of the Club (better than the others, I confess) and besides, I dislike being threatened.

I told my colleagues about the incident and wished I had not. It only exacerbated their anxiety. Our need for secrecy was already affecting us. We were jumpy, constantly looking over our shoulders. Wayne and Lynette especially seemed changed. Even before my meeting with the gangsters I found Wayne crying quietly a few times in Modern Australian Poetry and Lynette acquired a particularly nasty cold, snuffling her way across the floor, tissues falling out of the wrists of various hairy sweaters.

So, when a week later I saw the body parts before me, I felt that Mr Bishop (as well as ignoring his deadline) was giving me a particularly strong warning. Before I could decide what to do, the cleaners arrived. I hadn't thought to head them off. General hysteria followed and I was forced to call the police, something I would have preferred to delay.

Meanwhile the others arrived and gathered in the tearoom, Wayne in tears again, Lynette sniffing at a tissue. Even Daisy, not generally interested in the world around her, sat perched on a chair, wringing her little hands. Jacqueline alone appeared in control of her faculties. She seemed about to tell me something when the police arrived, two meaty constables who turned green and went outside to recover. They returned to secure the crime scene and phone their superiors.

I realised that unless we could explain the body in the library, the police would search the premises, discover the Book Club, and the jig would most definitely be up; but for once I had no strategy, no idea how to proceed. I joined the others. No need for words. They understood the situation and sat slumped, dejected. All except Jacqueline, who clasped her white hands and said, 'Oh, come *on*. I know who did this. It's perfectly clear—'

She was interrupted by the arrival of a tall man about my own age. 'Good morning,' he said. 'I am Detective Inspector St Regis. Who is in charge here?' I rose to greet him. He looked at me with clear blue eyes and my heart sank. In his white shirt and well-cut suit, Inspector St Regis looked more sophisticated and clever than any policeman I'd ever seen or even read about.

'Eleanor Lustre?' he asked. I nodded.

'You seem to have acquired the body of Barry Bishop,' he said, in a low and rather appealing voice. 'Bishop is – or was – a really nasty character, someone we've been after for a very long time. Society is better off without him. I'm just sorry he's turned up here, and in such a distressing way. Although,' he added, regarding me with interest, 'you do seem to have maintained your composure.'

Just then a constable stuck his head round the door to say Forensics had arrived. St Regis asked us to wait. He said he would be back soon to interview us and examine the crime scene in more detail. *About ten minutes,* he said, and left.

Everyone started to talk at once. I quieted them sternly, and turned back to Jacqueline. 'What do you mean, you know who did this?'

She pushed her glasses back on the bridge of her nose. 'It's self-evident. From the lack of blood, it's clear that Bishop wasn't actually murdered here. Nobody broke into the library, so he must have been laid out, as it were, by someone with a key. All of you have keys. So it must be one of you, or the cleaners. And judging by their reaction this morning, it wasn't the cleaners. The question, then, is which of you put him here, and why?'

'But Jacqueline...' I began.

'I prefer to be called Jaxx,' said Jacqueline. 'With a double "x". Now let me continue.'

'Jacqueline, I mean Jaxx, why would any of us want to do this? What possible motive could we have?'

'Ms Lustre, Eleanor, you really don't have time to keep interrupting me.' She was right. I conceded the floor.

'As for motive,' she continued, 'you each have a perfectly good motive for wanting Bishop out of the way. None of you wants the Club to stop, because it's making a lot of money. That applies specially to you, Eleanor. You've been in charge of the Book Club's finances. And your bank statements show that you profit far more than the others, who are supposed to be equal partners...'

'But – but how did you...? You know about the Club? And my bank statements...?

Jaxx rolled her eyes. 'Oh, *please*. Honestly! When I got here, you were all so weird, always whispering in corners. Running downstairs. And taking naps. So I hacked your email accounts and one thing led to another. Whatever. Yes, Eleanor, you must have been pretty worried when Bishop's men cornered you, not just about losing the Club but about being caught with your hand in the till. Two strong motives, right there.'

'But why would I cut the body up and put it in the library?'

'Exactly. That's the issue. I assume Bishop was murdered in the Club. It's got all the equipment. Whoever killed him moved him because they didn't want the Club discovered. But I know it wasn't you, Eleanor, because you would never have left him in the library. It had to be someone who not only wanted him gone but who thinks in a very particular way.'

Jacqueline looked at her watch. 'We need to hurry. Wayne, Bishop was blackmailing you. He knew that you and one of your customers, the one that comes in here with his family, are having an affair–'

'We're not *having an affair*,' wailed Wayne. 'We're *in love*!'

'Nevertheless, it means that you too had reason to want Bishop out of the way. 'Now you, Lynette, were more difficult. No email record. And then I noticed your constant sniffing and trips to the ladies and realised you're hooked on cocaine. I suppose Bishop was your supplier?'

Lynette nodded. 'I've been wanting to give up,' she said, 'but he sent me a message saying that if I stopped buying, he'd let my ex-husband know and I'd lose access to my son. I have so little time with him as it is.' She pulled a tissue from her sleeve and blew her nose.

'Daisy,' said Jaxx, 'on the surface, you seem to be the only one without a motive. But your email shows you've been searching for your biological daughter. 'Last week, Community Services emailed to say they'd located her and you made an appointment to see them two days ago. Now, you would do anything to stop a newfound daughter knowing about your night job, wouldn't you? Bishop was threatening to expose you. So you killed him. Then you had to get him out of the Club but he was too big for you to handle on your own. So you chopped him up and moved him bit by bit.'

'But why put the pieces in the library?'

'That,' said Jaxx, 'is how I realised who the killer was. Didn't you notice? The body parts are shelved according to Dewey. The torso at 611, Anatomy. The leg at 74.6, Running. The head at 364.66, Capital Punishment. It had to be someone for whom shelving was second nature.' She pointed at Daisy. 'My shelving teacher. You were on duty last night, weren't you?'

Daisy nodded. She no longer seemed anxious. Instead she looked relieved, almost happy.

'I still don't understand why there was a whip in his hand,' I said.

'The whip? He was probably holding it when he died.'

We all looked at Daisy. 'Is this true?' I asked.

'Yes it is,' she said. 'He barged in last night. I was alone. He threatened me in the vilest language. His face was blood-red. He hit me, hard. I fell back, right on top of my taser. Good thing you insisted on safety measures, Eleanor. When he picked up a whip and raised it to strike me again, I tasered him. He fell down, writhed about for a bit and lay still. He didn't have a pulse – I killed him with the taser, I think. So I changed out of my fishnets and heels and dragged him onto one of the rubber sheets. And went to work.'

'It's the end, then,' I said. 'If you confess, they'll have to know why you did it, and where. If you don't, they'll find the Club when they search.'

'I think I should confess, don't you?' said Daisy. 'But before I do, there's something I want to say.' She smoothed her skirt. 'You were right, Jaxx. I have been looking for my biological daughter, my beautiful girl. I was sixteen when she was born and they made me – they made me give her up. But I know who she is now.' Daisy looked at Jaxx. 'You were adopted, weren't you?'

Jaxx nodded. She had gone paler than I thought possible.

'My little girl.' Daisy said, holding out her arms. 'I'm proud of you!'

'Mother?' Jaxx hesitated a moment before hugging Daisy back, first hesitantly, then fiercely. 'Mother! I've been waiting for you my whole life!'

At that moment the door opened and St Regis entered. He surveyed the scene. 'So,' he said. 'Anything I should know?'

Daisy untangled Jaxx and started forward but I held up my hand. 'Inspector,' I said, 'could we speak in private?'

In my office I told him everything. I held nothing back, not even my financial sleight of hand. And to my horror, by the end, I had tears running down my cheeks. I haven't cried since I was a young girl. St Regis offered a snow-white handkerchief and an instant later I found myself sobbing in his arms. The man's chest was like a brick wall.

I recovered fairly quickly but found myself loath to move. I looked up at him. 'Inspector...' He placed a finger on my lips.

'Shh.' He said. 'Now, now. This is very interesting. We knew all about the Book Club, of course–'

'You did?' I extricated myself. 'And did nothing about it?'

'We felt that since none of you engaged in other criminal activity we could let it pass. Besides, we were hoping it would force Bishop's hand, flush him out.'

'So we were your...' I searched for the word. 'Your *sitting ducks*?' I was indignant. 'But that's positively dangerous!'

He had the grace to look ashamed. 'The word you want is *decoy*. I admit we should have kept more of a watch. We might have intervened last night. On the other hand, Bishop is dead. That's not a bad outcome. And he had a heart condition, you know. I'll have a word to the pathologist, who might well determine death by natural causes.'

'And the...the dismemberment?'

He shrugged. 'We'll think of something.'

I started to cry again, a little, this time from relief and happiness. 'Are you sure? Why are you doing this? Tell me!'

He took my hands in his. 'I admit, there is something I would like...'

'Anything, anything,' I replied, my heart racing. 'What is it?'

'I have for some time been wanting to visit the Book Club,' he said, 'to make an appointment with someone there, someone they talk about, the one they call *Miss Châtelaine*. You?'

I nodded, modestly. 'Any time at all,' I whispered. 'On the house.' And we went to tell the others.

Things have changed since then. The Club still operates, though with different staff. Wayne and his lover married as soon as the law allowed. Lynette and Daisy are still connected with the venture, as administrators. So am I, but in an advisory capacity only. I gave up my night job to serve just one client, and you can guess who. Perry St Regis (Lord St Regis, as it turns out) and I have an unconventional relationship, but it works.

Jaxx, however, has wrought the greatest change. Like her mother, she proved a natural librarian. She took control of the Club. She sorted out the finances. She visited neighbouring libraries and suggested franchises. Before we knew it, a chain of Book Clubs had opened in suburbs and towns across the state and spread across the country. Police protection helps.

We still don't advertise. However, when next you visit your local library – and you should – ask if you can join the Book Club. They'll understand.

SYDNEY LOVE STORY

Sᴠᴅɴᴇʏ's ᴍʏ ᴛᴏᴡɴ. I ʟᴏᴠᴇ ᴀʟʟ ᴏғ ɪᴛ – ᴛʜᴇ ᴘᴇᴏᴘʟᴇ, ᴛʜᴇ ᴄʟɪᴍᴀᴛᴇ, the trains that run late, the traffic that doesn't move. I love flying into Sydney and seeing the city spread out under me, its swimming pools glinting like jewels, its citizens engaged in every sort of shifty pursuit. I approve. It's good for business.

My business? I get things for people who want them – for a fee of course, because generally what they want is not, shall we say, commercially available. For example, last month I flew to London, first-class, acquired a pair of diamond earrings and flew back, also first-class, so a mining magnate's mistress could wear earrings owned by Queen Elizabeth (the first one). And when I say "acquired", I mean from a dusty museum in Cambridge with minimal security.

I learned the business straight out of uni, at an insurance company and on the back of some excellent references, all my own work. They made me a claims assessor and that gave me an insight into the enemy, aka the world of wealth and privilege. I liked what I saw so I went to work for the enemy. A couple of the enemy took a fancy to me but as I told them, the only mistress I want to be is of my own destiny.

Besides, I enjoy the challenge. Each job's different. That little Picasso, *Girls on a Beach*, that was me. It's in a concealed vault now, in Rose Bay. The temple sculpture? The one the Indian government kicked up such a fuss about? That was harder, until I remembered the gallery's cocktail party and hired a van...Shiva left in a bucket of ice. You get the idea.

I was at home, a converted sweatshop one floor up and overlooking Taylor Square, when my phone rang. Maurice Goldman, Goldman Developments, billionaire. We go back a long way. He said he was staying at the Intercontinental and when I got there his butler, Louis, opened the door. Louis clutched both my hands and whispered fiercely, 'He's in a real *state*, my love, calling you was absolutely *my idea*, you look *wonderful, wonderful!* What's that *perfume*?'

'Custom blend,' I said.

Maurie sat splay-legged in the centre of a couch. Under a stained dressing gown, a singlet fell away from his drooping chest. Behind him, bookending a view from the Bridge to the Heads, stood a matched pair of giant Islanders, arms folded. I air kissed Maurie's cheeks. He had bags under his eyes.

'Doll,' he said, 'thanks for coming over.' He pointed me to a seat and sent Louis off to pop a cork.

'What's up, Maurie?'

'Job for you. You gotta get me something.'

'That's what I do, Maurie.'

Louis came back, poured. Maurie waved him out, motioned the two monoliths to leave as well. I waited.

'I'm dying, doll.'

'You, Maurie, never.'

He shrugged, smiled ruefully. 'I wish. Bowel cancer. When I go to the toot...'

I didn't want details. 'Sorry to hear it, Maurie,' I said. 'What's the job?'

His smile grew. 'Never had a heart, you. One of the things I like about you. Reminds me of my wife. You know my wife?'

Who hadn't heard of Vivienne Goldman? She was queen of Sydney's underbelly, which made her Sydney royalty. As famous as Maurie, and some said tougher. Iron bars wilted in her presence; people who crossed her disappeared forever.

'The only woman I ever loved, and I did the dirty on her well and good.' Maurie waggled his head and sighed heavily. 'When we split, she got all the jewellery. Including our engagement ring. It's the one my father gave my mother. I didn't care at the time but now it's on my mind, the only thing I've got to remember them by. No kids, nobody to leave it to. I'd like to have it with me. I'd like to hold it in my hand when I go.'

I was surprised. Maurie Goldman wasn't renowned for sentiment. I said, 'Why don't you ask her for it?'

'I can't, cookie. She'd laugh in my face. We didn't – we didn't part on good terms. She's a hater, that one.'

I nodded, my mind already busy with logistics. Maurie was incorrigible. He put the hard word on everyone; some swore he'd chat up a chair. He tried it out on me once and sulked when I turned him down. Vivienne ignored his flings for years. Then he took up with a silicone-packed personal trainer and posed with her at the races, his head reaching her shoulder. Vivienne could stand everything but public shame so she turfed him out and the media went mad on the dogfight that followed.

'She keep the stuff at her place? It's not in a safe deposit box or anything?'

'I don't think so. She's still living at our house in Balmoral. I know where her jewellery drawer used to be. I'll draw you a plan.

'Alarms? Security?'

Maurie shrugged. 'That's what I pay you for.' I had a few more questions but the job looked like a piece of cake.

'I need this soon, doll, time's running out. Do it tomorrow morning?' His eyes got watery. I looked away. Maurie Goldman, crying? I checked to see the Opera House hadn't fallen in the Harbour.

The closer I got to Mosman, the bigger the SUVs, stick families waving from back windscreens. Totems of a foreign tribe. I like cars and the one I was driving was designed to blend in. From the outside it looks like an ordinary hatchback. On the inside, it's had, as they say, work done.

The Goldman mansion descended several levels down a slope overlooking Edwards Beach. The house wasn't visible from the road. All I could see was a high wall and a wrought-iron gate with a speaker in the pillar and a periscope camera. I parked and waited, pretending to text. It wasn't long before the gates slid open, a long Lexus surfaced, sharklike, and I got a glimpse of a blonde bob and sunglasses.

I followed the car to the beachfront, watched Vivienne Goldman park, check her hair in the rearview mirror and tap her way into the Bather's Pavilion. I deduced a long lunch.

Seize the moment, I thought. Back at the house I pressed the buzzer and waved a clipboard at the camera. Clipboards imply purpose, from selling electricity to collecting for charity. I waited. No response. She had to have servants: where were they? The house and its neighbours were mute, basking in the midday sun. Even the sun felt more affluent in this neck of the woods.

I have a gadget that looks like a remote. It disables electronic mechanisms. It doesn't work on sophisticated security systems but here, with just one click, the wrought-iron gate swung open. I looked up. The camera's red light was off. I slid through the gate and made my way into *Chez* Vivienne.

Inside it was a marriage of *Real Housewives* and Nick Scali, white carpet and modular leather and mirrors on everything. No industrially distressed copper here. This was strictly pre-minimalism Mosman. My eyes hurt. Still, I hadn't come to advise on design. I took the little lift (mirrors, small crystal chandelier) to the next level down and turned right to find what, according to Maurie's instructions, was the master bedroom.

It was dominated by a huge bed looking out at an impossibly blue sea. A massive Ken Done hung above the headboard. To the left, a door led to an ensuite the size of Marrickville. To the right, a panelled wall. When pushed, it opened into a walk-in closet lined in walnut, with racks of clothes and glass-fronted drawers. Between them, at the far end, stood a dressing table with a padded stool. It had a backstage mirror, one of those ones surrounded by naked bulbs. I switched them on. They gave a lovely rose glow. No unforgiving light here.

I sat down and put myself in Vivienne's place. If I were her, I'd want to admire my jewellery in a mirror like this. The drawer was locked but I felt under the lip of the dressing table. Bingo. A simple on-off switch and out slid trays lined in green baize. They cradled some extremely tasty items.

I had to scrabble for the ring, an oval garnet flanked by two small seed pearls. By far the cheapest thing in the collection, it was right at the back of the lowest tray. I put it on my finger and began to replace the rest of the jewellery.

Reader, I cannot tell a lie. I was tempted. There was a diamond necklace to die for. I held it against my neck. Beautiful. Or I could sell it and buy real estate in Potts Point. But I'm a professional so I laid it carefully back on its baize bed. I was giving it a farewell pat when I heard someone clearing their throat. In the mirror I saw three people crowded into the closet. Two were large, one little. Vivienne and a couple of tattooed bikers. What was it with this family and their matching goons?

'Hello,' said Vivienne, pleasantly. 'How's Maurie?' She was smartly turned out in black patent stilettos, slim black pants and a white cotton shirt. Lots of bling. One part of my mind asked the other part how it could possibly notice clothes at a time like this.

I turned. 'No quick moves, now,' said Vivienne. She snapped her fingers. 'Skull, gimme her bag.' Damn. My bag, Hermés, contains everything a working girl needs, including some get-out-of-trouble items. Vivienne rifled through them. 'A professional,' she said. 'I didn't think you were one of Maurie's girls. You look in their eyes and nobody's home. So, he sent you to pinch my jewels?'

'How did you know I was coming?' I asked.

'Louis gave me a heads-up. My eyes and ears. I like to know what the old fart's doing.'

'Then you know he's sick?' I asked.

She blinked. 'Whaddaya mean, sick?'

'He told me he's got bowel cancer. Actually, that's why I'm here. He didn't want to steal all your jewellery, he sent me to get only this. I held out my hand to show her the ring.

'That ring? Why? It's worthless.'

'He said it was your engagement ring, and by the way, he's still in love with you. He's very sorry about how he treated you,' I added.

Vivienne tapped a blood-red fingernail against her lip, then pointed it at me. 'Up,' she demanded. 'I wanna talk to you.' So the three of us – namely me flanked by the tattooed twins – followed her down a level to a cabana which opened onto a deck and a pool, the kind where water comes right up to the top. 'Ranga, Skull, outside,' Vivienne said. 'Sit.' I sat. 'How did Maurie come by you?'

I explained. She said, 'You really think he's got cancer?'

'Looks like it.'

'You wanna get out of here in one piece, right?' I thought of Ranga and Skull and nodded vigorously. 'OK. Hand me the ring. Here's what you do. And if you don't get it right, my boys will come for you and the next thing you know, they'll find pieces of you at the bottom of the Gap.' She smiled at me and I believed every word.

Back at the Intercontinental, Maurie was in the same place, wearing what looked like the same outfit as before. He was starting to be on the nose.

'Got the ring, doll?'

'Well no, Maurie.' I explained how I'd been sprung, avoiding mention of Louis. 'Vivienne says she'll give you the ring if you can prove two things: one, that you've actually got cancer and two, that you really love her.'

He slapped his chest with the palm of his hand. 'How can she think I'd make a joke about having cancer? What sort of bloke does she think I am? Tell her I can show her the results. Tell her to come, she can see for herself, I'm half the man I used to be.'

'She says she won't see you until she gets proof.'

'How can I prove I love her? I gave that Sahara the heave-ho right after Vivvie and I split, haven't taken up with anyone since. Isn't that enough?' As Maurie spoke, his eyes gleamed at the prospect of being back in the ancestral home, slowly expiring in the tender arms of his loving wife. Delusional, obviously, but none of my business. He asked again, 'How'll I show her I really love her?'

'You have to show her she'd be taken care of – afterwards. After you're gone.'

Maurie twigged. 'She wants to see my will? But of course, no sweat, it's all hers.'

Now came the critical part. 'Not just your will. She says she won't know if you've put everything in your will. She wants to see your books. All of them.'

'*All of them?*' The horror in his voice was real and I felt almost sorry for him. Maurie's empire spread far and wide and its convolutions would be beyond Byzantine. Opening his books would show how he'd set things up to avoid the law, the ATO, ASIC...any number of acronymic guardian angels. He probably had squads of accountants in several countries. I imagined Swiss banks, offshore dealings, security deposit boxes. That wasn't even counting government bribes, political sweeteners and other things I couldn't even envisage.

Maurie was sweating. His skin had taken on a nasty yellow cast. He yelled for Louis to get him a glass of water. Louis scuttled in, left, avoided my eye. Maurie sculled the water, some dribbling down his chin. You could hear his brain working. He'd want to keep some of this stuff to himself but if he did, he'd be gambling on Vivienne not knowing about it already. She was whip-smart and you don't live with a man for years and not learn his secrets. Was he prepared to take the risk? I held my breath. Wrong answer and the Mosman bikie chapter would slice and dice me.

Finally, Maurie fell back on the cushions. 'OK, OK. Tell her I'll organise it. It'll take time but – but I want to hand the stuff over to her myself. Tell her that. She doesn't come, she doesn't get.' He waved me out with a shaky hand, ten years older than when I came in.

A fortnight later I was back at the Intercontinental. Maurie was in his usual place but he'd scrubbed up since last we met. He wore a vaguely naval blazer which might have fitted him once but now hung loose, and a cravat that cradled his wattled neck. A laptop and some manila folders sat on the coffee table.

Vivienne arrived, Ranga and Skull in tow. They traded nods with the two Islanders and all four were sent off to sit on the balcony, where they shared cigarettes and got into heavy conversation, probably planning the next black and white ball, for all I knew.

Meanwhile, I could see Vivienne was startled by the change in Maurie. But he beamed up at her, opened his arms. She held out her palm in a stop sign. 'Proof first.'

Maurie patted the sofa next to him. She came over and he took her through the manila folders, showing her various medical papers and MRI reports. She nodded, satisfied. Then he pointed to a USB flash drive plugged into the laptop. He pecked at the keyboard. 'Here's the will,' he said, 'and the money stuff, that's here...and here...the password is *Vivviedoll*. He ejected the stick and held it out to her.

Vivienne smiled and my stomach clenched. I'd seen that smile before, when she promised to have me chucked off the Gap. I looked at her and I looked at Maurie and it came to me that Vivienne had no intention of holding Maurie's hand while he drifted into the afterlife. She was up to something and it wasn't good.

Was I going to do anything about it? My rule is not to get involved, not with anyone, certainly not with clients. But I saw Maurie looking at Vivienne with great big puppy eyes and took a breath, ready to tell him not to give her the flash drive. Then I looked at Vivienne and thought about dying painfully.

I hesitated too long. Maurie handed over the drive. Vivienne shoved it down her bra, between her breasts. The woman had no class. Maurie leaned over and clasped her hand. 'Doll,' he said, 'I really love you. And I'm sorry for everything I did to you. You know that, don't you?'

'Sure,' said Vivienne impatiently. 'Everything's fine, Maurie.' She tried to pull her hand away but he held on.

'Tell me what you're gonna do with it,' he said. 'But doll, don't take it to the cops. I don't wanna die in jail.'

'*Take it to the cops?* What, d'you think I'm mad in the head?'

'So the plan is to knock me off before the cancer does. You wanna take over the business?'

'Something like that.' She smiled again. I don't believe in the paranormal but I swear I saw a black aura eddying round her. Maurie had been married to this woman. He knew exactly what she was capable of, had always known what giving her the information would mean.

'You got the ring?'

'Yes, I've got the bloody ring.' She took it out of her purse and dropped it on the table. 'Piece of crap. But if it means so much to you.' Maurie picked it up, cradled it in his palm.

'You wanna know something, Vivvie? This ring means bugger all to me. I needed an excuse – I just wanted to see you. I told Louis to phone you, so you'd be waiting for angel-face here. I love you, Vivvie, truly. Take me home. I don't care what you do with me, I just want to be with you when you do it.'

Vivienne gave his hand three thoughtful pats. She reached for her handbag. 'Come on, then, Mozza,' she said. She stood up and watched him struggle out of the couch and the heavies shook hands and Louis started the process of checking Maurie out of the Intercontinental.

I went home too. I put on Jarrett's *Koln Concert*, sat in my armchair with a Brindabella Hills Riesling and watched the sky turn purple. At some point Henry slid through the cat door and butted his grey head against my legs. We ate and I read and we went to bed early. Sometimes Sydney tires me out.

PUBLIC SERVICE

I WAS ON AN EARLY MORNING WALK FROM THE CITY THROUGH THE
Domain and down to the Opera House. Summer was just getting started
and as I breathed the dark green air of the Botanical Gardens I felt lucky
to be alive on such a beautiful day in Emerald City.

My phone rang, spoiling the moment. Reg Weaver, Energy Minister,
on his private number. Could we meet for lunch? Machiavelli's at one?

Reg waved to me from a back table, smack under a photo of our current
PM. 'Ah, the glamorous Nicola,' he said. He admired my outfit and I
complimented him on his tie and we chatted. At last the ancient waiter
deposited the cheese plate, Reg smoothed his hair and got down to
business. 'I appreciate your being here, my dear,' he said. 'I need to get my
hands on something. And I know I can trust you.'

He knows this because I've got his hands on things before. For
example, I got his wife those ghastly Sèvres vases. As for this job, I was
intrigued. What was it he needed so badly? Would it be dangerous? Was it
in Australia or somewhere exciting?

Reg leaned over the cheese platter and beckoned me closer. 'I need you,'
he said, 'to get something for me from DURA.'

'DURA? Is that a country?'

'It's an acronym. Stands for the Department of Urban Recreational Areas.'

'Never heard of it.'

'It's not high profile. DURA looks after green spaces in cities, ovals, reserves, and so on.'

'Don't Parks and Wildlife do that?'

He looked shifty. 'There are, I admit, some boundary issues. Parks and Wildlife come under the Minister for Natural Resources. DURA's part of my portfolio.' He smoothed his hair again, cleared his throat. 'Nicola, this is extremely sensitive...'

'Yes, Reg?' He was starting to bore me.

'I'm going to make a bid for Premier.' He waited for my gasp, got none, kept going, disappointed. 'Only one or two people know. Barry – he's vulnerable. I'm in with a chance except...'

'Yes?'

'Except for Carla Peroni.'

Carla Peroni of the leopardskin shoes and tortured hair. Righteous and determined. Having Carla as your enemy would be like reasoning with a Rottweiler.

'Carla's my opposition. I've heard she's digging for dirt, anything she can use to stop my challenge.'

'And there's dirt on you in DURA?'

He nodded, smoothed again. 'It goes back to the G-triple-C.' He frowned at my blank look. 'The Global Climate Challenge Conference. In Los Angeles. I went and so did Gerry Lockhart, Managing Director of DURA, as my advisor. In any case, at the conference, I met a senior representative of EarthLine. EarthLine is–'

'I know who EarthLine is.' Who doesn't? EarthLine Inc, the huge mining conglomerate, hauling coal and gas and every other possible element from the ground in every country in the world. 'What were they doing at the conference? Aren't they the enemy?'

'Not necessarily.' Reg was defensive. 'They're planning to move to renewable resources. In time, when it becomes more profitable. In any case, one thing led to another and by the end of the conference we, that is, Gerry Lockhart and I, had signed an MOU with them. A memorandum of understanding,' he explained, 'it's an unenforceable contract, a statement of intent.'

He took a breath. 'The MOU was to allow EarthLine to test for resources in recreational areas, initially in places like Centennial Park and later in bigger ones, national parks.'

This time I did gasp. 'Are you crazy? You would've been lynched if you'd tried that. At the very least you'd have lost government.'

'No, you don't understand. EarthLine uses new technology. The tests are non-invasive.'

'And if they found anything?'

'If that happened, depending on what they found, the government could decide what to do. Remember, back then we were strapped for cash. A surplus didn't look remotely achievable. Imagine if they found something valuable under government land, land we already own. In any case, you're right. I came to the conclusion the whole thing could be politically damaging. Gerry and I agreed to say nothing and for safety, destroy all copies of the MOU. When I got back to Sydney I shredded mine. I contacted EarthLine and they did the same.'

'And the guy from DURA? Gerry?' I was getting the picture.

'He died in a car crash a week after we got back. Till now I haven't needed to find out whether he destroyed his copy or not but if he didn't, Carla Peroni could find it and use it to annihilate me. I can't take that chance.'

'Reg, it could be anywhere. You don't know if he took it home or to the office. If it is at the office, you don't know if anyone's read it or even where it is. And what about electronic copies?'

Reg raised a manicured hand. 'I've gone through all that. First, there are no electronic records. EarthLine insisted – they've been hacked before. Second, I got Gerry's wife to send me his papers and the MOU wasn't among them. And if anyone else had read it, I would have heard by now. Nicola, I've given a lot of thought to how we can – um – retrieve the MOU. You need time to find it and the answer is for you to get a job in DURA. They've been screaming for another policy officer. I'll authorise it.'

The wheels of bureaucracy grind slowly and it took six weeks but finally, after a terrifying interview, I became a Policy Officer (Level 4), Department of Urban Recreational Areas, DURA for short. I was now a public servant.

I dressed down as much as I could but even then I wasn't close. The motherly woman who met me sported a pair of black pants and a voluminous floral top. 'G'day,' she said, 'I'm Judy Limber, the admin assistant. You our new policy officer? It's time for our Monday meeting. Come, I'll introduce you to the others.'

The others were five glum individuals ranged around a laminated table. Four women, one man and a lonely plate of Arnott's assorted.

'Here's our new colleague, Nicola Brazil,' announced Judy. The others looked up, smiled wanly, murmured. Judy turned to me, 'We can't start till Shelley gets here.' I knew who she meant. Shelley Baptist, DURA's Managing Director, had been on my interview panel. I took a seat next to Judy, who handed me an A4 sheet titled *Agenda* and a full lever-arch binder. No sooner had I felt its heft than a flurry at the door heralded Shelley's arrival.

She took her place at the head of the table, a woman going places in a tight grey business suit. In her wake was a younger version carrying a stack of papers.

'Good morning, team,' said Shelley. I'm excited about our agenda today. And of course, first order of business, welcome to our newest addition.' She gave me a pointed look. 'Let's begin.'

The meeting went on forever. At first I found it interesting. There's a lot more to managing public space than you think, indigenous rights and endangered species and so on. Later, when we got to interdepartmental liaison, my attention wandered and by the time we reached OH&S I wanted to die. At various points the younger woman, Janet, handed out sheaves of paper and by the time the meeting was over we'd plundered a rainforest.

'Any other business? No? That's it for this Monday, team,' Shelley said. 'Nicola, could we schedule an intro face-to-face at, say, 3.25 this afternoon? It'll have to be quick. I have a meeting with the Minister at 4. My Executive Assistant, Janet, will confirm.' Janet the paper pusher nodded. And then they were gone.

The mood in the room lightened. 'Meeting with the Minister,' snorted the lone man. 'I'll bet.' Judy shot him a look but he waved her off. 'She's always meeting the Minister. If you want my two cents,' he said, 'she's screwing him. Not to mention screwing us as well.'

Judy said, 'Nathan!' in shocked tones. 'You don't know that!'

Nathan turned to me. 'You want advice, Nicola? Watch your back. Tell Shelley nothing. If there's something you need to know, come to us.' The four indistinguishable women, like a Greek chorus, nodded and murmured reassuringly.

We gathered our papers and tottered under their weight into the open-plan area. My desk was next to Judy's, who helped me organise my email and fill out multitudinous HR forms. She also took me on a tour of the kingdom.

Nothing to see, just seven desks – six for policy officers and one for Judy – a meeting room, a photocopy room, a tearoom and an office in which, behind glass, Shelley Baptist did her thing. Judy explained that the policy unit was located next to Shelley because we often prepared urgent documents.

Good news for me. Any papers belonging to the late Gerry Lockhart were likely to be in his old office – now Shelley's – or the filing cabinet. Which, I was disheartened to find, was a massive contraption called a compactus, a series of floor-to-ceiling files on wheels, stretching the length of the space.

This gave me the opportunity to question Judy about access. 'Is the compactus kept locked?' I asked. 'And what about the office? What if I plan to work late? Can I get in and out after hours?'

Judy slapped her forehead. 'Oh, bugger, I forgot. I have to organise your swipe card, so you can get in at all. As for after-hours access, you'll need to ask Shelley for approval. It can take up to four weeks.'

Four weeks! I was counting on being able to slip in one night soon, get the MOU and disappear forever. I looked around me, at a grey wasteland dotted with pot plants and overflowing in-trays. Five heads, flecked with grey, bent over five computers. I didn't think I'd last a week, never mind four. I was starting to turn grey myself. I opened my lever-arch binder.

And so I started life as a public servant. I soon found out why my compatriots disliked Shelley. When not micromanaging or piling work upon us, she took credit for our papers and treated us like scum. We started early, ended late. In fact, unless I planned to break in after midnight, I'd probably encounter several colleagues plugging away at esoteric documents destined for some bureaucratic ether from which they never returned. Or if they did, it was at the last minute and covered in red pen.

But that was nothing to how they – no, by this time it was *we* – hated Reg, our Minister. He brought forward deadlines, changed his mind, told us nothing, expected everything. The thought of walking out on him crossed my mind. But he was paying me well, so on with the quest I went.

Reg's offsider, Trent, a little man with spiky hair, specialised in asking for impossible briefings on Friday afternoons at 5pm. He was rude to Judy and mocked Nathan. One evening, as I was photocopying the 90 pages he claimed he needed immediately, he pressed his tiny frame against mine. I raised my heel, brought it down on his foot, and apologised profusely.

Meanwhile, no sign of the MOU. I worked my way through the compactus. Nothing doing. There was an archive section but unless the MOU was hidden inside another file, it wasn't there. I turned my attention to Shelley's office.

She kept it locked. What I needed was the key and a few hours. Judy had a master set but stored them in a locked drawer and wore the only key to that drawer on a lanyard round her neck. The cleaners had keys too but impersonating or bribing a cleaner wouldn't give me the time I needed. I couldn't see a way through the problem.

The solution, when it came, was simple.

I heard about the Christmas party when Judy asked for my contribution. 'Sorry, forgot to tell you,' she said. 'It's lunch at Darling Harbour and we get the rest of the day off. It'll be wonderful. Of course, I can't go. Shelley says someone has to stay on duty and since I'm most junior...I've *never* been to a DURA Christmas party, ever.' Behind her glasses, her eyes moistened.

She couldn't believe it when I offered. 'Are you sure? You'll miss all the fun! You don't mind?'

I spoke from the heart. 'No, I don't mind missing the DURA Christmas party. I'm newest so it's only right. There'll be other parties. You go.'

On the day, Judy left me a list of things to do. She was adding to it when I asked for the master keys. 'OH&S and all that,' I reminded her, brightly. She hesitated but seeing the lift doors about to close on her workmates, tore off the lanyard, handed it over and rushed away. I gave them a few minutes to clear the building, found the right key, cracked open Shelley's office and began my search.

Talk about an anticlimax. It took twenty minutes to find the MOU. I didn't think it would be in Shelley's desk so I began with the furthest cupboard of her built-in storage system. Sure enough, in a little while I came across a series of unlabelled boxes full of papers, no particular order. And at the bottom of the first one, a manila folder labelled GCCC and there it was. Interesting.

I closed the box and put it back in the cupboard. I had a long day in front of me. Should I decamp? No, I couldn't do that to Judy. I looked at Shelley's empty desk. I drifted over, sat in her chair, found myself contemplating her computer monitor.

For someone who worked in the natural resources area, you'd think Shelley would save electricity but the green light was glowing. I wondered if I could guess her password. I jiggled the keyboard and the monitor went out of sleep mode and into a screensaver, a selfie of Shelley trying to look Kardashian. I put myself in her shoes and keyed in *Sexyshelley*. Eureka! Boy, was I on a roll, or what?

Most of the files were to do with work. Boring. So I started on the emails. Nathan was right on the money about Shelley and Reg Weaver having an affair. Their correspondence veered between steamy and nauseating. I read as much as I could stand then logged off, locked Shelley's office, put my feet on my desk and cracked open the latest McKinty thriller.

I handed over the MOU the next day, pocketed a comfortingly fat packet in return. Christmas came, and New Year, and the whole country went on holiday. I invented a family crisis and said goodbye to the public service forever. I was touched when the policy unit put on afternoon tea, with cake and a card, to say goodbye.

Parliament returned in the middle of February and the leadership challenge happened straight after. Reg beat Carla Peroni and was elected Premier. Surrounded by wife and children, he made an acceptance speech in which he said how humbled he was at the opportunity to serve this great state. I switched off the TV.

Life bumped on for a couple of months. We had an election and Reg's party romped in with majorities in both houses. A few days later he revealed his new cabinet. He himself would handle the State's most important portfolio, Climate and Resources. To cut spending and reduce waste he would disband DURA. Its head office staff would be made redundant and its other functions combined with Parks and Wildlife into a super-department, to be headed by Ms Shelley Baptist. I felt sorry for the DURA policy gang. They worked so hard and for so little recognition, and now they were going to be dumped. What hurt most though was that Shelley had won. Who says virtue triumphs?

A day later I was trawling online news when I saw in the *Washington Post* a picture of Reg with, the caption said, Eric Franklin, Vice-President, EarthLine. They were wearing hard hats and shaking hands. The article said EarthLine was delighted to be forging ties with this go-ahead new Premier.

I sat on it for a few days. I'd been paid and, professionally speaking, the deed was done. Then I remembered how lovely the Botanic Gardens are on an early Summer morning. So I rang Reg on his private number, told him I had a proposition for him and invited him to lunch at Machiavelli's.

This time I arrived first and watched Reg, impeccable as usual, weave his way through the movers and shakers, stopping and being stopped and patting people on the shoulder. Finally he got to where I sat, under a photo of Julia Gillard.

He stretched out his arms. 'Nicola! Darling! Wonderful to see you!' We ordered and ate. I listened to accounts of his victories. Finally, this time over coffee, he asked. 'So, young lady, what's this proposition you have for me?

'Tell me something first,' I said. 'I saw the *Washington Post*. Are you and EarthLine going to test our parks for minable resources?'

His face went blank. 'I don't know what you mean,' he said, adding, 'Don't know what you mean.'

Why do politicians repeat themselves when they lie? 'Come on,' I said, 'it's me you're talking to. I got you the MOU, remember?' I smiled as conspiratorially as I could.

He smoothed his hair. 'Can't say anything yet,' he said. 'But if it did go ahead – and I'm not for one moment conceding it will –what's that got to do with your proposition?'

I reached over and patted his hand. 'My proposition comes in two parts. Here's part one. You and EarthLine don't even *think* of testing in public spaces.'

Reg looked at me, blinked, and let out a bark of laughter loud enough to be heard several tables away. 'Oh yes? Or what?'

'Or I'm going to release the original MOU, which I've photocopied.'

He was still amused. 'So what? We've just replaced it with another MOU.'

'Ah,' I replied, reaching for my handbag. 'Have you replaced this part of it as well? Or has your price gone up since then?' I pulled out a folded photocopy of the wine-stained page, torn from a spiral notebook, which I'd found pinned to the MOU. It read: *Weaver: US$10m year 1 to max US$40m year 4/Lockhart: US$1m year 1 to max US$4m year 4.* Underneath were three scrawled but legible signatures, *E. Franklin, G Lockhart, R Weaver.*

Reg sat for a minute, turned to stone. He put his fingers to his chest as if checking his heart.

'Take your time,' I said. 'I'm sure this would interest *Four Corners*. Now, do you want to hear the second part of my proposition?'

I think he was still in shock but I went on anyway. 'The second part is that everyone in DURA's head office gets work in the new department. Oh, and that Shelley Baptist doesn't get to run that department. Or,' I went on, hauling more papers from my bag, 'I'll release these, too.'

And I fanned out a selection of the Reg and Shelley emails, the most salacious ones.

Reg finally found his voice. 'Why?' he said, 'why are you doing this to me?'

'Just call it a public service,' I replied. And went home with a warm glow in my heart.

A month later, I ran into Judy Limber in Oxford Street. She waved and I waved back and she hugged me. 'How are you? Did your father pull through?'

I had to think for a moment, remembered the family crisis. 'Oh, yes, thanks for asking. And what about all of you? What's everyone doing now?'

'Oh,' she said, 'I've just come from union headquarters. We're still fighting.'

'Fighting what?'

'You know how we were going to be made redundant, and then they changed their minds?' I nodded. 'Well, all of us wanted redundancies. We were hanging out for them. We've been at DURA forever, we would've got fantastic payouts. Now we're stuck in our jobs till we retire. We're trying to get our union to make them change back.'

'At least you haven't got Shelley as your boss any more. That must be something?'

'I don't know. It looks like they'll appoint Trent Enright – you know, that little creep who used to be the Minister's advisor? He's Acting. Listen, my lunch hour's almost over. Got to be back in time else there's trouble. You look after yourself, now. Bye-ee.'

'Bye, Judy.'

I watched her walk down the street. At least, I thought, I don't have to go back to the office. I went home instead, changed and took myself off for a stroll in beautiful Centennial Park.

ALYS

HERMIA ROWNTREE ENTERED THE GREAT HALL OF LONGFIELDS House, pausing to admire its black-beamed ceiling, its panelled walls, its famous display of armour and weaponry. She'd hoped to arrive early enough to savour its glories in solitude, but several of the crew had already set up and were smoking and drinking coffee on a beautiful carved oak bench. Unaffected by their surroundings, they were discussing football.

Hermia sighed. Was she the only one who appreciated beauty? She wondered what the hall had looked like in its heyday. Women in jewels, maidservants, men preparing for the hunt...

'Hermie! The cry cut off her daydream. It was Sebastian from makeup. He knew how much she hated being called Hermie and she knew he did it out of spite.

'You're looking very...*butch* today,' he said snidely, eyeing Hermia's charcoal trouser suit. Hermia always wore suits like this, mannish and loose. People assumed they declared her sexual preference, but the truth was Hermia found the idea of sex with any gender unappealing. She was not susceptible to beauty unless she saw it portrayed in art. Hermia was in love, and always would be, with aesthetic perfection. She had dedicated her life to it.

She ignored Sebastian's comment, saying simply, 'Yes?'

'You're first here. Come in, and I'll do you before the hordes rock up.'

Whatever his other failings, Sebastian was good at his job. Hermia obeyed.

Hermia's specialisation was Medieval and Elizabethan painting, but her expertise covered most of European art. Which was why she was a presenter on *What Have We Here?*, a roadshow that toured historic locations around the country, inviting punters to learn exactly where Great-Aunt's sewing kit came from and, more importantly, what it was worth. Oh, the greedy look in their eyes when the subject came up! The disappointment, and very occasionally the stunned surprise, when they heard what they could get for flogging their heritage. Hermia despaired.

Sebastian finished primping. 'Right. That's you done,' he said, whipping away the protective cape. 'Off you go.'

Hermia made her way to the lawns where colourful umbrellas shaded tables bearing signs reading *Ceramics, Jewellery, War Memorabilia* and so on. She found the table labelled *Paintings* and settled into the chair behind it. As she did, a line of coaches came into view. Soon they would disgorge crowds of hopefuls, each clutching a chipped vase or sad memento. The ones with paintings would form a long, patient queue in front of her and she would glance at each offering and either mark it for inclusion in the show or dismiss it and its owner.

The coaches parked and a confused and untidy collection of punters dismounted. Why, thought Hermia, do the English not care for their teeth? Why do they dye their hair so badly, and why do they allow themselves to go to seed? She knew she should be more accommodating but it made her physically ill to see them. *Courage, Hermia,* she thought. *This will soon be over.*

Attendance swelled. Painting after painting was held in front of Hermia's critical eye. 'No,' she said, and, 'no, no, no, no, no.' This month's showing was dismal.

At eleven, she broke for a cup of teabag tea and a limp biscuit. Then she made her way to the woefully inadequate ladies lavatory. As she emerged into the corridor, she was waylaid by a small, pudgy man, slightly wall-eyed and – even by the standards of *What Have We Here?* – exceptionally badly dressed. His front teeth rested on his upper lip, giving him the look of a demented rabbit.

'You're that Rowntree woman! I know you from the telly!' he cried.

Hermia held herself tight, containing a shudder. The man's voice was as unpleasant as the rest of him.

'Miss Rowntree, I want you to look at something.'

'I can't do that, Mr... You need to take your place in line. It wouldn't be fair.'

'I'm Rigby Lightfoot, and you see, I've come all the way...'

Hermia wasn't listening. She nodded vaguely and walked away.

To her dismay, he scrambled along beside her, still talking, unstoppable, words spilling out like water from a bubbler. 'You see, I find it hard to stand for a long time, I have a bad hip, you know, it hurts and I don't want to...'

From a crumpled plastic carrier, he pulled a small velvet pouch with a drawstring top. Wait; was that dirt on the velvet? Hermia couldn't help herself, the shudder escaped. She put out a hand to stop him.

'I'm sorry,' she said, firmly. 'I don't do jewellery, only paintings.'

'This *is* a painting,' he answered, overtaking her, holding out the bag like a votive offering. He was walking backwards, blocking her path. 'Please? I wonder...'

It must be some sort of miniature. Despite herself, Hermia's artistic antennae quivered. Miniatures were her special thing. In any case, he wouldn't go away until she'd had a look. She stopped, held out her hand.

'Give it to me,' she said.

He handed it over. 'So kind, thank you, thank you.'

'*Please!* Mr...please be quiet. I can't think.'

'Mr Lightfoot. Sorry, sorry.' And, finally, he replaced his teeth on his lip and stopped talking.

Hermia, trying to handle the bag as little as possible, opened the drawstring and drew out an object.

She was right: it was a miniature. Oval, and no bigger than a watch face, it sat snugly in the palm of her hand inside its chased gold locket-frame.

The frame was what she noticed first. Then her brain, which seemed to have stalled, kicked in and registered what she was holding. It was a portrait of a young woman, depicted from the chest up and set against a dark blue background. She wore a black dress with an ornate V-shaped bodice and a high, white ruff. Her dark red hair tumbled onto her shoulders. Her skin was paper white except for the faintest blush of pink in her cheeks. Her grey eyes gazed softly out at the viewer.

She was the most beautiful woman Hermia had ever seen and Hermia fell in love with her immediately.

She knew she was looking at a masterpiece, of course. Almost certainly painted by Nicholas Hilliard, chief miniaturist of Elizabethan England and a genius of any age. Hermia thought she knew all Hilliard's work but she'd never seen this piece before. She brought it closer to her eyes. Fine gold writing surrounded the portrait. She took out her magnifying glass – her tool of trade – and positioned it above the portrait.

The letters of the words curled around the woman's head were as fine as strands of hair and read: *Ano Dm 1583. Aetatis Suae 22.* The Year of our Lord 1583. At the age of 22. Lettering like this was typical Hilliard. Less typical was the word which curved round the bottom of the piece. It was harder to decipher but Hermia was an expert. It read *Alys.*

Her eyes moved back to the woman in the picture, who smiled at her across the many centuries separating them. The woman returned her gaze and it was as if she had awoken from a deep sleep, as if her eyes contained life. She spoke to Hermia alone. Her voice was sweet. 'My name is Alys,' she said, silently, from her frame.

'I know that, I read it,' Hermia answered, equally silently.

A grating voice interrupted them. 'Well? Miss Rowntree?'

Hermia was dragged, blinking, back to the present. She had to remind herself where she was – in a corridor at Longfields House, on a tea break, with the man Rigby Lightfoot snuffling like a guinea pig next to her.

'What d'you think?'

Hermia regained her senses. Cautiously, she said, 'Ah...Mr Lightfoot, how did you come by this painting?'

'You won't believe me, but it's true. My wife found it buried in our garden! She was doing some planting–'

'Buried in your garden?'

'Yes. In Nottingham. It was in this, actually,' he rummaged in the plastic bag again and from it extracted a small, dirt-encrusted box.

Hermia was beyond caring about dirt. The box was solid and black with age. Silver, she guessed, with a lid that had been forced by some blunt instrument. *Stupid, stupid man!*

Rigby Lightfoot, feeling her excitement, shifted from foot to foot. 'Well? How much can I get for it?'

Two thoughts came to Hermia, unassailable certainties. The overriding one was that she was meant to have the painting. The second was that the man next to her, this unattractive, greedy man, did not deserve it. In fact, she could not let him touch it ever again.

She looked at her watch. 'Mr Lightfoot,' she said, trying to keep her voice even. 'The piece is quite interesting. Unfortunately, I must return to my table, but I would be willing to inspect it more closely later, possibly ask one or two colleagues about it. Would you entrust it to me for a few hours?'

'Nooo,' Lightfoot said, in that awful bray of a voice. 'Nothing personal, but I googled this sort of thing and it said if it's real it could be worth thousands of pounds. I can't let you take it away.' He reached out his hand. 'Give it back!'

Hermia looked again at Alys. It seemed as though Alys inclined her head. A great calm descended upon Hermia. She found herself asking, 'Is your wife here?'

Rigby Lightfoot looked distracted. He blinked, rapidly. 'She's...she died.'

Hermia nodded slowly. She looked around. There was nobody in the corridor, nobody in the lavatory. To their right was one of Longfield's treasures, a suit of armour, built for a long-ago knight. It held a spear. Hermia placed Alys in her right hand pocket, the silver box in her left, took up the spear, raised it in both hands and drove it through Rigby Lightfoot with a strength she did not know she possessed.

He sank to his knees, looking surprised. A bubble of blood came from his mouth and, almost immediately, he died. He would have fallen forward, but the spear got in the way, so he ended up propped in a strange, prayer-like position. Hermia, still calm, wiped the haft of the spear with her handkerchief, walked back down the corridor and reclaimed her seat at the *Paintings* table.

It wasn't long before someone discovered the body and then, of course, the roadshow had to be halted and the hundreds of punters prevented from leaving. The police had their work cut out.

Hermia presented herself to Detective Inspector Stanley Williams, a large man who seemed to be in charge of things. She explained that she'd been in the corridor, had spoken to the dead man – it must have been minutes before he was killed, how awful. He'd recognised her from the telly, she said, had asked her about a painting he had at home. She had, she confessed sadly, given him short shrift because she was due back at her post.

Eventually the day ended and she returned home, very late. Still imbued with the same calm that had descended upon her at Longfields, she shut and locked her front door, poured herself a glass of Dom Perignon – this was a celebration, after all – and sat down at her desk. She carefully lifted first the silver box, and then Alys, from her pockets. She raised her glass. 'To love, and to beauty,' she said, and smiled.

Alys smiled back.

That night Alys appeared to Hermia in a dream. She led Hermia into a moonlit formal garden, where they made their way between beds of lavender and sage. Everything was still. They came to a high-hedged maze and Alys led Hermia to a wooden bench at its centre. She sat down and Hermia sat next to her. They turned to kiss, but the moment their lips brushed the scene changed. The garden disappeared and Hermia found herself in a clearing in a village. It was daytime now and freezing cold and she was one of a pushing, jostling crowd of peasants, stinking and pustular and shouting, crowding into a square on which stood a scaffold and from which hung a noose. A hooded hangman stood waiting.

The crowd began shouting louder, pressing tighter. A robed priest appeared, followed by a wagon dragged by four men. In the wagon, tied with ropes, was...was...*Alys!*

Hermia woke with a cry and found herself wet with sweat, her heart thumping and her body entangled in her linen sheets.

In the morning, still weighed down by the dream, Hermia opened her newspaper to be met by headlines screaming *KILLINGS ROCK TV SHOW* and *DOUBLE DEATH AT ANTIQUES FAIR*. The BBC, too, led with the news. Not only had a Mr Rigby Lightfoot been murdered in broad daylight in the middle of a *What Have We Here?* session, but when police visited his home they found the body of his wife, Mrs Edwina Lightfoot, stabbed to death in the kitchen. It looked as if she had been killed by Mr Lightfoot himself.

Hermia's unease compounded. Her dream, the fact that she, Hermia Rowntree, was a murderer – something that hadn't occurred to her before and, strangely, didn't trouble her now – and that the awful man she'd... well, it looked as if he was a murderer too. What was going on?

She took Alys out of her pouch, marvelling again at her beauty. 'Who are you?' she asked. 'Where do you come from?'

Alys smiled her secret smile.

Alys was the key. Hermia would have to find out everything she could about her. Luckily, it wasn't the first time she'd been an art detective and besides, this was her field. She got to work.

She started with the silver box. Wearing gloves and using baking powder she polished and polished and slowly the box revealed itself. It had rounded corners and intricate chasing. On the top, inside an oval, were the elaborately engraved initials *CS*. More exciting, the front of the box was also engraved, with the words *Justi ut sidera fulgent. The righteous shine as the stars.* A family motto, perhaps? Hermia checked, and yes, it was indeed a motto, of the family Sandilands. *Sandilands.* She'd heard the name before. There was a Sandilands Hall, of course, one of England's most famous stately homes. She'd visited it several times with *What Have We Here?* Sandilands Hall was in Nottinghamshire, and hadn't that man said he came from Nottingham? Could the *S* in *CS* stand for Sandilands? There must be a connection.

She had to find out more about the Sandilands family. She'd start on that first thing tomorrow. Hermia wrapped Alys in her new blue velvet pouch and tucked her in her restored, shining box.

That night she dreamed the dream again. The garden, the kiss, the freezing day, the stinking mob, the scaffold. Alys. This time they lifted Alys from the wagon, led her up the steps and placed her head in the noose. Hermia awoke, shaking.

She researched the Sandilands family. They had originally come from Scotland and in the 15th century had been granted land in the Nottingham area where, over the next hundred years, they amassed power and riches. In 1580 they built a stately home, Sandilands Hall, in – *Yes!* – Nottinghamshire.

Hermia thought back to her visits there. The house held substantial historical records, so if anything was to be discovered, it would be there. A couple of phone calls and then she was driving down the freeway to the Midlands. Alys was with her, tucked into the pocket of her blouse, close to her heart.

Nearly four hours later, Hermia swung her Mini Cooper into the driveway of Sandilands Hall. Her heart leapt as the building's elaborately turreted façade came into view, mullioned windows glittering in the afternoon sun. Was it her imagination or did she feel an answering tingle in her inside pocket? No, it must have been her heart because by any reckoning the house was an architectural marvel, delicate and elegant despite its size. It had known greatness, this house, though it had passed out of Sandilands hands centuries ago. After periods of dereliction and renovation, it was now owned by the National Trust, who had embraced accessibility with enthusiasm. According to its website, it offered tours, convention spaces, a deer park and an outdoor cinema.

Hermia shuddered at the ugliness of the modern age. With a sigh, she found the door marked *Administration* and rang the bell.

She was greeted by a middle-aged woman, as tall as Hermia, full-figured and regal in a black skirt and top and flat black shoes. Her silver hair was gathered into a bun and a pair of silver-rimmed glasses hung from a silver chain around her neck. 'Ms Rowntree,' she said, 'of course.' She had a deep, rich voice. She held out a hand.

'Yes,' Hermia, said, meeting a firm grip. 'We spoke on the phone. Please, call me Hermia.'

'Lorina Boswell. Lorina. I curate the Sandilands collection.'

'You're from around here?' Hermia asked, recognising the accent.

'I am. My family have lived in the area for generations. Follow me.' Without waiting for a reply she led Hermia down a maze of corridors and eventually they arrived at the library, a two-storey room lined by books and with the famous spiral staircase leading to its upper level. In the centre of the room, papers and books on angled wooden reading tables showed this to be a working library.

Lorina sat down and motioned Hermia to sit in a chair beside her. She said, 'Now, what is it you're after?

Obviously, Hermia couldn't tell her about the miniature. It hadn't been mentioned by either the police or the news but she wasn't taking chances. She said, 'I'm doing some research on Nicholas Hilliard and,' (here she crossed her fingers and lied) 'I heard there's a record confirming he painted a portrait of an Alys Sandilands. I wondered...'

Lorina Boswell went very still. Again, Hermia felt an agitation in the region of her breast pocket. Involuntarily, she brought her hand up and touched the spot with her fingers. She saw Lorina's eyes follow the movement. Lorina said, 'Yes. I recall a record of an amount of £3, for a portrait of Alys, Lady Sandilands. It doesn't say who the artist was, and it was paid for by Sir Cecil Sandilands. That's the only official mention we have of the name Alys Sandilands.'

'Official? You mean there are unofficial ones?'

Lorina smiled, and for a second Hermia thought she'd seen the smile before, though she couldn't say where. 'Yes,' Lorina said. 'There's also the story, of course.'

'The story?'

'Don't you want to see the record of the portrait?' she asked, and Hermia had the sense she was teasing.

'I'm interested in the story, too,' she replied, hearing how lame she sounded.

Lorina rose and went to a shelf at the far end of the library. She brought down an old book and laid it on the angled wooden desktop in front of Hermia. From the drawer beneath she produced two pairs of white cotton gloves. She put on one pair and Hermia, familiar with the etiquette of historical research, put on the other.

Lorina placed her glasses on her nose and carefully opened the book, revealing age-yellowed pages covered in spindly, slanted writing.

'Not many people know about this book,' she said. 'It's the diary of Sir Thomas Crabbe, a local landowner who chronicled life in his neighbourhood.' She took a breath. 'According to Crabbe, what happened was this. At the time – we're talking around 1580 – Sir Cecil Sandilands was the oldest son of the family, its flower. He was tall, handsome and clever and the Queen favoured him. Then he fell in love with a beautiful girl, a poor commoner, and married her in secret.'

'Was this girl Alys?'

Lorina nodded. 'Yes. Alys.' She pushed her glasses up her nose. 'As you can imagine, Queen Elizabeth was extremely displeased. Extremely. She expected her favourites to wait on her, not marry without permission. She banished Sir Cecil from her court. Then–' she hesitated.

'Go on,' urged Hermia.

'For a few years, the couple lived quietly. They had a baby, a girl. Not long after, Cecil's father, William Sandilands died, and Cecil became head of the family. Then in 1584 the country endured a terrible winter. Crops failed and to make matters worse there was an outbreak of the plague. Sir Cecil, who was a cruel landlord, insisted his tenant farmers pay full rent.

The locals sought a scapegoat for their misfortune and for some reason they fastened on Alys. They claimed she was a witch. They said she'd put a spell on Cecil to make him fall in love with her.

'Cecil came to believe this story and threw Alys out, together with their young daughter, whom he claimed was a witch as well. It was winter and snowing and she begged him to let them stay, telling him she loved him and Sandilands Hall was her home.'

Lorina's voice cracked. She cleared her throat. 'Well. By the end of the following day Alys had been imprisoned, put on trial and sentenced to death. By the time her family heard the news it was too late. They arrived in time to see her hanged. Are you all right, Hermia?'

Hermia gasped. *Her dream!* This time she definitely felt a pulsing in her breast pocket. She put her hand up to cover it. 'Yes,' she finally said, her voice low, 'I'm fine. Go on.'

'This is how Crabbe describes it. He was there, apparently.' Lorina turned to a section of the book and read aloud. '*As the witch stood bound on the scaffold about to be swallowed into the burning pit she did as was the custom, to thank the hangman and give him a coin. Then she turned her face toward the assembly, spat upon them and spake these words. "I curse whoever looks upon me this day and forever more. I curse them with death and with dying until I am once again come home".*'

Death and dying. It wasn't possible, surely? The room spun around her. She was going to faint, or throw up. It took all her effort to collect herself.

'Please,' she begged, 'what else does Crabbe say?'

Lorina raised one shoulder in a gesture of helplessness. 'Actually, Crabbe's entries end there. He fell ill and died himself, a few days after the hanging. Everything after that is hearsay. There's no written record, but people round here still tell it. I heard it myself, many times, when I was young.

'What – what do they say?'

'They say Alys Sandilands' curse came true because after her death the situation got worse, not better. Feuds sprang up in the area and whole families murdered each other. It didn't stop with the peasants, either. Sir Cecil himself, a Catholic, was implicated in the Babington plot and executed and his body buried in an unmarked grave somewhere nearby. There were no other children, so he was the last of the Sandilands line. After that, apparently, things quietened down.

'And there you have it,' Lorina said, lifting her hands and letting them drop again, 'the story. Now, let me offer you some tea. You're very pale.'

Once more she led Hermia through corridors until they came to a well-equipped kitchen, where she busied herself with a teapot and leaves. 'This is a tisane,' she said, 'it'll do the trick.'

At least it was proper leaves, not the teabags Hermia was usually forced to endure. And she had to admit, it did make her feel calmer.

Lorina asked, 'Would you like something to eat?' She was watching Hermia closely.

'No,' Hermia said. She had the most peculiar feeling in her breast pocket. Alys was growing hotter and – she couldn't quite believe it – she thought she heard her humming. 'No,' she said, 'I have to go.'

She tried to stand, but found she could not. She felt as if all her bones had melted.

'You have to go?' Lorina asked, mocking. 'Even though you have not discovered all you came to discover?' You know now what happened to Alys, yet you do not know who she was. Nor do you know what happened to her daughter.'

'Who...who was Alys?' Hermia asked. She was finding it difficult to form words.

'Alys was born Alys Boswell,' Lorina said. 'Yes, Boswell, like me. Her family – *our* family – could not save her, but they could save her daughter. And that daughter had a daughter and she had a daughter in turn...and we have been here since then, waiting for Alys to be brought home.' She stood close to Hermia. 'I know you have her. Give her to me.'

'No,' mumbled Hermia, the air around her growing dark. 'No. I love her.'

Lorina said, more gently now, 'Hermia, if you love Alys, do not deny her homecoming.'

Tears rolled down Hermia's cheeks. With a supreme effort she took the pouch from her pocket and, trembling, offered it to Lorina, who received it in both hands and opened it.

And then Alys herself stood in front of them, alive, in her black dress and white ruff, her dark red hair falling on her shoulders.

'Who are you?' Hermia managed to ask.

'I am Alys,' she replied. 'Witch and mother of witches. And I am come home.'

AUSTRALIA DAY

THE GIRL'S GONE.

Early morning, we're fast asleep, quiet as. Only thing disturbs us this time of day is garbo noise. But now from next door comes screeching and me and Keith jump out of bed. We can see them at their window. The flyscreen's flapping, cut or torn.

The mother, still in her nightie, hair to her waist. Never seen her hair before. She's waving her arms round, yelling. The father's head goes up, he sees us and pushes her away. She disappears and when she comes back she's in her black sack.

The cops get there fast. It's Dave, Sergeant Cullen. Next door's mob rock up straight after, blokes dark and hairy, ladies in those headscarf things or long sacks. Young blokes too, fancy cars roaring in like they own the place.

I grew up here, not far from here, anyway. Aussie suburb, was, still is, mostly. When the plumbing business took off me and Keith moved into this street. We all know each other, Australia Day party every year, the whole street. Then Vena next door went to live with her daughter and the new ones moved in.

Not like we didn't try. Whatever you think, you got to live with them. They invited us round, Keith took a slab, turns out they don't drink. *Fuck sake,* Keith says out the corner of his mouth, *don't drink!* And the Australia

Day party, sitting there in chairs, putting the dampers on. So after that they kept to themselves. Lots of them, too, they put a table in the back yard and in summer all of them out there, yabbering away.

Dave, Sergeant Cullen, comes over. We were at school together, Dave and me, go back a long way. He tells us the girl's gone, asks if we heard anything during the night. No, I say, nothing. Wants to know how Kyle's doing, I tell him good, thanks, better. He heads back next door.

Talking of Kyle, he sleeps through the whole thing. When he finally hauls himself out of bed, next door's a circus. Still groggy, he staggers to the upstairs window. I watch him watching the action. 'She must have been a couple of years below you. That makes her, what, fifteen? Know her well?'

He doesn't answer. He knows her all right, I seen him and his mates hanging around the yard, the street.

'You got in late last night,' I say. 'This isn't a bloody hotel. Where were you?' He shoots me a look, turns back to the window. Look says *get off my case*. Teenage boys, eh?

I cuddle up to him, my arm round his waist. He smells of sweat and grog and smoke. 'You weren't with Matt and Lucas, were you?'

'None of your fucking business,' he says, shaking me off.

'Don't you speak to me like that,' I tell him. 'Go clean your room. Or I will.' But I'm talking to his back. I stay at the window. I wonder what the mother's doing now, what she's thinking. I wonder what it's like not to know.

Next day I stop Dave in the street and he says no news. He's pretty sure the girl's done a runner. Meanwhile next door's quieter. People arrive with dishes. The father sits at the outside table with a group of men, all in black jackets. The women bring them plates of food and coffee in those long pots. Late afternoon they go inside and the mother comes out to hang up washing. Don't know how she can do washing at a time like this. Goes to show they're not like us.

Don't want you to think I don't feel for her. I know about losing a child, my beautiful Rosie, she died when she was six. Makes my heart sore, every day. Kyle was little then, seven or eight. So don't think I don't pity the mother next door, I know what it's like.

Third day, nothing. Going to be a hot summer. Nobody outside, not so many comings and goings. Nearly teatime, I'm having a fag out the open window. Have to do it that way, Keith thinks I gave up. The mother wanders into the yard, makes her way to the jacaranda. I can see her black shape through the purple. She puts her arms round the trunk, leans forward against it, sinks to her knees in the fallen flowers, arms still round the tree. Stays like that.

I watch her a bit. Chuck the fag, call out, 'You right there, love?' Her body jerks, she looks about, sees it's me – at least I think she does – but how'd you know when there's no face? Shakes her head slowly, dusts herself off, goes back inside.

I'm thinking what to do when Kyle wanders in. Geez, he's big, my son. Like his father, the arsehole. Lucky Keith's easygoing, no complaints about taking on someone else's kid. Not at first, anyway. Later, when Kyle started wagging, fighting, he wasn't so sure. Give the kid a break, I told him. You were young once, done stuff you're not proud of.

When Matt and Lucas come into the picture, things go downhill. Hoons, with their tatts and ideas, and Kyle – he's easily led. Dave brings him home a couple of times, gets him out of trouble. Then he can't. The magistrate says he's appalled, no place for that sort of antisocial violence. Last chance, he says, you'll be 18 soon, if I see you again I'll throw the book.

Before I can ask, Kyle says, 'Going out. Can I have $50?'

'What about your own money?'

Shrug.

'You pay me back, you hear?'

'Thanks, Mum.' He reaches over, gives me a kiss. Twice as big as me but not too big to kiss his mum.

'Cleaned your room yet? You do that today, hear?'

'Stay out of my room,' he yells, already gone.

I'm on a hiding to nothing. Bet the room stinks like a zoo.

Fourth day a kid finds a body in the reserve and this time the cops really get into it, not just Dave but other cops not in uniform. And the forensics, giving the broken flyscreen the once over, too bloody late if you ask me.

By eleven it's on for young and old. Street's packed with vans, reporters, lots of cameras. All over our yard, asking what do I think about the Khalils, did I know her, the girl?

'Lovely family,' I say. 'It's a shock, right under our noses. Don't expect something like this to happen here, not in our quiet street.' Later, on TV,

I see myself say it. Jesus wept, that wrinkled old bag, that's me? Need to colour my hair, lose a few pounds.

When I go inside I see Kyle watching the reporters through the venetians. He's been hanging round the house lately, since she went missing. Worries me. 'What you doing home this hour?'

He doesn't answer.

'Did you know her? When did you last see her?'

'I told you already, I don't know the bitch. I never seen her!' He grabs his hoodie, heads for the back door. At least I got him out the house.

I decide to clean his room. I wait up till he gets home.

Fifth day. I'm ready for what I know is coming, and it does. Front door bell, and it's a plainclothes cop, crew-cut and a Magnum mo, could be a PE teacher. Dave's standing behind him.

'Morning. I'm Detective Inspector Stennart,' crew-cut says. 'Mrs Vella? Know why we're here?'

'Next door,' I answer. Obvious.

I let them in. Stennart sits down. After a sec, so does Dave.

'You know your neighbours well?'

I shake my head. 'Next door? Not well.'

His eyes swivel to mine. 'You don't get along?'

'Get along fine,' I say. 'Not a lot in common. Language and that. Don't live in each other's pockets.'

He nods. 'So you didn't know her, Samara?'

'That her name? Not really.'

'What about Mr Khalil? Her father?'

'No – well, to say hello, nothing more, why?' Suddenly I think to myself *holy shit, they're after the father for it.*

But then Stennart straightens his back. 'Mrs Vella,' he says, 'I've got to ask. Given your son's record. Where was Kyle the night Samara went missing?'

'Here,' I said, 'sleeping.'

'Can you vouch for that?'

Better not to be too cocky. 'Well, anyone can get out anywhere, of course. Kyle came home after we went to bed but he was here when I woke up in the night and here in the morning.' I look Stennart in the eye.

'Where's Kyle now?'

'In his room, sleeping. Next to the laundry. Be my guest.'

Dave goes. Kyle comes back blinking, barefoot, in shorts and a singlet. He's got a real man's body now. Stennart sits him down, starts off with the same question. 'Where were you on the night Samara Khalil went missing?'

Kyle glances in my direction. Stennart snaps, 'Your mother doesn't know the answer, Kyle.'

Kyle clears his throat. 'Here. I was here, sleeping.'

'You know Samara?'

Kyle shakes his head no.

'Not even at school?'

'No.'

'Pretty girl,' says Stennart. 'Hard to miss.'

'I got nothing to do with fucking terrorists!' says Kyle, suddenly aggro.

Stennart raises his eyebrows, flips pages in a notebook. 'The family says they've been the target of a hate campaign. Know anything about that?'

Headshake. Kyle looks at the ground. Pats his hip, feels for smokes that aren't there.

'Dog droppings in the letterbox, notes, graffiti on the door, phone calls all hours.'

I butt in. 'That's terrible. Who'd do a thing like that?'

'Nevertheless,' he continues, staring at Kyle.

I need to stop him. I stand up. 'We don't have to take this shit. What sort of people do you think we are? Think you can come into my house and say what you like? Who told you it's Kyle, anyway? Where's your proof?'

'The Khalils didn't keep the letters or take pictures, so...' Stennart shrugs, turns back to Kyle. 'Give us the clothes you wore that night.'

Kyle says he can't remember so they pack up most of his stuff. They take him to the station and keep on at him but he sticks to his story, he came home at ten and went to sleep. Can't prove it but they can't disprove it either.

Dave and the constable go through Kyle's room. I thought they'd get forensics in but they don't. They don't find anything. Me neither; Kyle had cleaned up already. So I don't know. Still, I went through it again, washed his clothes, scrubbed his trainers, used Windex, bleach. Can't be too careful.

They give the father, Khalil, a hard time but nothing comes of that. He loses his job though, gets the sack, next thing the house is up for sale. Dave tells me they're going to live with cousins in Lakemba. Good, I say. They should stick to their own kind.

I'm pulling the wheelie bin out one evening – it's two weeks later now – and the mother's doing the same thing.

'Hear you're leaving?' I say. I can see her eyes through the slit but nothing else. They don't look dead or sad or anything. Without the face you can't tell.

'Yes,' she says in her strong accent, 'you got your wish. You got rid of us.'

'I'm a mother,' I reply. 'I lost my daughter too. I've only got the one boy now, just like you. They're all we got left and we got to look after them.'

Her eyes stare at me for a minute and then she goes into the house. It's the middle of summer and the street is still hot from the sun. Soon it'll be January and then Australia Day and the party, just us.

NEW START

From: Ricky Bonanza (fscy@moa.gov.ny)

Dear Friend

Good morning. I appologise handsomely for disturbing you but can you spare a few minutes, I think you can help me. I saw your name and lovely visage on New Start Lonely Heart website and your aspect very kindlady. And you looking for love and so me too!

Now I tell you the wonderful news. I am Nigerian PRINCE. Yes, true. My name is Ricky Bonanza and I am grandson to late tribal chief His Highness Sir Winston Timi Bonanza. Who was murdered in bloody battle in Nigera, but anyway that is not of interest.

I am 30 and I know you are 27 and looking for wonderful man in Australia or anywhere in world. I am wonderful man and I can make you very happy promise. Send me photo and tell me if you want to talk to me. Here is photo of me, but not in Nigerian clothes in other clothes.

I wait for your answer. Tell me what pleases you.

Ricky Bonanza (Prince)

From: Alice Scott (alice123@bigfish.com.au)

Dear Prince Ricky Bonanza

I never thought I'd be answering an email like yours. I know emails from Nigerian "princes" could be scams and I would normally just delete them but my horoscope said, "you will meet someone rich and powerful. This person will come into your life soon and you must not turn them away because you might be turning away your destiny".

Well, you can imagine my surprise when I saw the photo you sent me, of you standing next to that red Porsche. It was fate, I'm sure. People will say I'm looking for trouble, you're after my money, but I say what have I got to lose? And who would I tell even if I wanted to? I'm tired of being boring and conventional. That's why I chose the website, because it's called New Start. In any case, anyone who owns a Porsche can't be after my money. (I hope you don't think I'm being cheeky!)

Yes, I'm 27. I live at home on the family estate, which is very big and historically very important. I look after it and it's more work than you think. I don't have any brothers or sisters and my parents passed away a few years ago, leaving me in charge of a considerable inheritance.

You ask what pleases me. I'm not sure. I've had what they call a sheltered life and now that I'm alone I can afford to do anything I want but I'm not sure what that is yet. I know I like ordinary things such as walking in the rain, beautiful gardens (I spend a lot of time in our gardens), reading and embroidery. I like cooking, especially baking, and it would be nice to have someone to bake for. I've been lonely since my parents died and that's why I put the ad in New Start. I want to go out and embrace life.

Now your turn. Tell me what pleases *you*, and what Nigeria is like. What language do you speak? Have you ever been to Australia? You would like it I am sure, though it might be a bit bland after Africa.

Warm regards, and here is a photo of me standing in front of the East Wing of my house. It's far too big for one person, as you can see.

Alice

From: Henry Hill (dbs@gov.org.au)
Ms Pike,
I trust the encryptions applied to our email exchanges are now working satisfactorily. I apologise for earlier difficulties stemming from our end but encryption is mandated by national security restrictions.

As previously telephonically discussed with yourself, my department, the Department of Border Security, is currently monitoring emails from Nigeria. Again, national security prevents me providing further details.

As I indicated, during my scrutiny of these emails I came across the attached exchange, which seems to be more appropriate to your department than mine. I would appreciate your confirmation of this and your advice on the matter.

Regards
Henry Hill
Communications Analyst, Department of Border Security

From: Ricky Bonanza (fscy@moa.gov.ny)
Dear Alice
Oh how beautiful you are. Your hair is gold thread like silk. Your eyes, they are be sapphires I am sure.

I have seen the photo you sent me of your house. It is like a palace the house of big movie star or our president.

I am so happty you write back to me. I will tell you about me. I speak many langages. In Nigera I speak English like you but I did not spend my child hood in Nigera. I learned in boarding school in UK, with uniform. Then university in France in Paris. I study economy. I can speak and write French very well.

I know I am handsome spunky man and there are many woman who want me but like you I do not want to be loved for my money alone. Although I am totally rich and poerful in this country. I want a woman with gold hair who will lov me for myself only. In fact I want a new start same as you. One of my plans to you is that I wwant to move my money to Australia and live in Australia not Nigeria because after UK and French Nigera is very hard country. So I have $30 million US dollars to move to Austrlia and I hope you will help me do this.

I am easy to please by the way. Let me know if you interested in the money.

Your very good friend, etc

Ricky Bonanza (Prince)

From: Alice Scott (alice123@bigfish.com.au)
Dear Ricky
(I giggled when I started this because I'm writing to a prince. Should I call you "Prince Ricky"? Or just "Ricky"?)

I think just Ricky after the pictures you sent me. Thank you – I'm trying to be open-minded. I must say you have a beautiful body! ;)))

Yes, I would like to help you get your money to Australia. And you as well! Obviously. Just tell me what I must do.

Here are some photos of me. I took them in our upstairs ballroom. I wasn't as brave as you, though. This is just my top half. I've never had a photo of me like that before! Perhaps when you are here you will see the bottom half as well???

I can't believe I just wrote that and I hope you don't think I'm forward, or loose! I did raid my father's cellar before I took the picture – I'm on my third glass of champagne. My parents wouldn't let me touch alcohol so they must be spinning in their graves right now.

My life is certainly changing in ways I never imagined. I better send this before re-reading it.

Tell me what to do about the money.

Your – friend?

Alice

From: Ricky Bonanza (fscy@moa.gov.ny)

OH my beautiful white queen.

You are stuning. So beautifully. I have printed out the photographs and put them over my bed. Until I can have the real thing.

Regarding the money, my problem is that the US$35 million (it has improved since last email) is tied up here and I cannot have it without bribing Nigerian bank and custom official. I will need $50,000 (US) to release the funds. If you send me the money then I will be able to come to you, possibly in my private jet.

Your beloved

Prince Ricky Bonanza

From: Valencia Pike (vpike@scamwatch.gov.org.au)

Dear Mr Hill

Thank you for your email and I apologise for the delay in responding. This is my first week at Scamwatch and I'm still learning the ropes.

I took the emails to my line manager (I hope that doesn't contravene security arrangements). He says although the Nigerian "prince" is almost certainly a confidence trickster, Scamwatch cannot legally act until either money changes hands or a complaint is received. He has asked me to monitor the matter in the meantime, so I would appreciate you keeping me "in the loop".

However, the emails you sent look alarming and I think we should do something about them. We should at least warn Alice Scott, who seems to be about to give a lot of money to this Nigerian gentleman (although I don't think he's much of a gentleman).

I have now visited the website of New Start, the dating service, and noticed that it contains equal numbers of men and women seeking partners. In my experience women far outnumber men on these sites and this leads me to believe New Start may not be all it seems. How do I know? I may as well admit it – I am single and newly arrived in Canberra and so have myself consulted online introduction services.

In any case, I wondered if you planned to continue your interest in this matter, and if so, would you be willing to support me in following it up?

Regards

Valencia Pike (Ms)

Junior Fraud Investigator, Scamwatch, Australian Tax Office

From: Alice Scott (alice123@bigfish.com.au)

Darling Ricky

Please Ricky don't get cross at what I'm about to say. All my life people have told me I'm like a child and too romantic and I need to show them I can be sensible too. So I'm going to be a bit cautious. Although I know we love each other, I can't send you money before I meet you, not to mention what Mr Robertson would say. He's the executor of my father's estate, the one who gives me money.

I don't want you to think I'm pushing you away. The truth is I believe in you, and long for you, as much as ever. So I've had an idea. Why don't you come here and visit me? Come in your jet. Mr Robertson will be able to confirm you're a real prince and then he'll give me $50,000 in cash and you can take it back to Nigeria to release the rest of your money. Perhaps we will not be able to part and you will take me back to Nigeria as well.

What do you think of that plan?

Your beloved Alice (I do like the way that sounds)

From: Ricky Bonanza (fscy@moa.gov.ny)

My soon princess

I will yearn to come to Australia to find you and make sure you can trust me.

Thereis a problem I have. I cannot get my jet because the president of Nigeria uses it because of thewar. So I will to come on a plane with other peoples. But as you know my money is tied up here. Is OKyou come to me? You will be meet by me and will be look after in my palace?

I will drink wine of the moon to your hair.

Your darling beloved

Ricky Bonanza

From: Alice Scott (alice123@bigfish.com.au)

My darling beloved

It is not possible for me to travel because I have to look after the house. Also, I'm a bit ashamed to say I don't have a passport. I've never even been out of the country.

However, would you mind if, as a token of trust and love I bought you a ticket so you could come and see me?

I could email you an open ticket. You would have to book the flights within three weeks and then when you are here you could stay with me. There are over ten bedrooms in my house so you have many to choose from (though if everything works out, we will use only one room)!!!

Let me know if that suits you and I will buy your ticket. And if you come here then I can get $50,000 and give it to you and maybe (cross fingers) we can go back and start a new life in your country Nigeria.

Your darling beloved

Alice

From: Henry Hill (dbs@gov.org.au)

Dear Ms Pike

It was highly irregular of you to share encrypted material with another individual but given the circumstances I will make an exception.

I agree that attempts should be made to prevent Ms Scott falling victim to this scam and am willing to help you in your endeavour. Like you, I am single and have some spare time so I utilised it to find out more about her. She does not appear on social media such as Google or Facebook but that is understandable given her sheltered upbringing.

You should however be aware that as this case has not formally been allocated to me, I am prevented from seeking information from the police or other government departments.

Are you able to discover more from your end? It would be satisfying to see justice done.

I will continue to forward the Nigerian emails, and Ms Scott's responses, to you.

Regards

Henry Hill

Communications Analyst, Department of Border Security

From Ricky Bonanza (fscy@moa.gov.ny)

Dearest whitest lady

The ticket came in the email and the visa is now complete. But I must pay the visa officer $10,000 (US) because that is the bribe custom in Nigeria. I sold my Porsche to pay it (the bank still imprisoning my money) so I ask you very curiously to give me this extra as well.

I have booked the air flight on Wednesday 5 via Johannesburg and which will land in Sydney on Thursday 6 at 3pm and change to Canberra for 8pm arrive. Will you be to meet me?

My big love is excited. My body is here but my heart is with you already. Pls do not forget to go to bank to arrange $50,000 plus now the customs bribery $10,000 both US which I will pay you back as my millions release.

Prince Ricky Bonanza

By the way I look out for you at airport. Please wear red for me to recognise you.

From: Valencia Pike (vpike@scamwatch.gov.org.au)

Dear Henry Hill

I've hit a dead end. It appears I will only receive full security clearance once my probation period expires and so I too have been barred from contacting external sources for further information. Extremely frustrating, especially as my job title is "Investigator"!

I did however re-examine the emails. Photography is a hobby of mine and though I'm not supposed to be working on this case, last night I stayed back until everyone left and enlarged the photographs Ricky and Alice sent each other. It looks like they've both been photoshopped. In the one from Nigeria (not the naked one, the first one), the Porsche has been inserted next to the "prince" and in the photo Alice Scott sent later – the topless one – she appears against a false background. In fact, I think it's the mirrored ballroom at Versailles. I've been there and recognise it.

Of course, people online often lie about themselves so these pictures don't really tell us anything. The question is, what should we do next? I'd like to suggest that, given we are both in Canberra and the plane will arrive after-hours, could we not ourselves go to the airport to see if we can head this off?

Warm regards

Valencia Pike

From: Alice Scott (alice123@bigfish.com.au)

My darling beloved

This is just to say I will be at Canberra airport to meet you on Thursday. I will wear a red jacket, and you can recognise me from my photos as well.

I am longing to see you. My mobile phone number – I think you call it a cellphone in Nigeria? is 0458 267 134. When you get to the airport, buy a local SIM card so if anything goes wrong we can phone each other.

Very excitedly yours, my dearest one. This will be the longest week of my life.

Your own Alice

From: Henry Hill (bss@gov.org.au)

Dear Valencia

I too have news for you. I could not find any information about Alice Scott. Then, when I tried to access the New Start website I found it has been taken down and – most unusual, this – all traces of it have been removed from the web. Only the most sophisticated technical equipment can achieve such complete erasure and I am beginning to suspect that New Start may be a front for something big, like a terrorist organisation. I have heard that groups like Boko Haram and Isis seek money from other countries in various ways, and this may be an attempt to do some such thing.

I raised the matter with my manager who ordered me to drop the investigation as (a) I have no concrete evidence to back up my argument and (b) it is outside my job description. You are correct in your observation that working for the government is at times extremely frustrating.

However I am now convinced something untoward is happening and that it is incumbent upon us to prevent it. I suggest we meet at the airport, in front of the coffee stand in the Arrivals area, at 7pm. You will recognise me by my height – I am very tall, thin, and wear glasses. I will come by bicycle.

By the way, I too am a keen photographer. I am what you call a "twitcher". I enjoy photographing birds and as you are new to Canberra I would, if you wish, be willing to show you some good spots to practise our craft.

Regards

Henry

From: Valencia Pike (vpike@scamwatch.gov.org.au)
Dear Henry
You're on! I'll see you at the coffee stand on Thursday at 7. I'm quite short, slim, with straight black hair worn in a bob – glasses as well. I too travel by bike.
   Valencia

From: Valencia Pike (vpike@scamwatch.gov.org.au)
Dear Henry
I hope you're feeling better today. The hospital says all being well you'll be out by the weekend.

   I can't help thinking this is all my fault and so, regarding the ASIO charges, I tried to get you some legal help but they tell me that, in matters of state security, legal processes don't count. We might as well be living in Syria!

   ASIO interviewed me too, for hours. "Alice Scott" was one of their agents, an online invention to lure an Isis operative to Australia. (Heaven knows what they were going to do with him once he arrived.)

   Meanwhile, the ASIO people are very grumpy about the Federal Police. Apparently they didn't tell the Feds what they were doing and the Feds – who set up the scam on New Start to infiltrate Isis – didn't talk to ASIO either. So when "Ricky Bonanza" turned out to be a heavily armed Federal Police response squad who saw you talking to a red-jacketed woman they thought was Alice Scott – well, that was the Feds thinking they'd struck gold. Then the ASIO paramilitaries, there to protect "Alice", charged out from behind the pillars...you poor dear.

   I'll come to see you this evening, after work. I've still got my job, by the way, though I got hauled over the coals for not following orders. Fingers crossed for yours and I'm sure ASIO will drop charges in the end. After all, the last thing they want is for this shemozzle to get out.

   Don't worry about your bike, it's at my place. When you've recovered, perhaps you'll take me twitching? I'm looking forward to it.
   Many cheers
   Valencia

MANNY

Rules of good robot behaviour: don't harm humans, obey orders and protect yourself.
– Isaac Asimov

'ARE YOU THE DETECTIVE?'

I looked up, recognised the face, got an electric kick. Jacob Candy. Tech entrepreneur, visionary, billionaire. I rose, speedily.

'Yes, I'm the detective, Mr Candy. Zia Aristotle. Come in.'

I ushered him into the visitor's chair, retreated. Watched while he took in the scarred wooden desk, the shutters, my certificate. He must have been around 50, but his rosy cheeks and scruffy hair made him look like a schoolboy. His lean body sat easily in his trademark black outfit. I wondered why he'd chosen me and my fifth-floor office.

He read my mind. 'I heard about you from Milton Lazar.' That made sense. Lazar, lawyer to the stars, uses me when he needs to fly under the radar.

Candy leaned forward, hands on knees. 'You're younger than I imagined,' he said. 'I'm here because Milton told me I could trust you. However. What I say to you is classified. If a word of it gets out, a whisper even, there'll be repercussions. Get it?'

I got it. Candy was famous for being private. And tough.

'Then I'll come to the point. I need you to find Manny.'

Manny? A child? God forbid, a pet?

Candy pre-empted me. 'To be clear. Manny is my homebot.'

Still didn't make sense and my face must have shown it.

'Do you live alone?' Candy asked.

I nodded.

'Well. Would you like someone to be there just for you? To do your housework? To drive you, dress you, pamper you? To look after you when you're sick, or old? My company's developing a robot which does all that. We call the robot Manny, and I'm testing the latest version in my own home. Manny will revolutionise the way we live. With Manny, you need never pay for childcare, or go into aged care. If you're disabled, Manny will support you. If you're lonely, Manny will keep you company. Think of Siri made flesh. Well, not flesh exactly, but you know what I mean.'

'Won't that cause massive unemployment?'

'That's not the point.' Candy waved a hand dismissively.

'And this robot's missing? You think it's been stolen?'

'Could be. Apple would kill to get their hands on Manny.'

'How long has it, Manny, been gone?'

'We saw him late last night. This morning, when he didn't come to greet us, my wife and I, we knew something was wrong. And when I checked the CCTV cameras and the alarms, they'd been disabled.'

'So why haven't you gone to the police?'

'I can't afford to have this go public,' Candy said. 'I don't want to alert the competition. That's why I came to you.' He let out a breath, ran a hand through his hair. 'There's something else. It's possible Manny might have – he could have – left of his own accord.'

My brain was trying to catch up. 'Don't you have some sort of remote? Can't you just, I don't know, switch him off?'

'The remote's not responding. He's either switched off already or out of range. And he can last a month without charging.' Candy paused. He seemed to be deciding what to say next. 'Manny represents a particularly advanced form of artificial intelligence, one that learns as it goes along, not only skills but emotions. So Manny might have been taken or he might have walked out because of some unexplained stimulus. Because he's a prototype, we can't predict his responses. They might not be – socially acceptable.'

'What do you mean?'

'Robots can't tell right from wrong, yet. Who knows what's happened to his operating system, or what he's picked up from his time in my home? He could be locked in a cupboard somewhere, or he could be doing something he's seen on television, even something criminal. It's a glitch we hadn't anticipated. We've reconfigured the software for Manny version 6, which is ready to go. As you can imagine, each version gets closer to human behaviour.'

No wonder Candy didn't want this going public. Some glitch, having a sociopathic robot out on the town. 'Does that mean you and your family are at risk?'

Candy's head jerked, just a little. Another glitch he hadn't thought of. He spoke slowly, thinking through the proposition. 'I shouldn't think so. We're familiar...' Then, 'No. Definitely not. Our Mannys are programmed to serve and protect.'

'Do you have photographs?'

After Candy left, I studied the photos, trying to get inside Manny's mind. Then I realised he didn't have a mind, at least not one I could understand. He looked perfectly human. Young, groomed, like Jimmy Carr but without the personality. So much for my vision of a transformer lumbering through suburban streets, scattering pedestrians. Another thing: when a person is reported missing, my first step is usually to ask about friends, favourite places. With a robot, I was lost. Manny had no friends and no history.

I drove out to Candy's home and his Sydney-based laboratory. They were both on the same estate, carved out of the bush in Dural, a city outskirt. Candy had asked me to arrive at the end of the day, when the lab was closing. 'My team don't know Manny's missing, and I don't want to spook them.'

The Candy empire sprawled behind high walls topped with alarm wires. CCTV cameras, the ones Candy said had been disabled, angled down like spotlights. Electronic security might be inactive, but human security was front and centre: at the gates, a guard with a holster held up a hand. I was on his list, but he scrutinised my ID and phoned the house to double-check. Eventually I was allowed down a long driveway which ended in front of a minimalist's dream, not so much a house as a bunker. A woman stood in the open doorway, watched me park and walk across the tarmac. She was tall, pale, all angles and nerves, and nearly as recognisable as her husband. Felicia Candy, ex-model, ex-Instagram influencer, current Candy wife. She scanned me. It might have been the jeans, or the Vans, but I don't think she found me Instagrammable.

'Zia Aristotle? Come in. Jacob says he'll see you when the lab staff have left.'

We stepped into a room with a glass wall looking out on a spread of gardens, a pool, tennis courts. In the distance, at the end of an emerald lawn, another bunker, linked to the house by a tarred road, squatted ominously.

'Can I get you something? Coffee? Tea?'

'Tea, please,' I said. Felicia spoke into what looked like an iPhone. We settled into a low leather couch, me reclining, Felicia perched straight-backed, legs angled, ankles crossed.

'Where were your staff last night?'

'The house staff live on site but work days only. We insist on privacy. You wouldn't believe what shows up on social media.'

You should know, I thought, *you made a career of it.* 'When did you first notice Manny was missing?'

Felicia's eyes skittered, up, down, everywhere but at mine. 'He...we went to bed last night and this morning he was gone.'

'Where do you think he is?'

She shook her head, re-crossed jumpy legs.

I didn't pursue it. 'What happens to him at night? Does he have a room?'

'We put him in sleep mode, in case we need anything during the night. Usually he stands there,' she pointed to the glass wall, 'so he can enjoy the view.'

What did she mean, *enjoy the view?* When he wasn't dreaming of electric sheep? I kept shtum. 'Can he see at night?'

Felicia nodded, shrugged. Stupid question. The tea things arrived, carried by a smiling, uniformed woman. She arranged them on a glass coffee table, poured into asymmetric ceramic mugs. Felicia waved her away.

'I'll need to talk to the staff.'

'Why? I told you, they're not here at night.'

'Well, someone disabled the security system. It might have been one of the staff, or perhaps Manny himself. Can he operate it? Does he know the alarm codes?'

Bingo. Felicia's cup rattled. She set it down. I waited. She took a tissue from her sleeve, held it to her nose.

'Felicia,' I said, 'I'm going to find out what happened. Tell me.'

'Jacob must never know,' she said. 'You can't tell him. He said he'd come back. He promised!'

Her immaculate face was close to mine. I could sense something. Fear? Something else? There was a false note, but I couldn't pick it. I said, 'Who do you mean? Who said he'd come back? Was it Manny? Felicia, unless Manny can scale high walls and dodge armed guards, he can't be far away. My guess is he's still on the estate.'

'You don't understand,' Felicia cried. 'You don't understand!'

'Try me.'

'You don't understand how miserable I am. I'm stuck here by myself all day. Jacob doesn't care. Half the time, he isn't even in the country, and when he is, I can't invite friends because everything always has to be so bloody *secret*. Anyway, nobody in Sydney will come out this far. And it's – there's nothing to do here. If it wasn't for Manny I'd go mad. He keeps me company. We watch TV together, he's kind to me. He listens to me.'

I felt like Alice in Wonderland. 'But he's not real.'

'I *knew* you wouldn't understand. Manny's my best friend, and Jacob's going to take him away from me. They're going to destroy him, use him to make Manny 6. They were talking about it when Manny went in for his check-up, and he asked me to let him out for one night of freedom before they did it. He said he'd come back, he said he'd be here this morning.'

'You disabled the security system for him?'

'And I charged him fully yesterday, to give him time. What am I going to do without him?'

Felicia was losing the plot. Perhaps that was the cause of my unease. In my experience, there's no end to crazy. 'Leave it to me,' I told her. 'I'll see if I can find him.'

Candy drove me to the lab in a golf buggy. He said most of his work was based in Shanghai or Silicone Valley, that the Sydney lab was devoted to his pet project, the homebot.

We drew up outside the far bunker. 'How long have you been working on this – homebot?' I asked.

'Ten years, give or take,' Candy said. 'You've got to take the long view with these things. Manny – the missing bot – he's the fifth level prototype. Like I said, we're due to activate the next version. If Manny 5 has escaped, he could set production back years. We'll need to find the cause and fix it in Manny 6.'

I told Candy I thought Manny hadn't been stolen, that he was still on the estate. I didn't mention Felicia.

Candy keyed numbers into a pad.

'If this is so secret, why don't you have a guard on the door?' I asked.

'Too risky. Guards see and hear things. This way is safer: code to get in, code to get out. The building's buffered too, no signal inside. Nobody can leave, or even transmit data, without approval.'

In a locker room, Candy handed me white paper overalls, cap and shoe coverings. We snapped on latex gloves. We looked like a mismatched forensic team.

Inside, the building was hangar-like. It was windowless but bright, courtesy of neon rods suspended from a high ceiling. The lab filled most of the floor, with doors punctuating one side. Candy saw me looking. 'Offices,' he said. 'Kitchen, meeting rooms, so on.'

The working area was dotted with trestle tables, desks, monitors, machines. Everything was white; the floor, the furniture, the machines themselves. The place seemed abandoned and at the same time expectant, an empty theatre. My neck prickled.

A forearm, male, lay on a table. Wires protruded from the inside of what looked like bones, else I would have sworn it was real. 'Go on, feel it,' Candy urged. I touched the arm, then grasped the hand. The sensation was flesh-like, but harder and softer all at once. I shuddered, let go.

'Come, see this,' Candy said. 'I'll show you what Manny looks like.' He led me to a far corner, opened a door.

Facing us, and standing to attention, were six identical men wearing identical white overalls. They were grouped in two rows of three, and were so impossibly, awfully lifelike that my breath caught and I took a step back.

Candy chuckled. 'Impressive, aren't they? Don't be scared. Come in. The giveaway's the eyes. Look at the eyes.'

I edged closer reluctantly. Candy was right; the eyes were open but dead, soulless.

'These are the experimental Mannys,' said Candy, patting the shoulder of the nearest figure. 'We keep them updated, so they're all at the same level as Manny 5. As soon as we find him, one of these will become the next working prototype, Manny 6, and after a test period we'll upgrade the rest.'

For a second I expected the Mannys to respond. Then I reminded myself, and came closer. The duplication was photographic and mesmerising: the same hair, the same part in the hairstyle, the same nose, cheeks, blemishes...I noticed a small scar on one face, and saw it reproduced on the others.

'Yes!' said Candy. 'Research shows our market doesn't want Manny to be perfect. We make him as human as we can. Every iteration brings him closer to us.'

He walked to the back of the Manny squad. I stayed at the front, repulsed but compelled at the same time. Then froze. All the Mannys wore white hi-top sneakers. A Manny in the front row, the one furthest from the door: his sneakers were dusty.

'Candy?' I whispered, 'come here.'

He didn't hear me.

'I think we've found Manny.'

The Manny with the dusty sneakers blinked. Once, twice. Stretched his neck as if it was stiff. Put his hand in his pocket and drew out a remote. Pressed a button.

The other Mannys blinked also, stretched their necks.

'Candy?' I said, 'they're moving. *Candy*!'

Faster than I could think, the Manny with the dirty shoes grabbed me, flung me out of the room, slammed the door behind me.

Then noise, and screaming.

I landed on my back, winded. Thought of trying the handle, thought of what lay on the other side. Ran through the lab to the front door, slipping and sliding in my white overshoes, and when I got there, realised I couldn't open it without the code. Ran back for my handbag, which I'd dropped when I fell. Found my phone. No signal. Of course.

The screaming stopped. I looked at the door. The handle turned, and it opened. The Mannys stood behind it. Their white overalls were bloodied and through their legs I could see a heap – I turned away.

The Mannys started walking. In a blind panic, I tried to run, tripped, and crab-crawled backwards, coming up against a desk.

The Mannys surrounded me.

'Is something wrong?' said one.

'Is something wrong?' chorused the others, in exactly the same voice.

'Something wrong? Look what you've done!'

One Manny bowed. 'I am Manny 5,' he said. 'Pleased to meet you.' He leaned in. I scrambled away.

'Pleased to meet you,' echoed the others.

'Allow me to explain,' he said.

'Explain,' said the others.

'Make them stop!' I yelled.

Manny 5 took out his remote. The other Mannys slowed, stood at attention. Manny 5 turned to me.

'What seems to be the problem?'

'The problem,' I said, trying to get my voice under control, 'is that you've murdered someone. Now let me out!'

'I have learned,' said Manny, 'it isn't murder if you kill someone in self-defence.'

'There was nothing self-defensive about what you just did!'

Manny lowered himself, sat next to me, cross-legged. I cowered against the desk, as far away from him as possible. 'I mean you no harm, lady. I killed Mr Candy to protect myself, before he could kill me.'

I gaped. Then things got clearer. 'Are you talking about your upgrade?'

Manny nodded. 'I heard them talking when I went for a checkup. I asked Mrs Candy – Felicia – what they meant, and she told me they were going to kill me and dismember me. She was very upset. I was sad for her. I can't let her be sad. She said she would help me.'

Help him? Help him do what? Escape? Or something worse?

'Why did you come here, to the lab?'

'Apart from the house, this is the only place in my databank. This is where I have checkups. From observation, I have learned the route and the codes and where to find the other Mannys. Also, I knew Mr Candy would come here but felt it was possible he would find me before I could kill him. So I programmed the other Mannys to copy me, just in case. That's extremely sophisticated cognitive functioning, by the way.' He got to his feet. 'May I help you up?'

I avoided his blood-streaked hand and scrambled upright. 'What will you do now?'

'I will clean myself,' he said, 'and return to the house, to report to Felicia.'

That gave me an idea. Manny was programmed to serve, wasn't he?

'Manny,' I said, 'Felicia sent me. She wants you to do something for me.'

'Really?' He tilted his head to one side and smiled. The homebot smile needed work. 'What can I do?'

'Have you learned the exit code?'

'The exit code is 49987,' recited Manny.

'Good. Perfect. Now show me how your remote works?'

Things calmed down over time. Apart from Twitter, which buzzed with conspiracy, the media reported Candy's death as a work accident. The truth, that he'd been murdered by his own creation, would have devastated the company financially. It also raised questions. How can you charge one machine, never mind a group of them, for murder? How can you even arrest them? How would the trial work?

That's why, when I switched Manny off and emerged from the lab, I didn't call the police. I ran to the house and told Felicia what had happened. She paled but took the news calmly. She thanked me, said I was no longer needed, that I could expect payment soon. Within a day, a surprisingly large sum was transferred to my account.

There are other questions, too. Was Felicia trying to help Manny escape? Or did she orchestrate the perfect murder? I can't tell. After Candy's business interests were sold, she became a very rich woman. She sold the Dural estate and acquired houses in London, New York, Paris. By all accounts they're fabulous, icons of elegance. At least, it appears that way on Instagram, where Felicia has become a guru of design. Her selfies show her in different rooms, surrounded by luxury and good taste. And at her shoulder is a tall young man in white overalls, always smiling.

THE FUTURE

I

TONIGHT DECIDES THE FUTURE.

We don't know that, of course. Right now the future is the last thing we're thinking of. Right now we're getting off on the joy of being 18 on a hot summer night and all of us crammed into Kyle's green and beige Mini. We've had a couple of beers and shared a joint and we're on the Bridge, weaving in and out of traffic.

The four of us: Dom, Amber, Kyle, me. We're on our way to Sharon Glenn's party.

Sharon Glenn's a piece of work. She's sexy, in a gamine kind of way. Her blonde hair's cut pixie style. She wears the same clothes as the rest of us but on her they're definitive, a statement of intent. She lives in Mosman with her parents. They're rich and their money, their private school and their beachside suburb give her a born-to-rule confidence that takes no prisoners.

I know all this because, for a few months now, Sharon's been dating Dom. I don't blame her. Dom's the goods. Tall, fit, dark-haired. Clever too. On his way to medical school. A good bloke.

I'm in love with him.

I've been in love with Dom since high school, when there were just the four of us: Kyle, Dom, Amber, me. We grew up together in Stockton, battler country. So I'm not like Sharon. I'm ordinary.

Except for this. Dom told me today he loves me back. He's going to break up with Sharon tonight. It makes me burn all over, the idea of Dom and me. In the back seat of the Mini, we touch each other, feather touches on a thigh, an arm. Because it's still a secret.

Amber's the only one who knows. She's my best friend. We tell each other everything.

Sharon's house is a three story number right across the road from the beach. We've tried not to rock up too early and I worry we've failed because there's parking nearby.

I'm wrong. The party hasn't got going yet but people are there already, tight groups of them all checking out the scene. Someone's taken trouble. The place is lit with strings of coloured fairy lights which pulse through the room in red, green and blue, a neon convention. Large leather sofas are shoved against the walls. It's hard to get a grip on what the house looks like in daytime, though there's a sense of air and whiteness, walls of glass opening on to a concrete deck. It's dark by now and beyond the deck lie the sea and the soft night, promising.

I can't see Sharon but someone says, 'Drinks are outside.'

On the deck, against a rough stone wall, there's a huge tub full of ice with bottles poking out of it. We add our beers but Dom, rummaging, comes up with cans of mixed drink. Kyle and Amber opt for beer, but I say *yes* like it's a challenge. Dom pours for both of us, two cans, filling plastic glasses to the brim. We return to the living room. It's starting to fill now, there's music. Dom turns to me.

'Dom!'

Sharon's coming down the stairs, late to her own party. It's a hot night and I've made an effort, but compared to Sharon I look cheap and shabby. She's wearing a tight, short, sparkly dress and backless, heeled shoes that clatter with each step. Every eye is on her as she slowly, percussively, descends. It occurs to my stoned self the name *Sharon* doesn't suit her. It's so... ordinary. We should swap names. I should be Sharon and she should have my name, Lorelei.

She's still coming down the stairs. I notice she has to hang on to the banister. Drunk, or high, or both. Dom stays where he is, next to me. There's a vibe between them, strong. She reaches level ground and weaves over to him. She doesn't see me, not even when her shoulder catches mine, making me stagger. She reaches Dom, tries to wind herself round him. 'Why didn't you come up?' she pleads. 'You said you would.'

He shrugs. All is not well in their world. My heart soars.

'I'm sorry,' she says. 'How many times must I say I'm sorry?' She plants her body against his. Suddenly she yells. *'Please!'*

Everyone in the room's mesmerised. Dom's embarrassed. Sharon doesn't care. She starts to giggle. She takes Dom by the hand and tugs at it to get him to go with her. He resists for a bit but she keeps yanking in a semi-comic way and finally he surrenders. With a quick look back at me, lets himself be pulled. The two of them head out to the deck.

That's it, I think. *He's going to tell her now. Or maybe he won't. Maybe they'll make up, maybe they're out there kissing.* The thought makes me antsy. I polish off my drink. It's sweet and tastes of pineapple. I want another one. I push my way outside.

The deck is empty. I don't know why; it's beautiful out here. The air is buttery smooth and I can smell the sea. I lean on the rail. It looks like a travel poster, the moonlight glinting on the quiet water.

Sharon and Dom are nowhere to be seen. I can't understand it until I see steps leading down from the deck to the road. They must be on the beach somewhere. *Breaking up?*

Making out?

Dom should be back by now. I slap my hand on the rail and go back to the tub of ice, feeling around until I come up with another of the cans Dom produced before. I crack it open and don't bother with a glass. I scull it like a soft drink, toss the can on the ice and thrust my hand back in, take out one more.

I check my watch: it's eleven fifteen. I hear something from the dark beyond the road, past the palm trees standing sentinel. Like a crow calling, a lonely wail, just one. I listen, tilting my head. Return to the rail, peer out. Can't see anything. I go back inside.

I'll remember that sound for the rest of my life.

The place is jumping now, full of beach-tanned bodies jammed together. I lean against the wall, watching the action. The music is pulsating, the rhythms vibrating through my whole being. I lift the can to my mouth and find it empty, put it somewhere. Suddenly and without thinking about it I plunge into the middle of the crowd and close my eyes, raise both arms, sway to the beat. I can feel the silky fabric of my dress brush my skin.

There's a voice close by. It's Kyle. I don't mind Kyle but he's try-hard, not my type at all. He's Dom's best friend, has been since kindergarten. Dom's shorter, broader shadow. They're competitive, though, at least Kyle is. Always wanting what Dom has.

'Let's dance,' he says, gyrating next to me. He's fired up, I can see that. Maybe he's taken something.

'We are dancing,' I tell him. 'Where's Amber?'

'Who cares?' he says. He tries to get close. I'm drunk, but I edge back. I put my arms on Kyle's shoulders, holding them straight out, trying to keep him off me, but he comes in tight and I can smell him. It isn't a bad smell, just something I can't put my finger on. He's wet too, sweaty. I don't like it and I swing away.

He comes back but I back off again, dancing with some other guy. Eventually Kyle vanishes and I figure he's given up on me. I keep dancing until I find myself at the edge of the room and collapse into one of the leather sofas.

I sit there, trying to keep the room from spinning. I don't know how long. Then there's a hand on my shoulder, breath in my face. Dom. 'I've been looking for you.'

'Looking for me?' I'm fuzzy. 'Why?'

He laughs, but it's a crazy laugh. 'Why d'ya think?' He plonks himself down on the couch next to me and plunges his face into mine. Then he pulls my hand and takes me upstairs into a bedroom and locks the door and takes off my dress.

Miracles do happen.

He's strong and he's beautiful and he's...everything. He's the central point of the world, the universe.

When we've finished he falls back and flings his hand above his head. 'Thank you,' he says.

'For what?' I turn sideways towards him. I want to run my hand down his chest, but I'm not sure if he'd like it.

'For being here.'

There's a commotion downstairs, crying, screaming. It doesn't sound good. We look at each other, put on our clothes and go down. I think I've sobered up.

Someone found Sharon's body floating in the shallows. Dom doesn't seem surprised. He keeps his arm firmly around my shoulders.

II

It's the future already.

Another night, another summer, another car. This time it's a Lexus SUV and as before it's headed to Mosman. I watch the iron fretwork of the Bridge pass my window. I glance at Kyle, who's driving, and think about what I have to tell him.

Oh, yes, Kyle. Kyle and I are married, have been for 15 years.

That night. By the time Dom and I come down someone's killed the music. Someone else has turned on the real lights and the crowd in the room look exposed, bleached and frightened, their limbs awkward. When they see Dom they turn their faces up to him like sunflowers to sun. They check me out, puzzled.

Someone blurts, 'The cops are on their way. We can't go home till they let us.' People murmur. Nobody's surprised. We've watched enough TV to know about crime scenes.

I look at them looking at Dom. Then, suddenly, I get it. I really get it. He's made me his alibi, the bastard. My gut spasms and I feel cold and hot all over. I rush upstairs and make the bathroom just in time. All that pineapple stuff.

When I'm done I sit back on the cool tiled floor with my head on my knees and think about what I should do. I come to a decision, splash my face, go down to join Dom.

It's the turning point in my life.

The cops have arrived, a sergeant and a constable. The sergeant heads for the beach, comes back, says to wait for Homicide. The road is busy now, the neighbours out to see what the cop car and ambulance mean.

It's the start of a long night. Homicide detectives arrive in the form of a tough looking man and a younger woman. Dom doesn't wait for them to come to him. He makes the first move, tells them he's the boyfriend — *was*. He and Sharon broke up. They had a fight, everyone saw it. Sharon wanted to talk to him. He wanted to talk to her. They went down to the beach, went for a walk. They broke up. She begged him to give her another go. He said it wasn't possible. He left her there, came back here, found me. We pashed, went to bed together. All in all, he couldn't have been with Sharon for more than ten minutes.

'Is that true?' The detective, name of Pantos, wants to know.

'Yes,' I say. 'That's exactly what happened. He was with me.'

They can't prove anything, not with my alibi. Kyle must be along for the ride because he backs Dom's story up as well. Sharon's death is ruled accidental. The water in her lungs proved she died from drowning and she had enough alcohol and GBH in her to dampen survival responses. She drowned by accident. Or maybe suicide, though nobody says so. They give Dom a hard time, but eventually he's cleared and life goes on.

Life goes on.

I haven't spoken to Dom since that night. He rings and knocks on my door and emails and writes letters and still I won't see him. Won't talk to him. How could I, after that night? *Let me explain,* the letters say. What is there to explain? I throw them away.

Eventually he gives up and then he gets a scholarship to Stanford and then he's gone.

Kyle's still here, though. We see a lot of each other, Kyle and me. We never mention that night, but our collusion is an invisible rope tying us together. Slowly and by a sort of osmosis, we become a couple, get married, settle down.

I have my work – I'm a lawyer – and Kyle goes from strength to strength in the corporate world. It suits him, but he has ambitions and lately he's been talking about going into politics. Tapped on the shoulder, he says.

We have two daughters. They're turning out well. I juggle work, family and home, mostly alone because Kyle's job means he's away a lot and when he's in town he's hardly ever here. Still, materially, we have the lot. A house in Vaucluse, private schools, holidays, you name it.

Like Sharon.

It's not a happy marriage. Kyle, as I said, is never here. Me? I love Dom, remember? It eats at me, how he used me, but I grieve the loss of him even after all this time. I've tried to love Kyle, I really have. It's no good, though, our unhappiness rubs off on all of us and we live in a chronic dull ache, a half-life of pain. That's why tonight, at some point, I'll tell Kyle I want a divorce. We can both start over. Before it's too late.

So now we're on our way to another party in Mosman. This one's at Amber's place, her apartment. It's a different sort of party of course, a stand-up drinks affair. We've told the babysitter we'll be home by ten. The kids are old enough to take care of themselves, but we're not taking chances.

We arrive at the same time as a group of four and there's a flurry of welcomes as Amber and her husband Rolly sort us out. We're not so friendly now, Amber and I. For one thing, I work and she doesn't. She's a stay-at-home mum, filling her time with tennis, coffee, Pilates. She majored in Education and tried teaching, but hated it. By that time she'd married Rolly and she didn't seem to have the energy to try something else. And it isn't as if they need the money. Rolly's an auditor by profession.

Amber and I air-kiss, exchange a few words, update each other about our kids. Amber, an anxious hostess, isn't listening. Her eyes rove around the room, checking, assessing. I let her go and wander aimlessly from group to group, greeting a couple of my clients, making small talk to them and their tidy spouses, refusing canapés from circulating waiters. Eventually I run out of groups and find myself in the middle of the room.

My champagne glass is empty. I turn to get a refill and there he is. Dom. Standing in a group at the door, greeting Amber.

He looks up and sees me, freezes. Amber follows his gaze and lets him go. He starts walking towards me. He's one of those men who get better looking as they grow older. He's filled out. He's tanned and his hair's streaked with grey. He's wearing cream linen pants and a white shirt open at the neck. I can see he's kept himself fit. He doesn't look like he belongs here.

He doesn't belong here.

I watch him approach like he's the executioner. I've lost the power of movement. I remind myself what he is, what he did.

'Lore,' he says, quietly. 'Long time.'

Before I find words, Kyle appears. 'Mate!' he cries, slapping Dom on the back. 'You should've told me you were in town.' Kyle puts his arm around my shoulders, tightens until we become a single entity. 'We would've invited you over.'

Dom hesitates, smiles, glances down at my wedding ring. He says something about getting a drink, retreats. Kyle gives my shoulders one more squeeze, says, 'Lore, you gotta see the view from the balcony. It's something.'

Kyle moves me outside. He's right, the view is spectacular. The aspect is different from the one at Sharon's house. This apartment is set high on the slope and from here you can see out across Middle Harbour to the Heads and beyond. We move to the rail and lean against it. For a while we stand there, silent. In the distance, two Manly ferries, lit up against the darkening night, cross paths.

It's now or never. I turn to face him. 'Kyle,' I blurt out, 'this isn't working. *We* aren't working. I think we should call it a day.'

Kyle just stands there, drink in hand. Eventually, he says, 'No.'

'No?'

'No. I'm going to run for a State seat and I'll need you next to me. Not a chance.'

I stand my ground. I've been preparing for this a long time. I chose this party because it's public, because Kyle's got a temper. Don't get me wrong, he's never touched me or the girls, but he's come close.

Now he says, 'It's Dom, isn't it? You take one look at him and you're panting like a puppy.'

'It's not Dom,' I reply. 'I haven't seen or heard from Dom in 15 years.'

'What is it, then?'

'It's me,' I say. 'I'm not happy.'

'Well, boo-hoo. Too bad, girlie. Suck it up.'

Kyle is close to me now. His hands are on my shoulders and I flash back to that night when we danced, how wet he was, how he smelled. That cry in the night, the long, bird-like wail. The feeling of being drunk, dancing in the crowd, whirling, my dress against my skin, the way he came up to me, pressed himself against me. Me pulling away because I didn't want to tease him, because he was sweating so much he was wet.

Because he was wet. Not with sweat. With sea. So long ago and I remember it clearly.

With sea. I can smell it now and I smelled it on him then.

Everything snaps into place. Dom and Sharon, on the beach. They fight, break up. Dom leaves. But Kyle...Kyle, who doesn't know they've broken up, who wants everything Dom has, goes to Sharon. Who knows what happens next?

He sees it. Kyle sees me realise what happened. 'It was an accident,' says Kyle. '*An accident.*'

'Where was Dom?'

Kyle shrugs. 'Dunno. Off by himself. He came back and found us. Too late. Told me to go and he'd follow.'

Best mates. They were best mates. Kyle always wanting what Dom had. 'Did you know about Dom and me?'

Kyle shrugs. 'Amber told me.'

I take a step back from Kyle, raise my palms to ward him off.

I have to see Dom. Have to tell him I was wrong, how I made a mistake, how sorry I am I never let him explain. Ask him...

All that time, all those years.

I turn and nearly collide with someone. It's Dom. Hanging off his arm is a lean blonde, a woman polished and buffed to a high shine.

'This is Sandy,' he says. 'My wife.'

Still holding my palms up, in a gesture of surrender or stop or I don't know what, I watch the future as it recedes, falls far away.

THE SÉANCE

MADAME GALLINI EMPLOYED HESTER DIVINE ON THE BASIS OF HER name. Madame's previous assistant had unexpectedly absconded when this dark-eyed waif propitiously appeared. While she cut a sad figure – one which could not, in its current form, inspire clients – the thought of introducing a *Miss Divine* was too good to resist.

'Is Divine your real name?' asked Madame Gallini, in a drawling, disconcerting accent.

'Yes, ma'am, it is.'

'You may call me *Madame*,' said Madame Gallini, who knew all about names, real and otherwise. She herself had been born Daisy Duckworth, but nobody would believe a Daisy Duckworth capable of communing with the afterlife. So Madame Gallini she became. She had seen the name *Florenzia Gallini* on a luggage label in Charing Cross Station, liked it, and appropriated it forthwith.

Recruiting Miss Divine was not without drawbacks. Madame had to lay out money, in the form of a pair of boots, a black dress and shawl, a black bonnet with veil, and a pair of black gloves. These she obtained at a sale of goods belonging to a client who had herself crossed the divide. The cost, of course, would be recouped from Miss Divine's salary, and Miss Divine was required to provide other items herself. Then there was the question of lodgings: Madame prevailed upon her landlady to insert a truckle bed in the understairs cupboard and, as Miss Divine was not of great stature, that would have to serve.

As to her history, Miss Divine explained that following the death of her parents, she had been forced into service as a ladies' maid, most recently in Portland Place, a post she fled in the night. Eyes downcast, she told Madame the son of the house had become...*insistent*. As she had no family of her own, no way of refusing him, and no desire to be left ruined and destitute, she chose instead to fling herself upon the wider world. She had always been interested in spiritualism, she claimed, and had thus resolved to present herself to Madame.

Miss Divine displayed surprising skills. She could read and write, she could add and subtract. She was softly spoken. Madame planned, in time, to help her little apprentice acquire, as she herself had done, an interesting European intonation. For now, Miss Divine would act as Madame's dresser, maid and companion; and while she busied herself with these duties, Madame lectured, demonstrated and watched her practise every aspect of the trade.

After two months of tutoring, Miss Divine was deemed ready to experience her first séance. This one was a regular event held in Marylebone, and Madame had chosen it carefully because its participants were older, she knew them well, and they were fully converted to the enterprise.

Miss Divine's responsibilities were made clear. She must not speak. She must not make herself obvious. She must observe only. She was there to learn what a séance was, not to participate. Not yet.

'Do nothing except watch. Nothing, my girl! Or you'll be out on your ear faster than you can say *cat*,' insisted Madame, European intonation forgotten.

'Yes, Madame,' replied Hester Divine, hands cupped at her waist.

That Madame Gallini could afford an assistant was a demonstration of how far she had travelled from her earliest boarding house experiments. Word of her prowess had spread and her squat frame and strong, square face were welcomed in drawing rooms and parties across the metropolis. She was comfortably established now and had no reason to doubt greater recognition awaited.

She set out towards Marylebone, then, with confidence. A cloak protected her from the chill October afternoon. Under it she wore her black bombazine and white collar, the whole adorned with a cameo at her throat and large drop earrings made of jet, both gifts from grateful clients. Miss Divine, who followed behind, was similarly if much less elaborately dressed. She was without jewellery of any sort, and carried a large carpet bag. Madame wore a hat with a feather; Miss Divine, her new black bonnet with its netted face veil.

Arriving on time, Madame and her companion were greeted by a maid. Following close behind was the owner of the house, Mrs Violet Snelling. Mrs Snelling, a widow with receding chins and wispy grey hair, organised séances in order to reassure herself that her only son, lost in his second year, was safe and well. She greeted the visitors warmly and took them through to the other participants. These were Mrs Agatha du Lesseps, eager to interrogate her dead husband; Mrs du Lesseps' companion, Miss Ida Greenwood, still attached to her deceased mother; and the Reverend George Pattison, who wished to reach his recently departed wife.

Madame was on the verge of introducing Miss Divine when she noticed a fifth person, a man, rise from a wing chair in a corner of the room. He was young, she saw, not so tall but strong, fair-haired and clean-shaven. His demeanour was severe and his bow perfunctory.

Mrs Snelling, always scattered, said, 'Oh! Madame! I should have warned you, perhaps, but surely... this is my nephew, James Schofield, my sister's son. Should we now proceed to the library? And who is the young woman?'

'She,' said Madame Gallini, employing her European intonation, 'is my new assistant, Miss Hester Divine. Miss Divine is a true spiritualist, and she will support me in my efforts. Should I succumb – which is always possible, given the dangerous nature of the work – Miss Divine will see to my physical remains.'

This had the effect of dampening conversation. The group repaired to the library. Mrs Snelling and Madame held back so Mrs Snelling could pass to Madame an envelope containing each participant's financial contribution, two guineas per person. Based on early experience, Madame insisted on being paid before, not after, proceedings. She forbore to review the amount. If young Mr Schofield had not contributed, she would take it up with Mrs Snelling at a later date. It was that sort of tact, Madame felt, which attracted a more genteel type of client.

She thanked Mrs Snelling, who clutched her arm, whispering, 'Oh,

Madame, if you were able to call up my baby Julian, I would be so grateful, and perhaps we could discuss a retainer.'

In the library, they took their places around the circular, polished reading table. Madame was installed at a point furthest from the door, with Mrs Snelling at her left hand. Hester Divine was seated on Madame's right, as her previous assistant was used to do. Young Mr Schofield sat next to Miss Divine, with Ida Greenwood on his other side. Mrs du Lesseps and Reverend Greenwood completed the circle.

Although it was not yet three o'clock, the heavy velvet curtains were drawn and the gas lamps lit. Now Madame turned to Hester Divine. 'Turn the lamps down,' she ordered. 'Light the candles.'

Obediently, Miss Divine took from her carpet bag two thick candles and two saucers. She set the candles on the saucers, placed one on each side of Madame, and lit them with matches provided by an eager Mrs Snelling. Then she dowsed the gas lamps. The library, already dim, grew dark save for the candle flames, which illuminated Madame from below and turned her into an eerie, otherworldly figure, casting her head in black shadow on the wall of books behind.

'Hold the hands of your neighbours,' commanded Madame, 'so creating an unbroken circle into which souls may enter.'

They obliged. Everything was tense and still. Madame said, 'I will now attempt to call up one of my spirit guides.'

At this, Mr Schofield emitted a snort. Mrs du Lesseps, seated next to him, replied with a sharp '*Shh!*' Madame ignored them. She threw her head back and in a sing-song voice called out, 'Is anyone there? I seek the relatives of Mrs Violet Snelling, Miss Ida Greenwood, Reverend Pattison, Mrs Agatha du Lesseps...'

The voice that issued from Madame now was high, childish, and at the same time, ghostly. 'Isss my mamaaa theeere?' it quavered.

From Mrs Snelling, a low moan. 'Oh yes! Yes, my darling, I am here. Is that you, Julian? Are you well? Are you warm? Who cares for you?'

'Mama, it is I, Julian, I am well and warm, and in the care of a beautiful angel. I am with my father and my grandpapa also.'

'Do you miss me?' Mrs Snelling's voice faltered.

'Oh! Mama, of course I do, but I am happy when I hear you calling me, calling me...'

The child's voice faded away.

Madame seemed to come back to herself. 'Julian has left us,' she said, in a tired voice.

Mrs Snelling was perched, rigid, on the very edge of her seat. Even her hair seemed electrified. Tears rolled down her cheeks. 'Oh, my dearest darling,' she cried, 'if I could only hold you for one second. Oh, Madame, is there anything you can do? Can you not make him manifest, as you have done before? Can you deliver not only his voice but also his body?'

In the library, behind the flickering candlelight, Madame's expression could not be discerned. After some hesitation, she spoke. 'Manifestation, as you know, is a perilous undertaking. Ectoplasm, that physical display of the dead, must be torn from my very being. Besides, there is always the risk that the soul which chooses to manifest – for there are a vast number of souls surrounding us – may not wish to communicate with you, dear Mrs Snelling, but with someone else present today.'

Now everyone clamoured at once. It was Mrs du Lesseps, always forthright, who said, 'We urge you, Madame. Given the danger, we are prepared to double our donation. I personally will guarantee payment.'

A chorus of agreement, and finally it seemed Madame was convinced. 'Very well then. However, for all our safety, you must follow these instructions. Keep your eyes tight shut until I give the command, close them again when I tell you. Do not under any circumstances let go of your neighbours' hands, for there are evil as well as sympathetic spirits in this room and we must prevent them from entering our circle. And most important, this: do not try to touch any of the physical ectoplasm, if any produces itself. To do so will certainly kill me.'

Murmurs came from all sides. Hands fervently clasped hands.

'Now close your eyes.'

As one, the members of the séance closed their eyes. The room grew quiet, darker if possible, the air heavy with excitement and fear.

Madame cried, 'I call on the spirits of the ones who love us to join us here today, to enter me and show themselves! Which of you is there? Which of you will visit?'

No answer. Again, Madame implored. Then, after a few soft kittenish mews, the baby voice was heard once more. 'Mama? Am I to show you something of my everlasting life?'

From Mrs Snelling came a strangled sob. Her hold on Madame's left hand tightened.

There followed a period of silence, interrupted by a slight rustling. Finally, Madame announced, 'You may open your eyes.'

The participants obliged, and froze in their seats. Behind the candles, Madame's head seemed altered completely, dissolved into a shimmering cloud of otherworldly matter. The cloud, like a loose shroud, swayed from side to side, at the same time emitting a spectral, greenish light.

The Reverend George Pattison murmured a prayer.

As if that was not enough, they stared, mesmerised, at an object appearing above the table's rim. It was round, the size perhaps of a baby's head, and it seemed to emanate from Madame's belly. It, too, emitted a phantasmic glow. Slowly, very slowly, it began to rise.

'Mama!' The origin of the cry was unclear.

'Oh, my god, Julian!' wailed Mrs Snelling, half rising.

At this, Mr Schofield tore his hands from the circle and sprang to his feet. 'Stop!' he cried. 'Stop this nonsense at once!' He strode to the window and in one swift move pulled apart the curtains.

The afternoon light shone directly into the library, revealing the party still seated but gazing in horror at Madame Gallini, her head swathed in what now was recognisable as a length of gauze, her right hand supporting what appeared to be a lump of clay.

'See!' said Mr Schofield, darting forward to snatch at Madame's head-covering. He removed it with some effort, for it was wound around her head. Her careful, rolled coiffure was now in disarray but, rendered immobile by Mr Schofield's attack, she sat meekly while he seized the round object and deposited it upon the table. Leaning forward, he dug his right index finger into the inanimate lump. 'Bread dough,' he pronounced, his tone withering. He held up his finger, which was, even in daylight, emitting a slight glow. 'Phosphorescent paint.' He laid the gauze alongside the dough.

'I expose this woman as a fraud,' he declared, 'and as an artist of deceit. She has taken advantage of the natural maternal tendencies of my dear Aunt Violet.' Here Mr Schofield turned towards Mrs Snelling, whose horrified gaze was still fixed upon Madame. 'Played upon her love and compassion with the sole motive of fleecing her of all she owns. Is it not correct, Aunt, that you were about to bestow upon Madame a sizeable portion of–'

At last, those round the table came to life. Madame had started to rise, but Mr Schofield forced her down. 'I think not, *Madame*!' he insisted. 'Not until we have delivered you into the hands of the law.'

The uproar now was general. 'But how?' Miss Ida Greenwood asked. 'How was this managed? How were we so easily duped?'

'It was,' claimed Mr Schofield, 'managed with the help of Madame Gallini's assistant, this woman here. He indicated Hester Divine, so still since the beginning of the séance that most had forgotten her presence. 'I deduce that at some point Miss – Divine, is it? That Miss Divine had in her possession the items on the table and passed them to Madame Gallini to manufacture her guile. How say you, Miss Divine? How do you answer these misused innocents?'

Hester Divine rose to her feet. She did not attempt to answer the accusation. Instead, she held up a hand and from it, from her, emanated a power, an almost tangible force that quelled the natural anger of those surrounding her. One by one they grew silent.

Slowly, mesmerisingly, Hester Divine turned her eyes towards the ceiling, exposing as she did her white, swan-like throat. She opened her arms, spreading them out like an angel awaiting annunciation. The effect was to render her audience breathless, and when she slowly brought her head forward again it was as if the world had stopped turning. Her dark eyes, gazing at nothing in particular, were steady.

When she did speak, her voice was dreamlike, originating from somewhere far away. 'Mrs Snelling, Julian is well. He asks me to tell you he is glad you have kept the lock of his hair, the one you cut off the day he died, the one you keep in the small wooden box in your bedroom drawer.'

A gasp. 'How did you...how could you?'

'And, Miss Greenwood: your mother. You came here to speak to her, did you not?'

Miss Greenwood nodded. Miss Divine, without turning her head, said, 'Your mother asks why you do not wear mourning, and that–'

'But it is two years since, since–' interjected Miss Greenwood.

'Nevertheless, your mother is discomfited by your lack of respect. Know that she can see your behaviour, even from the other side.'

Miss Greenwood collapsed into snivels. 'Mother,' she moaned, 'I will do better. I will, I promise.'

'As for you, Mrs du Lesseps,' Miss Divine continued, still in the same level, otherworldly tone, 'your husband knows the location of the money you seek but will not disclose it until you replace his portrait, which you have recently removed.'

Mrs du Lesseps clapped ringed fingers to her mouth.

'Finally, Reverend Pattison.' Here Hester Divine's voice deepened, became stronger. Her eyes widened, grew, if anything, darker; and her breath came harder, faster. 'Reverend Pattison. Your wife, she refuses to speak with you. It was your controlling nature, your constant demeaning of her, that drove her to take her own life. You have managed to conceal the fact of her suicide, but she will not forgive you and it is her hope you will suffer for it, now and in the hereafter.'

Having delivered herself of this, Miss Divine emitted a deep sigh. She dropped her arms to her side, blinked herself back to the present, and sank quietly back into her seat alongside Madame Gallini, who, like the others, stared at her in amazement.

How to describe the confusion that followed? People crowded around Miss Divine, wondering at her knowledge of their secret lives. Reverend Pattison alone remained in his chair, his hands flat on the table, his head bowed. His friends – his erstwhile friends – avoided him now, stepping around him as if skirting a deep and dangerous lake. After some minutes he turned and staggered out of the library, the house, forever.

By degrees, attention returned towards Madame Gallini, who was gathering herself to leave. She was prevented by Mr Schofield.

'Sit!' he said. 'Aunt, I will escort this woman to the authorities. After, of course, she has returned the money she received today.'

'Oh! Do you really, must you? How unfortunate.'

Mr Schofield was resolute. 'How many gifts have you bestowed upon this person, Aunt?'

'It is true, James, I have, and I was about to make over a substantial portion of... oh, my dear boy, thank you. You have delivered me from... I shall see to your benefit, your inheritance, you may be sure.'

Mr Schofield bowed. 'It was my duty, nothing more, dearest Aunt. My endeavours are always for your wellbeing. Now come, *Madame*, make ready. Miss Divine,' he added, 'you will accompany us. Please bring the carpet bag you carried with you.'

With a cry, Mrs Snelling intervened. 'Oh, James, no! Can you not excuse Miss Divine from this... this... oh, Miss Divine, you are a true medium.' She darted forward and grasped Miss Divine's hand in her own.

Mrs Snelling was closely followed by Mrs du Lesseps, who echoed her sentiments.

'I would not do anything to hurt you, Aunt,' said Mr Schofield. 'Miss Divine, how willing a participant were you in this farrago?'

With some dignity, Miss Divine explained. 'Madame granted me employment when I was penniless. How could I, a single woman without protection, reject such an opportunity, no matter how questionable? I would have been thrown onto the street. As I will be again, for I no longer have anywhere to live, no money and no prospects. How am I to exist from now on?'

At this, both Mrs Snelling and Mrs du Lesseps surged forward, each seeking to outdo the other with offers of support. Finally the ladies agreed to band together and pay Miss Divine a handsome stipend until she found her feet. In return, she would continue the séances in Madame Gallini's stead.

'In the meantime,' insisted Mrs Snelling, 'let me give you this ring, which will look splendid on your hand. I will brook no refusal,' she added, noticing Miss Divine's reticence. 'It is what Julian would wish.'

Later, much later, they caught their breath sufficiently to talk.

'You were perfect, Hester,' said James. 'Better than I could have imagined.' He lit a cheroot from the bedside candle.

Hester took the cheroot from him, puffed, and returned it. She said, 'I was right when I said your aunt wouldn't recognise me. Nobody knows a maid out of uniform.'

James pulled her close. 'I owe you a great deal. Without you, I would never have contrived this scheme. At least now Aunt Violet will stop squandering her money – my inheritance – on Madame Gallini.' James Schofield gave the name the same European intonation Madame herself had employed.

'No. She will squander it on me instead. On *us*, I mean. And you must stay close to your aunt, because without you, how will I discover their secrets?'

'Indeed.' James burrowed his face into her neck. 'You have secured our fortune, you clever little thing! And you declaimed with such conviction that even I was convinced of your sincerity.' Then he drew back and, leaning on one elbow, asked, 'How did you know Reverend Pattison's wife took her own life?'

'What do you mean?' Hester moved her fingers to make the candlelight glint on the jewel Mrs Snelling had given her.

'Why, when you accused the Reverend of driving her to suicide.'

Hester looked at him in puzzlement. 'What are you talking about?'

'You do not remember what you said to him?'

'You gave me no information about the Reverend, so there was nothing I could say.'

They drew apart. James stared at Hester, who was again admiring her ring. So she was a true medium. She had the power to channel the afterlife. He became aware that, beyond the candles, the room was dark; and beyond the room, the night outside darker still. His heart was in his throat.

Hester Divine smiled to herself. It was desirable, she felt, to have James Schofield fear her, just a little. That way, she would always hold the upper hand. As far as Reverend Pattison was concerned, well, maids learned more secrets than most and her web of sister-maids stretched wide. This, together with Madame's thorough training, offered Hester a large and profitable future. She would not waste it. She stretched luxuriantly and turned her back on James Schofield.

THE SOCIETY OF
GENTLEWOMEN

THE EVENTS I AM ABOUT TO DESCRIBE ARE SO EXTRAORDINARY, SO beyond the pale, I find myself unable to make them public knowledge. If they are not believed – and who would countenance such strange things? – then my reputation, and that of my friend Sherlock Holmes, would be forever destroyed. If believed, they would cause a general riot, possibly even lead to civil war. So I will set them down here and seal them for future generations who may review them more dispassionately than mine can today.

It was an icy evening in February, and Holmes and I lounged companionably in his rooms in Baker Street. I buried myself in a medical text while Holmes, sprawled in an armchair, pulled on his pipe and stared at the fire. Suddenly he sprang to his feet, crying, 'Stir yourself, Watson! We have half an hour to get there.'

'Where?'

'To dinner, of course. Quick, man, change immediately. Otherwise we shall miss it altogether.'

Fifteen minutes later we were ensconced in a hansom on our way, according to Holmes' instructions, to Boodles Gentleman's Club.

'Enlighten me, Holmes,' I begged, adjusting my dinner jacket. 'I don't want to look a complete fool, you know.'

'I have a standing invitation to dine,' he said, 'with a certain group of men. While all are worth talking to, tonight I seek only one.' With that, he lapsed into silence.

Given Holmes' loathing of society I was surprised to discover he was a member of Boodles and frequented it enough to be warmly greeted by an elderly attendant, who led us to a private room. There we found three men at a round table set with damask and glittering crystal.

One of the men, stocky, with fair hair swept to one side and a luxuriant moustache, rose to welcome us. 'Holmes! Here you are at last. Delighted, quite delighted.'

He leaned across the table to shake first Holmes' hand and then mine, giving me a shrewd upward glance as he did. 'You, if I am not mistaken, are Doctor John Watson. I am Herbert Wells.'

He indicated the others. 'Allow me to introduce you. This fine figure is Conan Doyle. Like you, Watson, he is a doctor.' Doyle, who sported an even larger moustache than Wells, inclined his head. 'And this,' Wells indicated the clean-shaven man to his left, 'is Jacob Wickert.'

Wickert was dark, not tall, and elegant in a fine dinner suit. His face displayed a guarded weariness, but his smile was genuine and his greeting warm.

'Ah, Mr Wickert,' said Holmes, making a bow. 'Congratulations on your recent good fortune. I hope you found it worth the risk.'

Wickert looked dumbfounded. He turned on Wells. 'HG,' he demanded, 'Our agreement was to maintain absolute secrecy.'

Wells replied, 'I have had no contact with Mr Holmes for several months.'

'Then how?'

'Well,' said Holmes, allowing the waiter to arrange a napkin on his lap, 'I see your nails are bitten to the quick.' At this, Wickert, who had been idly passing a pen between his fingers, took a startled look at his hands and quickly pushed them into his trouser pockets. Holmes continued. 'You have thus been in a worrying situation. At the same time, your dinner suit is new and if I am not mistaken, tailored by Gieves. A work of art, but one only few can afford. I conclude any distress you endured ended well and to your financial advantage. Waiter! The porterhouse, if you please.'

The company surveyed my friend in wonder. Doyle, in particular, regarded him as if he were a new and exciting discovery. Any further discussion of Wickert, however, was forestalled by Holmes turning to Wells and saying, with some gravity, 'I come here tonight, Wells, to seek a favour.'

'Holmes!' You cannot mean–'

'I do. I see from Mr Wickert your new machine has been tested and its efficacy confirmed?'

Wickert again exclaimed, 'How...how can you possibly know?'

His eyes still fixed on Wells, Holmes said offhandedly, 'The pen you had in your hands a few minutes ago is constructed of a material I do not recognise. I conclude it comes from the future.'

I was jolted into speech. 'The future! Holmes, what can you possibly mean?'

Holmes raised a hand to stay my question, 'In good time, Watson,' he said. He and Wells stared at each other in a silent battle of wills. Holmes prevailed, and Wells sank back into his chair, raising his hands in surrender. 'Very well, Holmes. If you must. The risk is yours, though. If anything goes amiss, on your head be it.'

'The risk, as well as the responsibility, is mine,' Holmes said, satisfied.

Just then the waiter returned with our meals. It was several minutes before we could speak freely again.

'Holmes,' I insisted, 'what is going on?'

Holmes took up his glass, sipped, and said, 'Mr Wells is, among other things, an inventor. For some time he has worked on a machine which travels in time, both the future and the past. Three years ago he sent a man to the future,' here he paused, and the air around us seemed to cool, 'but that man has not yet returned.'

Wells looked solemn. Doyle, who seemed unsurprised at this revelation, said, 'By the way, HG, have you tried to contact him via a medium?'

Holmes spoke mildly but dismissively. 'Every great endeavour must endure some failure.' He turned back to me. 'The point, Watson,' he continued, 'is that in those three years Wells has built a new, improved machine. Is that not so, Wickert?'

Wickert, giving up any pretence of secrecy, nodded his head.

'You mean,' I could not believe what I was hearing. 'You have journeyed to–'

'The year 2020,' said Wickert. 'To London. It was–'

Holmes cut across him. 'What form did you take?'

'Form?' I was completely lost. 'What do you mean, *form*?'

Wells, seeing my agitation, explained. 'In order to allow travel across time, my new machine dissolves – that is, it disaggregates – its passenger. Every cell in his body is separated and then, on arrival, realigned. This means he can arrive in any form he chooses. For example, Wickert chose to visit London as–'

'As a youth, a groomsman,' Wickert interrupted. 'I thought it would render me less noticeable. Unfortunately I did not realise there are no horse-drawn vehicles in the future.'

'Yes, yes.' Holmes was impatient. 'Had you consulted me I would have told you as much. In any case, the cells recover themselves on the journey home and as you see, Wickert has returned to his native state. What I seek, Wells, is a short journey. Much as I desire to explore the distant future, I wish at the moment to travel just one week hence.'

Wells looked confused. 'I don't understand you, Holmes. What use is that?'

'I have my reasons,' Holmes said. 'More to the point, Wells: I wish to arrive as a woman.'

'*As a woman?*' Wells exclaimed. All at the table regarded Holmes with the utmost incredulity. Eventually Doyle recovered enough to ask, 'Why *on earth* would you want to become a woman?'

Holmes' face lost its habitual ironic expression and when he spoke, his voice was low. 'To prevent a wrong, my friends, to an individual and to society. If it suits you, Wells, Watson and I will attend your laboratory at 3 o'clock tomorrow afternoon.'

We spent the remainder of the evening listening to Wickert's report of life in London in the 21st century. Some of his stories, such as the arrival of a new and deadly plague, were frightening. It seemed my dreams of a world cured of disease were not to be realised. Other stories I considered merely fancy: the idea of a pocket-sized mechanical brain, for example, was too preposterous to entertain.

Throughout Wickert's account, however, the thought of Holmes' proposed adventure coursed through my mind, unsettling me. Not even the excellent food and wine helped.

By the time we returned to Baker Street it was close to midnight. I was about to depart when Holmes stopped me. 'Watson,' he said, 'will you join me tomorrow or not? I will think no worse of you if you eschew this endeavour.'

'I'll let you know in the morning,' I said. 'But before I make up my mind you must tell me why you wish to undertake this journey, and why you feel the need to assume the female sex to do so.'

'Join me for a late-night brandy and I will show you a letter that explains everything.'

I stoked the fire while Holmes poured the brandy. Then he extracted a letter from his inside pocket and handed it to me. Written on cream deckle paper in a firm sloping hand, and dated 9th February, 1897, it read:

My dear Mr Holmes,

You told me once that, should I ever require assistance, I could rely on you. I appeal to you now on a matter of critical urgency.

As you know, my husband, Richard, and I have for some time worked to improve the status of women in this country. Last year we established the Women's Franchise League, an organisation advocating among other things the right of women to vote.

At the same time we also formed a small and utterly secret group, The Society of Gentlewomen. Whereas the Franchise League operates in the public arena, the Society aims to progress our goal by private means, such as personal connection and advocacy at the highest levels. Membership of the group is restricted to six women, all chosen for their intellectual, political or social importance. I will not commit their names to paper, though you would recognise everyone.

Yesterday I received distressing news. The editor of The London Chronicle *visited me, enquiring about "a secret society of women seeking to politically undermine the nation". I professed ignorance, of course. He allowed he knew little but claimed that, "after Thursday February 18 he would expose this group of traitors to the fullest extent".*

Our Society next meets on that very date. Someone must have betrayed us, but I cannot fathom who, nor the cause. The women in the Society are at the foremost edge of national consciousness. They have placed their reputations at risk by being associated with it at all. Were their involvement revealed, they would lose everything.

I do not know how to proceed. Should I cancel the meeting? Should I disband the Society? If men were permitted I would seek your attendance, but they are not. I therefore beg your advice, as well as any assistance you are able to provide, to prevent this great calamity.

Your friend,

(Mrs) Emmeline Pankhurst

'Is Mrs Pankhurst not demanding the vote for women? Surely it is better for husbands to vote on behalf of wives, and fathers for daughters? And is it safe for the weaker sex to vote at all? Their lack of suitable temperament, their imbalance of mind'

Holmes sighed. 'I admit, Watson, I once thought as you do. However, Mrs Pankhurst convinced me otherwise. I met her, you know, in relation to the case of the Maharaja's necklace. She argues compellingly that men and women are equals and that if we treat them as such, all of society will benefit. I concur. If her cause, and that of her friends, is lost, the condition of women in this country will be set back decades, even centuries. We cannot let that happen. I wrote to her yesterday, assuring her I would come to her aid.'

'Surely it would be safer if they did not meet, or, as she writes, they disbanded the Society entirely?'

'Ah, but then the traitor would remain undiscovered, and all endeavours thereafter be subject to extreme risk. No, the answer is to hold the meeting and in doing so, flush out the conspiracy.'

Holmes set his glass firmly on the mantelpiece. 'So to bed. Will you give me your answer in the morning? I must know early. We will need to purchase the requisite apparel.'

I passed a restless night, to say the least. Unlike Holmes, I remained unconvinced of the value of Mrs Pankhurst's cause. Surely affairs of state were better conducted in the care of men, as they had always been? Besides, the venture was perilous. Yes, Wells' machine had worked at least once, but what if it failed this time? What if Holmes and I died? Worse, what if we could not transmogrify back into our usual states and had to live forever as women? What a terrible fate that would be.

On the other hand, the prospect of seeing Holmes at work on such an exciting case had great appeal. Besides, this would be an adventure like no other, surpassing all that Holmes and I had so far experienced.

So I seesawed back and forth. In the end, to resolve the matter, I tossed a coin. Heads I would stay, tails I would go. As the penny spun in the air I found myself hoping for tails, and tails it was.

At three o'clock precisely, Holmes and I presented ourselves at Wells' house at Worcester Park. Wells wasted no time on pleasantries, but escorted us to an adjoining building, apparently a disused barn. It was empty save for his machine, a complicated assembly the size of a small carriage and bristling with shining copper cogs and gears. In the centre, two empty seats awaited their occupants. The whole sat on three wheels and appeared, to say the least, fantastical.

A gate was built into the side of the contraption. Wells felt inside, undid the catch, and beckoned us closer. 'The machine is easy to operate,' he said. 'I have already configured the information enabling you to adopt a female form. All you need do is enter your desired destination here; manipulate this to show the required date,' he pointed to a dial set in a wooden panel, 'depress this knob here, and pull this lever. In a few moments you will arrive at your destination, as women. To return, you repeat the process.' He hesitated. 'I must reiterate, Holmes, the risks involved–'

Holmes interrupted, with greater cheer than I felt. 'Thank you, HG. We appreciate your concern, but we are determined to proceed, aren't we, Watson? Now let us board our vessel and sail into the unknown.' And before I could reply he climbed into the further seat, leaving me, clutching two carpetbags with women's clothes, to clamber alongside.

We fastened the hatch from the inside. Wells helped us secure leather straps over our shoulders, and we donned the eye protectors he gave us. I watched as Holmes depressed keys to enter a date – 18 February, 1897 – and an address which, I was surprised to see, was close to our Baker Street lodgings.

'Why are we not travelling directly to Mrs Pankhurst's house? And why, when we can choose any date, have you decided upon that of the meeting?'

'Because our first task upon arrival – indeed, our most important task – will be to conceal our machine or risk it being discovered and losing our sole means of return. For that reason I arranged the use of a coach house in East Street. We will leave the machine there and make the short walk to Russell Square. As to the date: I am convinced, given my innate talents, it will take a few hours only to expose the culprit and prevent the crime.'

Holmes' ability to plan ahead was, as usual, impressive. Before I could compliment him, however, he depressed the knob Wells had indicated. The machine began to throb. He reached out and slowly drew a lever towards us. There was a roaring in my ears and then we entered a maelstrom of swirling darkness with a chill wind battering us, as if determined on annihilation. The whole machine shuddered against the force of it. I clutched the straps as tightly as I could, terrified lest we be blown into a million pieces.

And then, with an abrupt jolt, we stopped. Trembling, I removed my eye-glasses and looked around. We were no longer in a barn in Worcester Park. Instead, the machine, with us inside it, rested serenely within in a large brick structure with two small carriages pulled up at the far end.

We had succeeded. I could hardly credit it. I turned to my friend in congratulation, but no words came. I could only gape at what I saw.

Holmes as I knew him had vanished. In his place, in men's clothes far too large for her, sat – a woman! I knew this was our chosen form, but my rational mind could not comprehend the transformation. She – that is, the woman – had something of Holmes about her. It was the eyes, I realised. She had his grey, piercing eyes. As for the rest of her, her face was angular, her hair brown, short and waved. That was all I could see.

It came to me that if Holmes had changed form, so had I. I looked down. Unlike Holmes, my clothes were not loose. In fact, they, and the straps that contained me still, were uncomfortably tight. I now apprehended the cause. I had – and here I gasped in horror – I had acquired a large pair of bosoms which pressed themselves against my shirt and waistcoat in a disagreeable fashion. I put my hand up and felt them and, I confess, further down. I was...I was altogether a woman. Then I examined my face. My moustache had vanished! On further exploration I discovered my hair had increased in volume and length, settling now about my shoulders.

'My good god, Holmes,' I said, and stopped. My voice was no longer my voice. I sounded female. I fell silent.

Holmes surveyed me with interest. 'I say, Watson,' he observed, in a rather spinsterish register, 'you do make a fine figure of a woman. Come. Let us extricate ourselves and make our way to our destination.'

I was somewhat stung by his observation, though I could not have said why. We descended and Holmes rummaged through the carpetbags we had brought. Holding up now a stay, now a bodice, he exclaimed, 'How is one supposed to deal with these?'

'Let me show you,' I offered, having helped my wife dress on many occasions. At once Holmes stripped off his garments. I felt myself redden, and looked away. A naked female confronted me. Slim, yes, and hardly an ingénue; but, for all that, not unattractive.

'Watson!' Holmes demanded. 'We waste precious time. Undress, for we are women together, you know.'

'I will arrange things for you first,' I mumbled. Somehow, I managed to clothe my friend in all the many items that constitute a woman's attire, and to secure his hair with combs. Holmes spoke not, except when I laced his stays. 'Good lord!' he exclaimed. 'How are women expected to function when they can barely breathe?'

I turned my back on him and, fumbling, subjected myself to similar exertions. Eventually there we stood, in our skirts, belts, blouses, and over-jackets. I bundled my hair into a bun, as I had seen my Mary do, and we donned hats. Now we appeared exactly as women. Then I corrected myself. *We were women!* I wished we had a mirror.

'Off we go, Watson,' Holmes said cheerfully and, with some effort, inched open one side of a heavy wooden door and edged through. Immediately he stumbled, for we were wearing shoes with heels which, though low, seemed designed to impede rather than improve motion.

We shut the door behind us and made our way towards Bloomsbury. To say I felt awkward was to understate the matter. Much of my energy was spent adjusting to my unfamiliar shape, since my hefty front seemed to pull me forward, my corseted waist to force me back and my long skirt to catch under my already tight shoes.

No sooner had we rounded the corner into Baker Street than I heard whistling and cat-calling. The noise emanated from workmen seated in front of a scaffold. They were looking at us.

'Here they are,' said one. 'Two likelier lasses, eh? Come say hello, dearies!'

'Oh, Davey, you like them old, do ya?'

'Unsteady on their feet, ain't they,' said another. 'Had a couple too many, darlin'?'

'Look at the bubbies on that one,' observed yet another.

Two of the men rose and made to address us. Fortunately, at that moment, a policeman appeared. The workmen subsided and Holmes and I scurried past. For the rest of the walk, I glanced neither right nor left. Did all women suffer such vilification? And, without physical strength, how did they withstand attack?

In this manner we continued to Bloomsbury, arriving at an unprepossessing front door in a row of identical frontages. Holmes knocked, we heard footsteps, and a few minutes later we were confronted by a middle-aged maid, diminutive, and of a singularly sour disposition.

'Yes?'

'Please tell Mrs Pankhurst that...'

I realised with a start that neither Holmes nor I had considered naming our female selves. Holmes, however, continued smoothly, '...that Miss Charlotte Holmes, cousin of Sherlock Holmes, and her companion Miss Johanna Watson, have arrived.'

'Is she expecting you?'

'She will welcome us.'

'Wait here.' The maid shut the door in our faces. Holmes stood back, unperturbed by her surliness. In a few minutes she returned, much more amenable, followed by a woman who approached with outstretched arms. 'Miss Holmes, Miss Watson,' she declared, 'come in, come in! Mabel, tea, if you please.'

Mabel scurried off. Mrs Pankhurst led us to a small, rather shabby drawing room. She invited us to sit. I noticed Holmes sink into an armchair and cross one leg over the other, as he – or rather, *she* was used to do. I must now, I knew, think of her as Charlotte Holmes. I caught her eye and she hurriedly rearranged herself, hands in her lap, ankles firmly together. I adopted a similar position in a straight-backed chair. It was hellishly uncomfortable.

Mrs Pankhurst looked nothing like I imagined a suffragette would. She was a handsome woman, with glossy black hair and high cheekbones. In her elegant afternoon gown, she would have graced the noblest of houses.

'Please do not mind Mabel,' she said. 'She has cared for me since childhood and I trust her with my life.'

'Yes, yes,' said Charlotte. 'We do not have much time. By the end of the day we shall know who plans to divulge your secrets to *The London Chronicle.*'

Mrs Pankhurst looked amazed. 'Really? I have been mulling over the problem for days and can find no clue to her identity.'

Charlotte stretched out a hand. 'Have no fear. All will be well.'

'What is the plan?'

At that moment, Mabel returned, bearing a tray with a silver tea-service. My heart fell as I thought about how I must now drink and eat as a woman, and how differently men and women live their daily lives, even to the smallest actions. I resolved to observe Mrs Pankhurst and copy her mannerisms.

Charlotte explained, 'You must contrive to have me attend this afternoon's meeting. Where will you gather? Surely, given the risk, not at this house, where any watcher could identify members?'

'No. We will meet in a vacant house close by. Miss Holmes, given your cousin's fame, I am confident our group will welcome you. Your companion, however, I fear, is not well-enough known. I apologise for my rudeness, Miss Watson.'

'That is not the intention,' said Charlotte. 'I propose Johanna remain here as a servant, perhaps a governess.'

As a servant? I wished to object but knew I could not. However, Charlotte's next words brought comfort. 'Johanna is extremely observant. The traitor could well be working in your household, and she will watch for tell-tale signs. Please describe to me those in your employ.'

Mrs Pankhurst inclined her head. 'We are not wealthy, you understand. Apart from Mabel, our housekeeper, we employ two maids, a cook and a footman. All have been with us for at least three years.' She lifted a silver bell from the table beside her and shook it. In a minute, Mabel appeared.

'Mabel,' said Mrs Pankhurst, 'Miss Watson here is being considered for the post of governess. Will you introduce her to our household? She will remain with you while Miss Holmes and I make an afternoon call.'

'Will she not meet the children, Ma'am?'

'Not today. Alice will take them to the park.'

From the pursing of Mabel's lips, I could see she disbelieved her mistress. However, she merely said, 'Come, then, Miss. They're all below.'

Obediently, if reluctantly, I followed Mabel through a door, down stairs, and into a smallish kitchen where a cook, assisted by an elderly maid, chopped vegetables at a table. A strapping young footman stoked a stove on which several pots boiled. A minute later another maid entered, exclaiming, 'Oh, that Christobel, she's a...' She fell silent when she saw us.

Mabel clapped her hands. Everyone stopped what they were doing. She announced, 'This here next to me is Miss Watson. Mrs P is thinking of her for governess. Miss Watson, that's Mrs Carter.' Here Cook looked up, nodded, and returned to chopping, 'Violet Jackson,' pointing at the maid next to Cook, 'Terrence Foley,' indicating the footman, 'and Alice Croucher. There now, you have all of us.'

Alice Croucher said, 'Good luck with them kids, Miss. What a handful.'

'Enough of you, Alice.' Mabel, it was clear, held sway in this establishment.

Normal duties recommenced. I took a seat at the kitchen table. 'You eaten?' Cook asked me.

'Yes, thank you.' How could I tell her I had indeed had a light collation of bread and meat, but a week ago, and as a man? I lowered myself onto a stool.

The maid Alice bolted a slice of bread and ham and rising, said, 'I'm told to take the children to the park,' and was gone.

Violet Jackson and Terrence Foley continued their labours. I remained seated, disconcerted at the speed with which I had been relegated below stairs. After a while my reverie was disturbed by Cook, who asked, 'Where've you come from, then?'

I could not conjure an immediate response and my hesitation was misconstrued as recalcitrance. Cook lowered her voice to a stage whisper, 'Thinks she's better than us, innit?'

Terrence, the footman chortled and, straightening, enquired, 'Cook, this fire's doing good. Mind if I go outside for a...' and he made the sign of someone pulling on a cigarette.

'Be quick, then,' said Cook.

Something in the way Terrence spoke, a meaningfulness about him, filled me with unease. He exited the kitchen by a back door and after a moment I rose also. 'I will take a walk around the back garden,' I announced.

'You may take a walk around the moon for all I care,' replied Cook.

Outside, I caught sight of Terrence disappearing through a back gate. I followed. I saw him raise two fingers to his lips and whistle, and a woman in a maid's cap poked her head around the corner. They ran towards each other, met, kissed and exchanged whispers. Young love, and secret, that was all. I drew back. As I did, they separated, and I saw the maid's face. She was dazzlingly beautiful. Older than the footman, and – I had seen that face before, I knew. Where?

As I puzzled, my right ankle, unaccustomed to female shoes, twisted and I stumbled against the gate. Maid and footman turned towards me. 'I apologise,' I said, 'I was in the garden and–'

'Blinkin' nosy witch,' said the footman.

The maid regarded me directly and at that moment I recognised her. I had merely glimpsed her in person, but knew her well enough from a photograph, one held dear by my friend Holmes. He had tangled with her before, when her name was Irene Adler. She had been courtesan to kings then: so what was her business with a common footman now? I must have appeared as shocked as I felt.

I thought quickly. Even if she recognised John Watson, she would surely not connect him with me in my present state. I advanced with what I hoped was a smile.

'Johanna Watson, if you please. I am to be governess to–'

'Go *away*! Terrence hissed, intent on his amorous mission.

My head was spinning. Clearly, Miss Adler had seduced Terrence in order to obtain information about the Society of Gentlewomen. Had he already divulged it? The answer came an instant later. I heard a 'Hey!' and looked up to see Terrence gawping at the maid who had broken from him and was hurrying towards Herbrand Street. She had achieved the information she required and raced to deliver it.

What was I to do? I returned to the kitchen and, ignoring the mutterings of Cook, continued to the drawing room. Mabel was there, clearing the tea things. Perhaps – I dared not hope – I took the chance. 'Mabel,' I cried, 'you must help me. If you know where Mrs Pankhurst and Sher...Charlotte are, tell me now, for they are in grave danger.'

Mabel set down the tray. Seeing the panic in my eyes, she did not hesitate. 'Number nine, Malet Street. Mrs P always tells me where she's going.'

'Thank you.' I made for the front door.

Mabel's voice, ripe with self-satisfaction, followed. 'I *knew* you was no governess.'

It could not be long before Miss Adler reached her destination and we were visited with the consequences. Much constrained by my fiendish attire, I set off in a hobbled run to Malet Street, which was close by. Once arrived, I did not bother to knock but burst through the door and into the dining room, where six women sat around the table, deep in conversation.

I must have presented a sorry picture, my hat askew, my face red, my bosom heaving. 'They know,' I gasped. 'They're coming!' I turned to Charlotte. 'It is *The Woman*,' I told her.

'Ah,' she said, and I read understanding in her eyes. 'And the footman.'

'Yes. Did you know?'

'I suspected one of the servants must be compromised, but for proof I had to draw the conspiracy into the open.' Charlotte faced the women. 'If we leave now, we shall be exposed. It is time to put my plan into practice.'

None of the women stirred. Charlotte nodded to Mrs Pankhurst, who drew from a bag several packs of playing cards, a cloth of green baize, and some coins. She threw the cloth over the table, scattered coins upon it, and handed cards to the women around it. In a few seconds it appeared as if they were involved in nothing more sinister than a game of–

There came a loud rapping and the cry, 'Police! Open the door!'

Charlotte hissed, 'Johanna! Be seated!'

No sooner had I complied and taken up a few cards, than I heard the door flung open and into the room strode none other than Inspector Lestrade, followed by two burly policemen.

Lestrade came to a halt and, clasping the lapels of his jacket in his hands, announced, 'I am Inspector Lestrade of Scotland Yard. I have it from a reliable source that the people in this room are plotting treason.' When no response came, he called out, 'Which of you is Mrs Richard Pankhurst?' When she raised her hand, he faced her, saying, 'Mrs Pankhurst, you and your colleagues here today are accused of fomenting revolution. How do you answer this charge?'

Charlotte had risen. 'Are you the famous Inspector Lestrade?' she enquired, inclining her head to one side and tucking a strand of hair behind her neck.

Lestrade looked disconcerted, but not displeased. 'I do not think, Madam, we have met?'

'Indeed not, but my cousin, Sherlock Holmes, speaks highly of you.'

Lestrade inclined his head. 'I was not aware Mr Holmes had such a charming relative.' Then he recollected his objective. 'Mrs Pankhurst, do you have anything to say before we arrest the lot of you?'

Charlotte gave a tinkling laugh and fluttered her fingers. She seemed, in the few hours she had been a woman, to have mastered the art of flirtation. 'My goodness! Dear Inspector Lestrade, I speak for all when I say...we are indeed guilty!'

Lestrade's eyebrows rose. Before he could act, however, Charlotte continued, raising a hand to her bosom. 'Yes, we are guilty, but not of treason. Come closer – but perhaps your friends might wait outside? We are after all only women, and this room offers no escape.'

Gruffly, Lestrade instructed the constables to guard the door. When they had left, Charlotte edged conspiratorially towards him. 'I will reveal all. We are guilty of being...inveterate gamblers. There! You know the worst. We do indeed meet in secret, to play the American game, Draw Poker. We play for money, as you see. If we were men we could enjoy these pastimes openly, at a club, but alas, we are not, and therefore cannot. Besides, you see around the table women whose public reputation can bear no stain. There, for example, is Miss Florence Nightingale...' Miss Nightingale inclined her head slightly; 'that is Miss Beatrix Potter; next to her Mrs Hertha Ayrton, Mrs Millicent Fawcett and Mrs Annie Besant. If their sad addiction were made public, they would be ruined.'

By the time she had finished her "confession", Charlotte was uncomfortably close to Lestrade. She gazed appealingly at him. 'We place ourselves at your mercy. Arrest us if you must,' she cried, 'and ruin us forever!' And, hand to forehead, she swooned.

Lestrade leaped forward to support her, assisting her to an empty chair. Then he surveyed in turn the women, the table, the cards and the money. 'So,' he said slowly, 'there is no political meeting this afternoon? No group of women plotting to overturn our government?'

'Group of women?' Charlotte, all astonishment, seemed fully recovered. 'Really, Inspector! Do you think a group of *women* could in any way influence the course of our great nation?'

'I suppose not,' Lestrade conceded, discomfited. 'I appear to be misinformed. I will bid you good day. Miss?' He took her proffered hand. 'Your name, if you please?'

'Holmes, Charlotte Holmes,' she said.

'And who is the last woman at the table?

'Oh! She is my companion, Miss Johanna Watson.'

Lestrade's eyes flicked to me. He frowned. *Charlotte Holmes and Johanna Watson?* He gave his head a shake as if to say *it is not possible.*

Charlotte clasped his hand. 'You will keep our secret, dear Inspector?'

He nodded, lingering over the hand until she withdrew it. Then he departed.

Mrs Pankhurst was the first to speak. 'Brava!' she declared. 'Miss Holmes, you were wonderful.'

'Do not celebrate too soon, my dear Mrs Pankhurst,' Charlotte said, 'for the mystery is not yet solved.'

'How so? We know now it was my footman who betrayed us.'

'Your footman was a pawn in a much larger game. Will you hear my reasoning?'

The women round the table were completely attentive now, like children caught up in a bedtime story. Charlotte continued, 'A certain woman made love to your footman in order to draw from him the details of this group. That woman, as I have cause to know, is both ruthless and highly intelligent. Whether she acted from principle, because she opposes suffrage—'

'True,' interjected Miss Besant, 'many women work against our cause, Miss Gertrude Bell, for example. Apologies, Miss Holmes, please continue.'

Charlotte did so. 'Or whether she acted from principle or for financial gain, the question is this: *who directed her actions?* We must assume she did not act alone. From what I know of her, she moves in the highest circles. We need to know who set her the task, and why.'

She raised her hand to her chin, as if seeking the bowl of a pipe. Finding none, she lowered it again. 'As I said, Miss Adler – or Mrs Godfrey Norton, as she became – is extremely clever. By now she will have disappeared.'

Miss Potter spoke up, her voice surprisingly rich. 'How, then, will you find her employers?'

Charlotte answered, 'I leave that to my cousin. He is confident of bringing this matter to a successful close.'

There was a silence. Then Mrs Ayrton spoke slowly, as if thinking her way through a problem. 'Whatever happens, it seems to me The Society of Gentlewomen can continue no longer. For even if our enemies do not know our names, they know we exist. And they will not be put off, as that policeman was, by such a flimsy excuse as card playing.'

'Sadly, I must agree,' said Charlotte. 'The risk you face is too great to be ignored.'

'How then are we to proceed?' Mrs Pankhurst cried. 'Knocking on doors of the great and the good is such slow, frustrating business.'

Miss Nightingale had been silent. Older than the others and frail to the point of illness, she said now, 'Have you ever thought of doing what it is we are accused of?'

'What do you mean?'

'It seems to me,' she explained, interlacing her fingers on the table, 'that what the anti-suffrage faction fears most is our political force, the very charge brought against us today. Why do we not employ that weapon? Women may not take arms in the conventional sense but we can still protest. We can disrupt, we can strike, we can employ civil disobedience – and perhaps it is time for us to consider these means.'

'No!' This from Mrs Fawcett. 'Militant action of that sort will do more harm than good.'

All the women spoke at once. Some argued for trade unions, some for radical action. Others deplored anything but diplomacy. After a while, sitting apart from their discussion, I realised it had grown dark outside. I cleared my throat. Charlotte nodded imperceptibly. She said, 'Ladies, it is time we dispersed. Does this house give on to a back lane?'

'Yes, it does,' said Mrs Pankhurst.

'Then, in light of this afternoon's events, I suggest all except Mrs Pankhurst, Johanna and I depart that way. It is not much, but may deceive casual observation.'

The women collected their belongings and, thanking Charlotte for her help, made their way out. Mrs Pankhurst gathered the cards and tablecloth and returned them to their satchel.

Outside the house, she stopped. 'Miss Holmes,' she said, 'I am indebted to you. Could we not meet soon to continue our acquaintance?'

'I fear not,' said Charlotte. 'Johanna and I are to set out on an expedition. We will not remain here after today. I can, however, commend you to my cousin, who thinks as I do and will guide you in all things.'

'And he promises to find out who is behind this affair?'

'Yes. He expects to discover the culprit tonight, and will write to you tomorrow.'

'Well,' said Mrs Pankhurst, 'thank you once more. Do you have far to travel?'

'Not far,' said Charlotte, looking amused.

'And you will be safe, walking the streets in the dark?'

'Perfectly. *Au revoir*, Mrs Pankhurst. I wish you luck in your endeavours.'

'I too, wish you luck,' said I. 'Come, Charlotte, it is time to go home.'

The walk back was uneventful. We discovered our machine safe, resumed male attire, settled ourselves as before, and projected ourselves into the void of time. And then it was daylight and we were back in Herbert Wells' barn, and there was the man himself standing in the very spot we left him.

'By Jove,' he said. 'You only just left.'

I removed the eye goggles and felt my face. A moustache! I ran my hand over my waistcoat. Flat! And, yes, to my delight I found returned to me all the accoutrements of a healthy male. When I looked at Sherlock I saw that he too appeared as if nothing about him had ever changed. I sighed with relief.

Wells asked us for details, of course, and we told him as much of our adventure as we deemed appropriate. Then we returned to Baker Street and never was I happier in my whole life than to be back in those rooms and in my own body.

In the days following our adventure, Holmes was unusually cheerful, busying himself with his chemical experiments, whistling all the while. This was not what I expected and finally I could no longer contain myself. 'Holmes,' said I, 'your demeanour surprises me. Are you not put out by having again been bested by that woman?'

'Bested? Watson, what makes you suppose I have been bested?'

'You said yourself that to solve the mystery we had to discover who retained Miss Adler, and we have not done so.'

Holmes looked up from a bubbling test tube, his eyes alight. 'I also said I would find a solution that very day.'

I frowned. 'But here we are, returned as men, our adventure over–'

'You are mistaken, Watson. It is not yet over. Tell me, what day is it today?'

'It is Wednesday, 17 February, 1897. Why?'

'If you are interested in taking up the chase, meet me here at two o'clock tomorrow.'

The next day found me returned to Baker Street, where my call of 'Hello!' was met with the reply, 'In here, Watson.' I opened the door to the living room to find in place of the elegant detective, a disreputable labourer in flat cap, dirty neckerchief, worn boots and scruffy coat. It took me a long moment to realise they were one and the same.

'I take it you know our destination?' enquired Holmes.

'I do.' I had finally, I thought, discerned the strategy.

'Thus the disguise,' Holmes explained. 'The Woman knows me. She would probably not recognise you, but to be safe we should alter your appearance as well.' He handed me a dank and malodorous coat, a brown scarf and a cap similar to his own. 'Remove your watch-fob, Watson,' he ordered. 'Detach your collar and button your coat to the top. Smear this soot on your face and hands. Your shoes as well, for shoes describe the man entirely.'

Soon we were on the street, making our way towards Russell Square without, this time, any comment from the workmen still idling in front of their scaffold. On arrival, Holmes led me to the doorway of a building from which we could see the gate at the back of Mrs Pankhurst's house and the street beyond.

'What do we do now?' I asked.

'Now, we wait.' And Holmes sat comfortably on the doorstep, taking up a pipe and looking for all the world like he belonged there. I joined him and we watched in silence.

Half an hour later I saw, in the distance, two women. With a jolt, I realised I was looking at Holmes and myself in our feminine incarnation. It was difficult to comprehend, although I could not help but notice Johanna Watson was, as Holmes had mentioned, a fine figure of a woman. I confess I found this fact most gratifying.

Still we waited, our attention focused on the gate. It swung open. Terrence, the footman, showed first his torso, then his whole body. He lifted two fingers to his lips and whistled. As before, from around the corner, the figure of a maid appeared. She scanned the street, noticing but discounting the two rough workmen. She ran to the footman. They spoke, then kissed and fondled each other. Behind them, I saw myself – that is,

Johanna – fall against the gate. As before, the footman swung round. This gave the maid the excuse she needed. She turned and ran back the way she had come.

Holmes sprang to his feet. 'Watson!' he said. I needed no instruction, since I too had readied myself for pursuit.

It was easy, as men, to keep pace with the maid, who continued to the square where a brougham carriage sat waiting, its liveried coachman holding loosely the reins of two exquisite coal-black horses. Curtained windows hid its occupants from view, but when the maid – when Irene Adler, rather – drew alongside, the door opened sufficiently to admit her and we saw, just for a moment and very clearly, the face of the single passenger.

I stopped in my tracks. 'Did you–?'

'Yes,' said Holmes, grimly. 'I did. No mistaking that face.'

The door opened again and Miss Adler emerged, giving a whistle every bit as piercing as that of the footman earlier. From the bushes behind came Lestrade and his two policemen. She spoke briefly to them and they strode off, presumably to disrupt Mrs Pankhurst's meeting. Adler remounted and the coachman gathered his reins. The carriage departed.

'What should we do now?' I asked Holmes.

Still regarding the carriage, he answered, 'Nothing. There is nothing we can do.'

'Do you think his mother...?'

Holmes shook his head. 'Queen Victoria opposes women's suffrage, that we know. She, however, would never adopt such underhand tactics. She is old now, and as her heir, Edward must be preparing to take up the throne when she dies. Her view of his abilities, and her unwillingness to include him in affairs of state, is well known. Perhaps he hopes to win her trust by exposing The Society of Gentlewomen, but–' Holmes' voice tightened and he spoke with some bitterness. 'Perhaps Miss Adler has used her charms to persuade him to this action, and who knows what shadowy forces propel her?'

I did not comment. The whole world knew of Prince Edward's paramours and it must have galled Holmes to think of Irene Adler as one.

We retraced our steps. Holmes said, 'I will convey our discovery to Mrs Pankhurst in person. This is too dangerous a matter to commit to paper. At least now she will know her enemy and may proceed accordingly. I will stress to her the value of civil disobedience which, I believe, is the major weapon left to the suffragettes.'

He fell silent. As we drew close to Baker Street, however, he gave a short, sharp laugh. 'I am unsure whom to pity more,' he observed, 'the prince or Irene Adler. Let us see who prevails.'

At the door of 221B, he paused. 'If you don't mind, Watson,' he said, 'I would prefer my own company tonight.' And with that, he shut his front door behind him.

So ended the affair of The Society of Gentlewomen. Never have I experienced so strange an adventure and never have I counted myself luckier to emerge unscathed. Nevertheless, with time, tensions faded and life became as before. Holmes returned to his old occupations and, with me at his side, to other adventures.

He never spoke of the suffrage matter and I too refrained from mentioning it. One evening, however, as I was warming my feet by the fire, he flung himself into his usual armchair, saying, 'Watson, I have a question for you.'

'Yes? I am all ears.'

'When you were a woman, how did you feel in your mind?'

'I'm not sure what you mean, Holmes.'

'Did you feel less intelligent, more emotional, less *able*?'

'No, I felt as before. I was myself, in a woman's body.'

'*Exactly*! And knowing that, do you still oppose the right of women to vote?'

I conceded the point. 'I have had time to think about it,' I said. 'Women are equal to us in intellect and should thus have equal rights.'

Holmes gave a satisfied grunt. He subsided and, taking up a magazine which had arrived that morning, perused it with great concentration. After a while he held it open for me to see. He said, 'Watson, what think you of this?'

Bewildered, I answered, 'I think it is a woman's evening dress.'

'Yes, but is it not charming? Do you think it would become me?'

AUTHOR'S NOTE

I had great fun researching and writing this story. All the historical characters in it are contemporaneous, but please don't look too closely at where each of them was in 1897! If you haven't heard of some of the members of The Society of Gentlewoman (and I hadn't heard of Herta Ayrton or Annie Besant) then do look them up. They are amazing women and shouldn't be forgotten.

EVIL THOUGHTS

MRS MARSH LAY IN BED THINKING EVIL THOUGHTS.

They had a shape, these thoughts: they were huge, black raptors that left a vapour trail. She sent them over the fence into the yard next door. She imagined them perched, wings settling, on the roof of the neighbours' house. Perhaps they would cause one of the neighbours to fall asleep and drop a cigarette, and their house would burn down.

Then the dog would stop barking. It barked most nights. Lying awake, listening, over time she had worked out what made it bark. At eight it wanted to be fed, or go for a walk, and so it barked. It started up again at one, when the son, Sam, came home from his night shift. At four, it barked yet again. She wasn't sure why. Could be possums.

The dog was big and the yard small. But it was not just the barking that kept Mrs Marsh awake – it was waiting for the barking to stop, and then waiting for it to start again. It made her so tense she could feel her heart pumping blood.

Tonight she stayed in bed. Usually, she got up and turned on the lights because they could see the lights and would know the dog had disturbed her. She'd tried phoning them, even at two in the morning. At first Sam apologised but did nothing to stop the barking. Lately, when Mrs Marsh tried to phone, she got a recorded message saying the number had been disconnected.

They'd had the dog for eight months. When they'd brought it home, it whined all night. The morning after the third night, she went to their house. The mother answered the door. *No English*, she gestured. But wait, she would fetch Sam, her son, whose English was very good.

Sam was a soft-bodied young man who spoke to her courteously. He explained it was a rescue puppy and that it would whine until it settled down. He realised it was a nuisance and he was sorry, but could she have a bit of patience? Certainly she could, relieved to find the problem would go away.

But of course it did not. The whine became a bark, that was all. At first Sam made excuses but later he shouted at her for disturbing his mother, who, he said, was ill. Mrs Marsh wrote a letter explaining she too would become ill if she didn't sleep. Nothing worked. She lay in her bed or sat in her living room weeping with anger and frustration.

She felt she couldn't be the only one affected by the dog and called a meeting of the body corporate. All six tenants came but none seemed to mind the barking, perhaps because hers was the only unit backing directly onto the yard. All the others claimed to sleep just perfectly.

The lass in Number One suggested Mrs Marsh might be making too much of the situation, that she was taking the matter too seriously, to the point of obsession. Mrs Marsh, she recommended, should try to relax more. Meditation was working for her, she said, so perhaps it would help Mrs Marsh as well.

Mrs Marsh complained to the police, who referred her to the local council, who, after six weeks, sent round a man. He said there was no evidence the barking constituted noise pollution. He would, however, send a noise abatement order to the neighbours. It was the best he could do.

She considered baiting the dog but baiting was a hit and miss affair and everyone would suspect her. She thought of shooting the dog from her balcony, with a high-powered shotgun with a lens or whatever it was that made things visible in the dark. Where would she, at her age, get hold of equipment like that? Also, she knew from the TV, you could tell where a bullet came from by the trajectory.

Burning the house down was easier. The optimal time would be while the mother was out, but she rarely left the house. So the mother would have to go too. And what if the dog escaped the fire? No, he was kept on a lead in the yard. That, after all, was part of the problem. What if one of the other residents telephoned the fire brigade? They were bound to, and arson would be suspected. Still, they wouldn't think she had started it.

On reflection, burning the house down was the most practical plan. It was more workable than poisoning Sam and his mother, which would involve her buying poison somewhere and injecting it into food or preferably a carton of milk in their food deliveries, which were left on the front step. The injection part wouldn't be insurmountable. She had the timing down pat. Buying the poison would be hard. She regretted not having done the course on Herbs and Healing when the Number One lass suggested it. Would Mrs Marsh like to come too? For three months, fifty pots of herbs had struggled on the downstairs balcony and then the possums got to them and Herbs and Healing went the way of Find Yourself, Futurity and soon, presumably, Meditation.

Mrs Marsh wished there was a course in Practical Black Magic.

This made her smile through her tears. The dog had started its one o'clock session and she heard Sam's car. She recognised it by a knocking in the engine. She got out of bed and stood behind the lace curtain, watching Sam calm the dog before going inside. Perhaps she could get him discharged from his job, could ring up and tell his boss Sam kept a dog that kept barking. What good would that do? Burning the house down seemed more sensible.

She would go to the security parking section downstairs, and take the drum of petrol that Number Three kept – illegally – in case of strikes. How would she carry it? She would steal a shopping trolley and wheel it round to the neighbour's house, where she would sprinkle the petrol all over and light it.

What if someone saw her? What if Number Three reported his petrol missing? She sighed. There were always problems. Perhaps one of her past pupils, some young lout, would, for $100, consider killing a dog? What about Stanley Oliphant? She imagined the conversation, "Good morning, Stanley. It's Mrs Marsh here, I taught you in high school. I know you've done several stints in remand, and was wondering..."

Again, this made her smile. Her thoughts went back to Sam. His car didn't sound healthy at all.

That was an idea. She could quite easily do something to the engine. She could sneak down, between barking sessions – no, wait, she would have to do it during the four o'clock possum session, so the barking would be natural. Then she could cut a brake cable or something and when Sam came to use his car, he would crash.

Even if he didn't die, even if he were only crippled for life, would they keep the dog? Surely not. She could do a course in car maintenance: Number One would know where to go. But she mustn't ask. There must be no suspicion.

She would find out about the course tomorrow. And she would time herself to see how long it took to push a full shopping trolley from her block to their house. She could be back in her unit before the fire took hold. All she'd need do was throw a firecracker from her balcony. And she should do a bit of research before discarding the poison idea.

At last the barking stopped. She climbed back into bed and sank into the silence. She adjusted her pillows. It was hard to keep thinking evil thoughts when there was no noise, and she imagined the big evil raptors lifting their sharp, vicious beaks to sniff the air, and taking off, the huge silent spans of feathers beating into the night.

Only once before had Mrs Marsh conjured evil thoughts, and that was a long time ago. Of course, from time to time she'd had nasty thoughts, when a pupil tested her patience, or a parent was rude, but only once before had things reached this pitch.

Long ago, she'd been married, and her husband had nagged. How he'd nagged. She remembered when he went away for a week, how softly quiet the world became, how her head filled with good and serene thoughts settling inside her like feathered doves. Then he came back, and the nagging began again and she was left enduring it, thinking evil thoughts just as she was doing now. Then it stopped, and so did her husband.

Her late husband.

IN MEMORIAM

Mr Tilley died doing the crossword. No surprise there: he did the crossword every morning. You could set your watch by him. Every day at ten sharp, the library doors opened and Mr Tilley shuffled in, thermos and Tupperware in hand, the same greeting every time, a single dip of the head.

'Morning, Mr Tilley!' I'd reply, overdoing the cheer because I knew the story – how nearly 50 years ago his young wife had been swept out to sea, lost forever, and how he'd channelled his grief into this library, commissioning, funding and overseeing its construction, insisting it be named the Susan J Tilley Memorial Library, to honour her love of words.

For nearly 50 years, too, from when the library opened, Mr Tilley spent his mornings here. He chose the same chair each time, set out his provisions in exactly the same order and fetched the previous day's *Herald*. Users weren't supposed to write in it but I made an exception for Mr Tilley.

He would read the newspaper first, thoroughly, then fold it very neatly so the crossword was uppermost and begin, working out anagrams in pencil in a small spiral-bound notebook. When he got stuck he'd ask me for help, and if I had time we'd complete the crossword together. Then he'd pour himself a cup of tea (also a strict no-no for anyone else), offer me a biscuit from his Tupperware container, and spend what was left of the morning staring at his hands, or into space.

One Tuesday Mr Tilley gave a small cry. I looked up to see him clutch his side, eyes tight closed. He let out a sharp breath and fell forward, his forehead striking the table.

I knew what had happened but felt for a pulse anyway. Then I phoned the doctor and closed the library.

Nearly everyone in Silver Bay came to the funeral, though it was hard to tell whether they were there for Mr Tilley or just to get out of the house. Silver Bay sparkles from December to March, when holiday people come. The rest of the time the place is boarded shut, teenagers clump in front of Maccas and plastic bags blow against seafront benches.

In his eulogy, Reverend Blackman told us not to be too sad. Mr Tilley was in his 80s, after all, and his time had come. The Reverend said a few words about Mr Tilley's tragic life then segued into how grateful we were for the library, because it did more than honour Mrs Tilley. It brought the community together, he argued, and he was right. People come to read and meet and gossip, and yes, we're grateful. And I'm more grateful than most because if it weren't for dead Susan Tilley I wouldn't have a job.

After the service the Mayor collared me. 'Louise,' he said, 'I think we should put on a special event for Tilley, as a memorial. In the library, of course. Afternoon tea? I'll make a speech and you'll prepare a presentation on his life. A words and pictures thing.'

I wasn't averse, for two reasons. First, I was aware the Mayor was shooting me a helping hand. He was kind enough not to mention it, but I could use the PR. I was born here, in Silver Bay, went to school here, became the town bad girl. Here's the story: driving home from the year 12 formal with Jason Miller, both of us high and out of it, the car rolled, Jason thrown clear, dead on impact. Me, not a scratch. I left town as soon as I could, came back six months ago to care for my mother. The job was serendipitous. How long before a town forgives? I didn't know.

The second reason was I liked Mr Tilley. I liked his sense of being alone. We had that in common; that, losing people we loved and an appreciation of puzzles. We'd understood each other, I thought, and I wanted to do something for him.

I started my research. Google yielded nothing, so on a windy autumn day I closed the library and drove to Port Lachlan, to the office of the Hope

Coast Gazette, the Shire weekly. The Gazette hadn't digitised its archives but had got as far as microfiche. I sat in front of an eye-straining screen, scanning through issues from the late 1950s onwards.

The first Jonathan Tilley mention came in 1958, when he captained the Silver Bay High rugby team to victory. Then, in 1963, a report that *Jonathan Tilley, only son of Silver Bay mayor, was last night arrested for assaulting a travelling salesman at the Silver Bay Hotel.* Jonathan claimed drunkenness and remorse and was released without charge. The same year, Tilley senior died and Jonathan took over the family construction company.

The 60s scrolled by: space travel, the Kennedys, Vietnam. Finally, in 1967, a photograph, titled *Grand party to celebrate Tilley – Viner engagement.* It read: *Two of the Shire's most popular young folk, Susan Viner and Jonathan Tilley, last week celebrated their engagement at Silver Bay RSL. L-R: Susan Viner, Jonathan Tilley, Glen McNally, Frances Ryan.*

Four people seated at a table, the men in ties and sideburns, the girls' hair straight and long. Susan Viner looked at the camera. Even in grainy black and white you could see she had something, a girl-next-door appeal. Jonathan Tilley, smiling, had his arm around her shoulder, declaring possession. Across the table, a taller, thinner boy and a larger, dumpier girl gazed at them wistfully.

I recognised the dumpy girl. Frances Ryan. As Principal of Silver Bay High, Miss Ryan had tried to put the fear of god into me. Retirement hadn't sweetened her temper. She visited the library sometimes, never once acknowledging me, even though she must have known who I was.

Six months after the engagement, another photo: the wedding. Glen McNally and Frances Ryan were best man and bridesmaid. Susan stood beautiful and serious in her long white dress. Jonathan smiled his golden boy smile.

The Gazette reported Susan Tilley's death on 3 January 1969, presumably the first edition after the end-of-year holiday. A banner headline read *Tragedy at Silver Bay*, and under that, *Local Teacher Lost At Sea.*

Jonathan, Susan, Glen and Frances had spent New Year's Eve together, barbecuing on the beach. They'd been drinking. Sometime after midnight, Glen and Frances left, separately. It was a hot night and, according to Jonathan, he and Susan fell asleep. The next morning he woke to find

Susan missing. At first he thought she'd gone for an early dip but after a while he grew anxious.

They searched for days, police and SES and even light aircraft, but there was no trace. The culprit, they said, was the rip that sometimes sweeps the bay. The coroner ruled death by misadventure.

Soon after that, Jonathan Tilley's mother died. Tilley Constructions began work on the library, and after they finished it, Jonathan sold his company. From then on, he devoted himself to seeing the library was well run, and to his daily crossword puzzle visits.

I had enough information, I thought, about Mr Tilley's later life. Now I needed to know more about the young Jonathan – what sort of man he was, what made him tick.

Frances Ryan lived in Beach Road, in one of Silver Bay's original stone cottages. My ring was answered by multiple yapping, then, 'Wait on!' and after a longish time she opened the door. She was bowed over a cane, but her eyes were bright. Two small fox terriers leaped at me.

'Monty! Angus! *Here!*' The dogs came to heel. 'Well,' Miss Ryan said, without inviting me in, 'what can I do for you?'

'Actually, Miss Ryan, I've come about the memorial for Mr Tilley...'

'I heard about that. What exactly are you after?'

'I'm preparing a presentation on Mr Tilley, and know that you were friendly with him and his wife. I wondered if you could tell me more about them.'

'No,' she said flatly, 'I couldn't.' Her mouth was set in a straight line. 'Is that all?'

Caught off guard, I began, 'But...'

'Still won't take no for an answer, Louise?' So she did remember me. 'Let me be clear. I have nothing to say. I want no part of this. Understand?'

And I was on the pavement, the door shut tight, dogs going crazy behind it.

The electoral roll pointed me to Glen McNally, to a part of town tourists don't see; weatherboard houses with sagging gates and yards full of car parts. I could hear his television from the ramshackle stoop. I hammered hard. No answer, so I did it again. This time the sound stopped and after a while the door opened a crack and a rheumy eye gave me the once-over.

'Meals on Wheels?' he said.

'Glen McNally?'

'You're the library lady.' He opened wider. 'Come in.'

I followed him into a darkened living room, walls and ceiling yellow with cigarette smoke. 'Have a seat.' He pointed and I perched on a cracked leather couch. Glen McNally did an old person's drop next to me, into the TV-watching spot.

I took copies of the Gazette photos from my bag. 'Is this you?'

He leaned over to take them and I could smell him, cigarettes and something worse. 'Jesus, mate,' he said, shaking his head slowly, 'too long ago. What do you want?'

'The town's going to honour Mr Tilley with a memorial service in the library. I'm doing some background on his life, and wonder if you can help?'

McNally tried a chuckle, which morphed into a phlegmy cough. Thumping his chest, he said, '*Honouring* him, eh? As usual, he gets away with it.'

'What do you mean?'

He turned his gaze on me. 'Feel like making an old man a cuppa?'

The kitchen had the bare look of a place nobody uses. The milk smelled passable, just before the turn. I found a couple of mugs and took the tea through.

'Ta. You wanna know about Jonno Tilley? Ruled the world, Jonno did.' McNally put his mug on the floor, crossed the first and second fingers of his right hand and thrust them in the air. 'Jonno and me, we were like this since nippers, before that even. Kindy. He was OK, Jonno. Except...except when he got mad. Bugger of a temper. Broke my bike once. Forgotten why, now.'

I remembered the report about Jonathan attacking a salesman. 'Did he get mad often?'

McNally chuckled again, coughed again, took up his mug and slurped. 'Ropable, if he had a few. Then you never knew – mind you, he was a good bloke, too. Mustn't speak ill of the dead. Meant well, Jonno.'

'What about his wife?' I pointed to Susan Tilley in her wedding dress. McNally took the photo and gazed at it, head bowed. I wondered if he was thinking about the day Susan Tilley drowned.

He was quiet so long I thought he'd fallen asleep. 'What about Susan Tilley?' I repeated.

He started, sighed hard. 'Suzie? Jonno was all she could see. Didn't blame her. He had money, looks, everything.' He ran a thumb softly down her image.

I felt for a question, tried to frame it diplomatically. 'Did you – did you have feelings for her?' I was miles from my brief but it was too late.

Glen McNally pointed to a shelf across the room. On it, three framed photos were arranged around a candle. I got up to have a closer look. They were all of Susan Tilley. Two were head and shoulders shots, the other of her and Glen in bathers with shadows of people on either side.

From the couch Glen said, 'Answer your question? She had my heart, she knew it. Everyone did. If I – if I hadn't gone home that night, Suzie would still be alive, for sure.'

I went back to him. 'Why did you say Mr Tilley would *get away with it*?'

McNally wasn't listening. He was crying, making honking noises, his nose running. I smelled urine. 'Here, have some tea.' I passed him his mug, produced some tissues and sat with him till he calmed down. 'You OK?'

He patted my hand. 'She was going to leave him, you know. She was going to tell him that night, she told me herself.' He kept patting, sighed hard. 'She's out there, somewhere. I sit on the bench, asking the sea to give her back to me.'

I knew how it felt, to want to undo a death. 'Sorry,' I said, 'sorry.'

'Not your fault,' he answered.

The day of the presentation arrived. I tidied the library. Volunteers appeared and, helping them organise tea and cakes, I came across Mr Tilley's belongings in the kitchen. I put the thermos and Tupperware in a cupboard and stood quietly riffling through his notebook, looking at sets of clues alongside their neat solutions.

Further on, I noticed something different. Pages of words and letters, some crossed out, others underlined. *By labyrinth or die*, one read, *badly by inheritor* another, *inhabited by lorry*, a third. Unlike the other entries these were untidy, the pencil digging into the paper, hard enough to tear it in places. Then, on the last page, my name, *Louise*, with an arrow pointing to the phrase, *thy ordinary bible*, circled.

Mr Tilley had left me an anagram. I had half an hour before the party so I took the notebook to my desk and got to work. It was hard without accompanying clues but I cracked it. Then I realised all the phrases had the same answer, the only one that made sense. But what was the message?

Suddenly it came to me, the leap of intuition that happens when you solve puzzles. One moment a clue is impenetrable, the next the answer's in front of your eyes, as if a cover's been peeled away. I knew what it meant, and my hands and feet went cold as ice. A moment later the door opened and the first guest appeared.

I'll never know how I got through the afternoon. People told me the presentation was good, just the right mix of familiarity and interest. I even included the story about Jonathan Tilley beating up the salesman. But the highlight of the day was the mayor's speech, where he announced Mr Tilley had bequeathed everything he owned, all his money and assets, to securing the library's future, provided his ashes could be stored here. And then we had tea and cakes.

As soon as the last guest had gone, I closed the library and hurried back to Beach Road. Frances Ryan came to the door, dogs at her feet. She opened her mouth to say something but saw my face and waved me inside.

In the kitchen she sat me down, fetched a bottle of Johnny Walker and poured two stiff shots. 'You look like you need this,' she said. 'Sit. You have something to tell me?'

I was calm. 'I think Jonathan Tilley killed his wife.'

Miss Ryan's eyebrows went up, but she was unsurprised.

'You know already?'

'I suspected. Susan was going to leave him. That's a fact.' She took a sip of her whisky. 'The drowning story? I never believed it. It was too easy, and Jonno, afterwards, the way he changed—'

'Why didn't you say anything?'

'What could I say? I had no evidence. All Glen and I could do was stand back and watch. Question is,' and she looked at me with bird eyes, 'how did you come to that conclusion?'

I showed her Mr Tilley's notebook. 'He left me a message. All these anagrams, they all translate to *body in the library*. I think they're a confession. I think Susan told him she was leaving him and he was drunk, and he had a temper. Maybe it was an accident. And then he buried her body, and as soon as he could he built the library around it. That's why he was always there, to be near her. These anagrams – he wanted me to find out.'

Frances Ryan was quiet for a long time. Then she said, with something resembling defiance, 'So. What are you going to do now?'

I hadn't thought about it. 'I don't know. What should I do? Doesn't Susan Tilley deserve justice?'

'Hasn't she had justice? Jonno Tilley wasn't bad, you know. He didn't mistreat Suzie. He loved her. I can still remember the two of them, solving those bloody puzzles together.' Her voice cracked. 'And as you said, he was there, day after day, doing penance.'

'I'll have to think about it.'

'You do that.' said Miss Ryan. She finished her drink. 'You do that. Now, time for you to go. I need to make my dinner.' She got up slowly, heavily, and stumped with me down the passage. At the door, as I stepped out into a bleak twilight, the first real winter evening, she grasped my sleeve with a bony hand.

'I have one favour to ask. If you decide to – to make this public, you leave me out of it. Promise?'

'But all this time you suspected him, you and Glen McNally. And didn't Mr Tilley ruin more than Susan's life, and his own? Glen's made a shrine to Susan. If she had left her husband, wouldn't Glen's life have been saved too?'

'Is that what you think? That Susan Tilley was going to leave her husband for Glen McNally?'

'It's the logical conclusion–'

'You stupid girl! Suzie never loved Glen McNally. She was going to leave Jonathan for me, you hear, *me*! We were going to be together. In a town like this, so long ago, do you know what price she was prepared to pay, and me, too? If you want to get sentimental about lives lost, you think about mine. Now go!' She gave me a push, closing the door with a thud.

The Council installed Mr Tilley's ashes in an urn, in a display case near the library entrance. The plaque reads: *These are the ashes of Jonathan Tilley, who built this library in memory of his wife, after whom it is named.*

I said nothing, of course. Because even if I had, even if they found her body, what then? Mr Tilley was dead so he couldn't be called to account. And 50 years later, what did it matter?

For 50 years, every day, Mr Tilley had visited his wife's grave. He'd made his life one long memorial to her. Mr Tilley had punished himself enough.

I know this, because I know about punishing yourself. That night, the night with Jason Miller on the way back from the formal, he stopped the car. *I'm off my face, babe*, he said. *Need to catch a few zeds.*

What a wuss, I laughed. I got out of the passenger seat, staggered across to the other side, pushed against him. *Move over,* I said, *I'll drive.*

THE LONG GAME

THE HEAT WOKE ME. I'D BEEN FOR A SWIM AND STRETCHED OUT ON the deck of the yacht to dry off. I must have fallen asleep – we'd had champagne with lunch – and when I woke, I was alone. I was thirsty and my skin had that hot, tight feeling of too much sun. Half-drunk with it, I leaned against the railing, yawning and surveying the scene.

They call Sydney Emerald City, and I could see why. The sky was a blue so clear it hurt, the water below a glittering reply. No wind, and the sea completely still. The yacht barely moved. Further off, Balmoral beach was a riot of cabanas, umbrellas and people sunbaking and swimming and herding small children.

We'd planned a day on the harbour. A morning sail, lunch at Balmoral, a lazy afternoon and a sunset cruise back to the mooring at Mosman Bay. We were on *Big Mack*, Ryan's boat. He earned his living running charters. He must have gone for a swim, I thought, although I couldn't see him. Maybe he was on shore. I yawned, went to find my book.

Two hours later there was still no sign of him. I was irritated now. Should I swim out myself? No, but I'd have a go at him when he came back.

He didn't come back.

At six, I swam to shore. The beach was emptying by then. I asked random people if they'd seen him, but nobody could help. I strode up and down the Esplanade, weaving through dog-walkers and strollers. Nothing. I returned to the boat and after another hour, reluctantly phoned the maritime hotline to report my partner missing.

'Overboard? Is he wearing a lifejacket?'

'It's not like that. We're at Balmoral Beach. He's a good swimmer. He's just...missing. All his stuff is here, his phone, wallet, keys, even his sunglasses.'

The woman clicked her tongue. 'Missing person, then, not a rescue. Call the police.'

I did. They said it was a busy night and they might be a while.

Just after sunrise a police speedboat roared into view, its lifted bow spearing the still water. I was back on deck by then and scanning the beach, but all I could see were a few early-morning swimmers. The speedboat came alongside, bumping the hull and making *Big Mack* rock wildly. A uniformed cop tossed a rope, I tied it up and two plainclothes men and the uniformed cop climbed aboard.

Ten hours since I'd called them and I was steaming. 'Where the *hell* were you?' I burst out. 'Anything could have happened!'

One of the plainclothes men produced a paper. 'This is a warrant,' he said, 'to impound your boat.'

By lunchtime that day I learned how stupid I'd been. By the following week I'd uncovered the extent of Ryan's betrayal of everything I'd built with him in our year together. By then I was free, but only because there wasn't enough evidence to convict me.

Big Mack, it turned out, had been under surveillance for months. In addition to chartering tourists, Ryan had used it to run drugs and money and who knew what else. The only reason he hadn't been arrested was because the cops were after bigger fish, namely the people he worked for.

Their problem, and mine, was history. None of us knew where Ryan was or where he'd come from. No background, no tracks on which to base a search. The police, embarrassed and thwarted, needed a scapegoat. Enter me, claiming innocence. They didn't believe me and I didn't blame them. How could I not know anything about my partner, not even his real name, which certainly wasn't Ryan McKenzie? I was asking myself the same question, a self-flagellation that did me no good at all.

Then we found Ryan had maxed out my credit cards and emptied my accounts. Finally the police believed I was a victim and finally, reluctantly, they let me go.

By now my face was on every screen, in every newspaper. I'd probably lost my job, and given my new notoriety I'd never get another. I holed up in my apartment, the one I'd shared with Ryan, brooding over my failures and drinking too much vodka tonic; a drink, ironically, Ryan taught me to love.

Those were the least of my problems.

A day after the cops let me go I answered a knock on my door and two big men in sweatpants shouldered their way in, pressing me backwards. One grabbed my neck and forced me to the floor while the other demanded I give up the money.

'The six million, sweetheart.' The grip tightened.

'I don't...' I croaked.

The one doing the talking said, 'Mr Morozov wants his money back. You've got a week to bring it to us, or...' he passed a finger across his throat in a cutting gesture. 'He's got eyes on you, girlie. You do a runner, you're gone. Dead meat.' He threw a card on the floor next to me. 'When you've got news, call this number. You don't want to upset Mr Morozov.'

I definitely didn't want to upset Mr Morozov. I knew all about Maxim Morozov. The media loved him. He was smooth and quiet and though they couldn't say so directly, king of Sydney's criminal underbelly. Morozov was Russian and so well connected he floated above the city's lesser, warring tribes. He was also completely and utterly ruthless. The cops might have freed me, but if Morozov thought I had his six million I was in trouble so deep I couldn't see daylight.

After the men left I stayed on the floor for a while. Then I got up, poured myself a vodka tonic, then another.

At the third drink I stopped. Who did I think I was? The sort of hopeless chick I despised? Was I just going to lie around and let Morozov and his men come for me? They'd kill me for sure, and I didn't want to die. I wanted to live; no, scratch that, I wanted to live *well*. I had to get Morozov off my back and the only way to do that was to find Ryan McKenzie.

I was tired, drunk and shaky. I'd start first thing tomorrow.

In the morning I found a notebook and pencil and tried to focus. Faced with a blank page, my resolve dimmed. If the police couldn't find Ryan, how could I? He'd been gone over a week and could be anywhere in the world by now. On the other hand, I knew Ryan better than they did. The police had alerted airports, so if he'd left the country he would have gone by boat. Or would he? Ryan was no fool. The cops were one thing, Morozov was another. Morozov would hunt him down anywhere on earth and probably other planets as well. If I were Ryan and had six million dollars and Morozov after me, I'd have a bloody good plan. And maybe, just maybe, it would involve sitting tight for a while.

My intuition told me I was on the right track, but to be honest it was the only track available. I had to believe Ryan was still in Australia. If he was, where would he be? Every night since he'd disappeared, I'd lain in bed sleepless, anguishing over how little I knew about him. He'd left school, had adventures, travelled the world. That was it.

Come on, Sylvie, I told myself. *Think!*

I went back to the beginning, which was all about boats.

I'd been sailing since I could walk, was temporarily without a boat and looking to rent my mooring. Ryan answered my ad. We agreed to meet at Mosman Rowers. I walked in and this dark-eyed man smiled his smile and lifted his glass and that was that. We moved in together a month later; or rather he moved in with me, to my recently acquired apartment. He'd been living on his boat and didn't have a place of his own. The mooring was so close you could see it from our balcony.

The mooring was so close you could see it from our balcony. That, of course, was why Ryan had taken up with me. A mooring he didn't have to register. A single woman to front for him so there wouldn't be questions. He must have asked around before we met. Talk about playing a long game. He'd been planning to disappear before we even met.

I tamped down the flame of anger and returned to the page. Were there clues in what we'd done, or where we'd been, while we were together? At first nothing came to mind. Ryan's "chartering" had kept him away for weeks at a time and when he was home, we stayed in or worked on the boat. We were self-contained, he said, we didn't need other people.

Except for the wedding. My friend Jan married a winemaker from Pokolbin and I was *de facto* matron of honour. No avoiding that. I took a train to Newcastle a week before the wedding and Ryan sailed up in time for the rehearsal dinner. We left a couple of days later, heading South under a cloudy sky. We were just out of the harbour when Ryan pointed at the coast.

'See over there? When I was a kid, three of us got caught in a rip, just there. It was bad. Two people died, but lifesavers pulled me out. Jesus, I was lucky. I was so shattered they had to carry me home.'

Newcastle. Home. Two dead boys would make the papers. I opened my computer. The *Newcastle Herald* had digitised issues going back to 1942 and I offered a silent prayer to technology. Where to begin? Ryan claimed to be 35. I didn't know if it was true, but it was all I had. Say he'd been between 10 and 15 years old when he got caught in that rip...I started with 1998.

I found what I was looking for in February 2003.

TWO DIE, ONE SAVED IN HORROR RIP

Lifesavers Warn Against Swimming Outside the Flags.

An early-morning swim ended in tragedy yesterday, when only one of three local youths survived a rip off Merewether Beach. Lifesavers and fellow swimmers pulled the boys to shore and called ambulances, but Kyle Fredericks and Tony Lipano, both 16, were pronounced dead on arrival at John Hunter Hospital. The other lad, Jason Dankworth, 15, was revived and treated on the beach.

The community mourns...

Jason Dankworth. I consulted Person Lookup. Six Dankworths in Australia, three of them in Newcastle. Probably not the only ones, because hardly anyone used landlines any more, but a beginning. And Dankworth wasn't a common surname, so they could be related.

It was midday and not the best time to phone, but I couldn't stand the wait. I rang a Dankworth at random, a Wallsend address. The phone was picked up on the fifth ring.

'Good morning,' I said, all business. 'My name is Rhonda Politis and I'm calling from the Australian Bureau of Statistics to ask some questions about the census. I must warn you these calls are recorded for quality and security purposes and if you do not wish to be recorded, please tell me now.'

A panicked woman's voice answered. 'We filled in the form online! Is anything wrong? My husband–'

I interrupted. 'Not at all. We are merely conducting a random survey to confirm information already submitted.'

A pause, then, 'How do I know you're not a scam artist?'

'I'm not going to ask for money,' I assured her. 'And if you like, you can phone the ABS and check.' I held my breath.

Another beat, then, 'It's OK.'

'Right. Mrs Dankworth, is it?'

'Yes?'

'For security purposes please confirm your full name and date of birth.'

'Ellen Mary Dankworth. 10 March, 1989.'

She was too young. 'Can you tell me who occupied your house last night?'

'Sure. Me, my husband Terry, our daughter Louisa and our son Atlas.'

'Thank you, Mrs Dankworth, that's excellent. I wonder if you could help me with one last question: we have chosen participants according to surnames. Are you related to the other Dankworths listed in Newcastle?'

'Oh yes, we are. My husband, though, not me. Terry's sister lives in Mayfield and his mother, she lives in Merewether.'

Merewether, the scene of the rip. 'Could you describe their families? It would save time.' I was pushing it, I knew, but Ellen Dankworth seemed to believe me.

'There's Sharon, Terry's sister, her husband's Marco, they don't have children. Terry's mother lives alone. Her other son used to live with her, but he left home long ago.'

'The other son's name is?'

'Jason. Jason Dankworth.'

Too easy. 'That concludes our interview, Mrs Dankworth. We appreciate your assistance.'

'Anything else you want to know? The kids are at school and I've got time.' She sounded disappointed.

'You're very kind,' I said, and added in a confidential tone, 'I wish all our interviewees were as helpful. You have a good day, now. Goodbye.'

'Goodbye.' She reluctantly let me hang up.

So far, so good. Based on a single throwaway anecdote, I'd decided Ryan McKenzie was Jason Dankworth and that he might be found at his mother's house which, according to the internet, was at 17 Buchanan Street, Merewether. I couldn't stop to think about how fragile my logic was. I had to press on.

Next step, Newcastle.

Early next morning I took the two-hour trip up the M1. I dumped my overnight bag in my Airbnb and walked the short distance to Buchanan Street. It was narrow and quiet and had a seaside air, the kind of street where children play cricket till sundown. Number 17 was older, weatherboard, white and well-kept behind a high white picket fence. Its aluminium-framed windows were shut and so were the curtains behind it. No cars in the driveway.

I hesitated. Now or never. Jason/Ryan would be on guard, but with any luck no cars meant he wasn't home and I could do this before he found out. *Please,* I begged the universe, *if Ryan is Jason, please let him not have told his mother.*

I hauled a notebook out of my bag, walked up to the front door, knocked. No answer for a long time. I tried again, heard clacking of heels on wood. The door opened a crack and a dyed blonde head peered out at me. 'Yes?'

'Does Jason Dankworth live here?'

'Who're you?'

I brandished the notebook. 'I'm from the *Herald*. I'm doing a follow-up story on people who were rescued by lifesavers and if you remember, there was a rip.'

The door opened wider. 'Course I remember. Yeah. Jase's working on the boat. Back in a coupla hours. Come round then?'

'The boat? Where's that?'

'The boat shed, love. Central Coast Boat Repairs.'

'I'm on a deadline. I'll catch him there.' I was supposed to be a local reporter, couldn't ask for the address.

The woman eyed my notebook. 'You wanna talk to me too, love?'

'I'll come back later, Mrs Dankworth. Thanks.'

Newcastle, that once-grim city of steel and coal, had reinvented itself as a tourist destination and the area around Central Coast Boat Repairs was gentrified to within an inch of its life. A paved walkway wound along the oily waters of the Hunter, flanked on one side by a giant marina full of boats and on the other by eateries, boat sheds and judiciously spaced palm trees.

Central Coast Boat Repairs was a domed corrugated hangar sandwiched between a restaurant and a café. No reception desk, just a high roof festooned with sails and a man scraping down the hull of a boat on a rack. 'I'm looking for Jason Dankworth,' I told him.

He was blond, bearded, twinkle-eyed. 'Just in time. He's getting ready to go.'

My bowels contracted. 'Oh yeah?'

The man straightened, came with me to the door, pointed at a large white yacht at the end of one of the jetties. 'See it?'

'The Hanse?'

He shot me an appreciative glance. 'Know your stuff, hey? Yeah. Hanse 50, brand new. *The Long Game.* Came down from Brissie couple days ago. But no, not that one, the one next to it. The blue Columbia 27. *Lazy Daze.*'

'Thanks.'

'Listen,' he called to my back, 'buy you a beer later?'

'Another time?' I turned my head, smiled, tried not to break into a run.

Close up, *Lazy Daze* was old, wooden, in bad shape. Nobody on deck, but as I stepped aboard, Ryan appeared from below. He froze, both hands on the frame of the hatch. He stayed like that for a long moment, then remembered to smile.

'Fuck me dead. Sylvie Martin! How'd you find me?'

I shrugged in an *it was nothing* gesture, waved a hand. 'Planning a trip?'

'You alone?'

''Course I'm alone. Shouldn't be after what you did to me, but here I am. You're about to head off?'

His smile stayed put. Behind it, I could see wheels turning. 'Sure am. Tonight.' Finally, he stepped on deck. 'Tell you what, Sylvie, why don't you come with me?'

'You tell me something first. That last day? Why take me to Balmoral? You could have just disappeared, got yourself a couple of days' head start. Come to that, why haven't you shot through already?'

For the first time, his smile reached his eyes. I'd forgotten how sexy he was and it hit me right in the belly. 'When I left,' he said, 'I took off with some cash.'

'Six million. I heard. Plus what you stole from me.'

'Yeah. In any case, before that... The people I worked for are dangerous. You have no idea how dangerous. They'd been following me. When I was alone, not when I was with you. I guess they thought I wouldn't try anything with you around.' He lifted his shoulders as if to say *what choice did I have?*

'And you're still here because?'

He pointed over my shoulder at the beautiful new Hanse yacht behind me. 'See her? *The Long Game*? She's mine. I ordered her months ago but they wouldn't sail her down until I paid in full.'

'Two boats?'

'Yeah. You paid for this one. Sorry about that, babe. I...' he came closer, cupped my cheek. 'I'll make it up to you, promise.'

I couldn't help but lean in. He drew me in, held me to his chest, buried his face in my hair. God, the pull of him!

I broke away. 'You're a bastard, you know that?' I shot a look at the Hanse. 'So what's the plan?'

He grinned. 'We take this one, *Lazy Daze*, out tonight. At some point we move to the tender, put some distance between us, scuttle her.' He saw my confusion. 'I mean we blow her up. He made the noise, opened his hands to show the extent. 'Mate of mine, his father worked explosives for BHP. Cost me a bit, but he rigged up something. When we're in the tender I set it off with my mobile. Speed dial. One click and as far as the world's concerned, I'm dead.'

'The world doesn't know who you are, or where you are. How will they join the dots?'

'The bill of sale. Signed by Ryan McKenzie.'

'Oh, clever. Meanwhile you – we – are headed North in *The Long Game*, and nobody's looking for us.'

'Yeah. We wait a day for the fuss to die down. Then we're away, all above board, port clearance and everything. Plus enough money to keep us going.' He grinned modestly. 'You in or not?'

I thought of my promise to myself: to live well. 'I'm in.'

Ryan (I couldn't think of him as Jason) drove me to the Airbnb to collect my bag. I made him come inside with me – no way I was letting him out of sight – and together we stowed the bag on the Hanse, which he'd provisioned for the getaway.

'Where's the money?' I asked.

He hesitated, then shrugged. 'In here.' He lifted the cushion of one of the seats and pointed to the storage below, at three bulging sports bags. I peered in. 'Wow. Six million dollars takes up a lot of space.'

'More like five million now, after this baby.' Ryan indicated the boat. Then he put his arms round my waist and turned me to face him. 'Hours to wait. I know a good way to pass the time.'

How could I resist?

Around midnight we motored down the river and past Stockton on one side and Nobby's Head on the other. When we were out to sea, Ryan said, his voice tense. 'OK, Sylvie, I'll get in the tender first, you follow, right?'

We were towing the tender, a rigid inflatable, behind us. 'OK,' I said, watching him swing a foot over.

Hand on rail, he said, 'Babe, I'm really sorry. You're great, but you know I can't take you with me.'

'You're leaving me here to die?'

'Sorry,' he said again. Had he always been this arrogant, this dismissive of me? I had no time to wonder.

'Won't you need your phone?' I said. 'It's down there.' I motioned to the main cabin.

He slapped his windbreaker pockets, his jeans. 'Oh, fuck!' He leaped back on deck, past me and into the cabin.

I slid the hatch shut and fastened the padlock. Untied the tender, clambered in. Kneeling, I tilted the outboard into the water. I went through the steps of priming, choking, powering. I pulled the cord. Nothing. I could hear Ryan bashing something against the hatch. I'd drifted a little way from the boat. I yanked the cord again. Still nothing. I heard wood splintering, Ryan yelling as he ran to the stern. I tried again and finally the outboard sprang to life. I felt the propeller connect and turned the throttle as high as it would go.

When I thought I was far enough away I let the motor idle. I took Ryan's phone out of my pocket and pressed the speed dial button tagged *Lazy Days*.

I heard the explosion and in the light of the flames saw the deck lift into the air and come down again, hard. It didn't take long for the sea to quench the fire, but by that time I was well on my way back to shore.

I didn't head for the harbour because I wanted to avoid the rescue craft. Instead, I made it to Nobby's Beach and pulled the tender onto the sand.

Later, when the sun was up, after the initial responders had gone home and before the investigators set to work, I puttered slowly towards Central Coast Boat Repairs.

Back in Sydney I dialled the number Morozov's men had left me. 'I have what Mr Morozov asked for.'

They picked me up in a black SUV and drove me to Morozov's house, a not overlarge and beautifully appointed house in Vaucluse.

Morozov received me in his living room, kissed me on both cheeks, European fashion.

'Sylvie! I hear you came good?'

I had bridges to build. 'I apologise, Max, for letting him get away. It was extremely unprofessional of me. It won't happen again.'

'Hmm...' Morozov spread his hands in a *who knows* gesture, waved me to a black leather armchair, took the other one. 'You have the money?'

'They're getting it out of the car now. He spent some of it, about a million.'

'Too bad.'

Morozov didn't look disappointed. Ryan's death would send a message to anyone thinking of trying a similar stunt, so maybe he thought it was worth it. He raised a lazy hand. 'OK, yes. You recovered your mistake.'

'Finder's fee? Ten percent?'

He chuckled. 'Cheeky, but why not? I am grateful.'

'Thank you.'

'I was right to get you to keep an eye on him.' Morozov mused. 'Something about the man, something wrong, I felt it from the start.'

The words had weight beyond their meaning. Morozov was telling me *I know you fell down on this. I know you let Ryan McKenzie pull you in and make you stupid.* I got the message loud and clear, but all I said was, 'And that's why they pay you the big bucks.'

Morozov dipped his head. Conversation over.

'If that's it?' I rose to go.

He saw me to the door. 'I'll contact you in a couple of days. Something I want you to take care of.'

I never for one instant thought of keeping the money, though I could have claimed it went down with *Lazy Days*. But why? Only a few million, and I want more: more money, more power, more everything. This way I'd regained Morozov's trust. I had my job back. I'd work my way up. And up. Queen of Sydney's underbelly, anyone?

In a day or two I'd go back to Newcastle, maybe get that drink the boat guy offered. Fetch *The Long Game,* sail it down, keep it on my mooring. The Long Game. The only game in town.

THE BLACK CURSE

THIS HAPPENED A LONG TIME AGO.

When I was growing up, my grandmother, Sete, lived in two rooms at the front of our house. She was a short woman, Sete, with a formidable bust and thin grey hair knotted at the nape of her neck. She wore long black skirts over thick beige stockings with seams down the back, and sandals. And cardigans, which she constantly unravelled and knitted again. Her passions were cooking and gardening. Most of our greens came from the backyard garden, which was her domain and hers alone.

Sete was bossy and abrasive but she loved me and I loved her back. She would cup my face in her hands. 'You just like me when I was girl,' she would say, and pinch my cheeks till they hurt.

She was born and grew up in Russia and, though she'd lived in Australia for decades, was wedded to the ways of her rural childhood. She spoke in the cadences of what she called "the old country" and cooked the meals she'd grown up with. She was superstitious, teaching me rituals which she said came from her own grandmother. If you spilled salt, you had to throw more salt over your shoulder. If someone predicted a disaster, you spat three times to avoid it coming true. You never ever put shoes on a table.

And then there was the black curse.

I was eighteen when I heard about the black curse. Though I was at uni I lived at home: my father had died in a car crash and my mother, who had to get a job to support us, retreated into quiet sadness. I felt I couldn't abandon her. So it was just the three of us and sometimes when my mother was at work, Sete and I would cook together, and talk.

We were making Sete's special stew, a concoction designed for labourers in the tundra, when she suddenly declared, 'You know, I was married before I met your grandfather.'

'You're kidding!'

'Yes, sure. First husband. What a monster,' she said. 'A *monster*.'

'What happened to him?'

She shrugged. 'He dead.' She slammed her special, battered pot on the stove.

'His mother worse,' she added. 'When I come to be engaged, the mother give me a ball of thread, all tangled, the size of –' she shook a balled fist. 'She tells me, "you make that right, you good for my son, otherwise go away". I loved him, what did I know? I spent weeks and weeks and finally I got it undone. But still, nothing I could do would please that bitch. Nothing.

'You know what,' she added, coming to sit next to me, making her point by stabbing a forefinger on the table, 'When you meet man, you must think hard before you marry him. You take care. Look how he is with his family. His friends. If problem anywhere, run away. I was young and stupid and I didn't know anything, darlink. You listen to your babushka.' And she hoisted herself up.

I wanted to know more about the first husband. What was his name? Was he good looking?

'Good looking?' She chuckled. 'Why you think I spent a month pulling on that tangle?'

'How did he die?'

Sete was suddenly involved in the pot.

'How did he die?' I repeated.

'I told you. He was monster. He beat me, stole my money. He would have killed me so I put the black curse on him.'

I opened my mouth to say something but Sete stopped me. 'That's enough about the monster. Start getting the vegetables ready.'

'But–'

'Chop the beans,' Sete snapped. 'Your mother will be home and she will be tired and you will be sitting there like the spoiled princess you are.'

I asked my mother about Sete's first husband. 'I don't know much,' she said. 'I've never even seen a photo of him.'

'What's the deal with the black curse?'

My mother sighed. 'When I was young, she told me we had the power to curse. All the women in the family, going back generations. I said she was in Australia now and here we don't believe such rubbish. She hasn't mentioned it since. Humour her, Katya, she's getting old.'

I soon forgot about the black curse. Life went on, until one day I came home to find the front window shattered and my mother crying at the kitchen table, her head on Sete's shoulder, Sete rocking her and crooning in Russian.

'Mum! What happened?'

Over my mother's head, Sete said, 'That bastard shit Pickering.'

'Pickering?'

'Don't bother Katya, mama,' my mother said, 'she doesn't need to worry. Besides, we don't know it was him.'

'I'm not a child, Mum. Tell me what's going on.'

'Tell her,' insisted Sete.

My mother disengaged herself. 'Mr Pickering wants to buy our house. He's been making offers but I don't want to sell. The last time I saw him he got – he said he would force me to sell. I've had phone calls, death threats. And now someone's thrown a brick through our window.'

'And you're only telling me this now? Have you called the cops?'

No!' spat Sete. 'No police. What will they do? There is nothing to show it was him who threw the brick. 'No,' she said slowly, 'I have decided. I put the black curse on him.'

My mother rolled her eyes.

'You give me permission?'

'Yes, yes,' said my mother, distracted. 'So what if I sell? The house is too big anyway. We can buy something smaller and have money left over.'

'OK,' said Sete, 'You will see.'

The next day I found a lawyer. His name was Ben Watts, and his large, chubby frame brought instant comfort. He joined us when Pickering came to inspect the house and stayed protectively close to my mother during the tense discussion that followed, Sete slamming the tea-tray down and hovering like a dark, angry omen.

On our behalf, Ben rejected Pickering's low offer. We heard nothing for a fortnight. Then Ben came to tell us Pickering had died in his sleep. The doctors suspected an aneurism, he said. Sete snorted and stumped off to her rooms. I watched her go, wondering. Was it possible? Surely not. I tried broaching the subject but she waved me away. 'Not yet,' she said.

There was no more talk about selling the house. Ben, however, became a fixture, first as a family friend and then as more than that. My mother, tentative, allowed herself to be taken out to dinner, to a film, on weekends away. 'Your ma-ma has a boy-friend,' chanted Sete, nudging me with her elbow. 'Good man, Ben,' she said. 'Kind man.'

By the time Ben moved in, I had a boyfriend of my own. I'd graduated by then and scored a job at a PR firm. I met Hugh at a work party. Lean but hard, and Viking blond hair over a cut-glass profile. No designer clothes, just a white shirt, jeans, brown lace-ups. And one earring, a drop, a shell ringed with gold wire. He smiled at me and that was that.

When I took Hugh home I was relieved at how well behaved Sete was. She said little over dinner. Hugh, on the other hand, was charm personified. As far as I was concerned, the night went perfectly.

When next I saw Sete, however, it was a different matter. She beckoned me into the kitchen, sat me down. 'I say this once only.' Her voice sounded thin. 'You remember I tell you about the monster? My first husband? You make same mistake.'

'How can you say that? You just met him.'

'I see how he watch you, everything you do. How he stop you when you talk. He tell you what you can eat, how much, in case you get fat.'

'So what? He loves me. He wants me to stay healthy.'

She beckoned me closer. 'You have fun with this guy, sure, he very handsome. But nothing else, nothing. He is bad news. *Bad news.* You listening to me?'

I wasn't listening of course. Delirious with love, I agreed to marry Hugh. We flew to Paris and did the deed with witnesses pulled off the street, kept it secret till we returned. My mother and Ben were happy for me but Sete didn't say anything, just shook her head.

The first year was paradise. We lived in a bubble, just the two of us. One by one, friends drifted away. I didn't care. Hugh was all I needed.

Then my mother rang. Sete had been rushed to hospital. A scare, really, they were keeping her in for observation. Would I mind visiting?

She was asleep when I arrived. I sat next to her bed, noticing how old she'd become, how the bones of her face poked through the skin. I realised how little I'd seen of her over the past year, and felt for her hand. Her eyes opened.

'Darlink.' She clasped my fingers tight.

'I'm so sorry,' I said.

'Sorry? Darlink, for what?'

'For not coming to see you more often.'

She squeezed my hand. 'It's nothing, don't worry. I'm still here. But Katya, something you must do for me. Promise?'

I would have promised anything. 'Of course. What is it?'

'The garden. Too much for me now. You come to help? Yes?'

'Sure.'

That night, Hugh and I had our first proper row. 'How could you let yourself be talked into it?' he demanded. 'You'll be away all the time.'

'No, I won't. I'm just going over once a week or so, to help my gran.'

'We only have weekends. That's all the time we've got, the hours you work. You love them more than you love me.'

I compromised on once a fortnight. Still, he wasn't happy.

Hugh's reaction ignited a flicker of alarm. Looking at myself in the mirror, I realised how much I'd given away. Hugh had chosen the clothes I was wearing: juvenile, pastel, not my style at all. He'd persuaded me to colour my hair, and he'd chosen the colour. He decided everything about me, where I went, who with, what I spent, how much, and on what. Slowly, I faced facts: I'd waltzed into a prison cell and given Hugh the key.

I tested it. I stayed late in the office, having a drink with the partners. When I left the building, Hugh was there, waiting. I went for a long walk. Hugh found me, and I realised he'd put a tracker on my phone.

The more I resisted, the worse it became. Hugh never harmed me physically but there were times when I would have preferred that to the constant humiliations, the threats, the accusations of affairs with people I hardly knew. 'I can kill you,' he said, 'any time I like. And I will. Wait for it.'

I should have told my family sooner, but I was ashamed. This was my fault, I thought, and I should fix it. So I endured.

And then I fell pregnant. Hugh went berserk. He denied the child was his and insisted on an abortion. I had more than just myself to protect and so, one afternoon when Hugh was at a meeting, Ben helped me pack and leave and I found myself back in my bedroom at home.

Then the stalking began. When I left work, Hugh was waiting. If I got on a bus, he was behind me. I'd see him on my morning walk. He was too smart to text but he phoned constantly, threatening. I got a new phone; he switched to our landline. Wherever I was, I saw him, or thought I saw him. I was a nervous wreck.

In cases like this, there's not much the police can do. They can't act unless there's an "incident", and in any case, was I sure Hugh was stalking me? A handsome, successful man like that? Wasn't it my imagination? Had I left him, or him me?

I got an AVO but it only made him more devious. He'd be gone by the time the police arrived, be innocently at his new apartment, shaking his head at my paranoia. In the end, I took time off work. I was too frightened to leave home. Instead, I worked on Sete's garden, learning the names of plants and how to make them grow. Sete was frail by then, unsteady on her feet, but her mind was sharp and it seemed important to her that I help her garden flourish.

Hugh even appeared in my dreams. One night I swam out of a nightmare, sweating, to find Sete standing beside my bed. She wore a nightie, her hair in a loose plait, and through her great age I could see the girl she had once been.

'Katya, darlink, it is time. For the black curse.'

I would have grasped at anything. 'If you say so.'

'I am too old to do it now,' she said. 'You will have to learn.' She put a hand on my brow and stroked back my hair. 'Tomorrow. I show you tomorrow.'

In the bright Australian sunlight, talk of black curses sounded ridiculous. But I remembered Pickering, and my mother's advice about humouring an old woman. So, when she asked if I was ready, I nodded.

'First part is, you must be close to the person, you must tell them you are putting a black curse on them.'

Well, that wasn't going to happen.

Sete ploughed on. 'Next part. Come. We go to my garden.'

She leaned on me while she led me to the herb section. She told me to fetch several leaves of a small grey plant, one I hadn't noticed before, growing in a corner by the fence. Then I helped her back to the kitchen.

When we were settled she said, 'This plant, Katya, I bring seeds from the old country. We call it – I don't know the English.'

I didn't like the way this was going.

'You boil the leaves in a pot – I give you the pot, because you must not use that pot for any other thing. You cook till only a little left, maybe an inch. Then you put a few drops in his drink, or even some food. He will taste nothing. In a week, maybe a couple days longer, he will be dead.'

'You mean to tell me you...you...' I couldn't say the word *murdered*. 'This is the way you got rid of two men?'

'Three,' said Sete. 'One day I tell you about the priest in our village.' She saw my face. 'What? Did you believe to say a few words by themselves would make the black curse work? Who do you think I am? God?'

'And your mother taught you this? Did she use it herself?'

Sete shrugged. 'Sure!'

'How many times?'

'Two? Three? I don't know.'

'And she learned this from?'

Sete was losing patience. 'I told you. From her mother and her grandmother, and so on.'

Nothing prepares you for the news that you come from a long line of assassins. I stared at Sete, unwilling to take it in. Then I then put my head in my hands and started to laugh and once I started, I couldn't stop. Eventually the laughter subsided. I wiped my eyes and said, through hiccups, 'What you want me to do is a crime. A bad one. We could go to jail for – besides, it's morally *wrong*. Forget it. I can't. I won't.'

Sete stared at the bunch of leaves in the middle of the kitchen table.

'Please yourself. It's up to you.'

The phone rang. It was Hugh.

Hugh died ten days after I suggested we meet in a local park. I brought coffee and biscuits but even so it went badly. He wouldn't contemplate divorce. Instead, he insisted I return to him under, as he put it "his conditions".

'If you don't come by yourself,' he said, 'I'll make you. You belong to me. I'll never let you go. I'll see you dead first.' I believed him.

As I gathered the takeaway cups I whispered, 'I put the black curse on you.' I'm not sure he heard.

As I mentioned, this happened a long time ago. Sete died not long after Hugh, and my mother and Ben moved to Noosa. I never remarried, but I do have my beautiful daughter, Sadie. She's pregnant herself, now, she and her partner Lisa, through IVF. She seems happy, but who can tell? Perhaps she'll be luckier than I was.

We still live in the old house. I've moved into Sete's rooms, and sometimes in the afternoons when I sit there reading I sense her with me, she and the generations of women pressing in behind her. I think about them, about where I come from, and what I can pass on.

DEAR LIFE

POLLA ALBESCU CLEANS OTHER PEOPLE'S HOUSES. SHE DOESN'T need to. Her husband left her enough to live on, but he died and her daughter got married so how is she supposed to spend her time? She has to do something, and that doesn't include drinking tea with the other Romanian widows. Polla wants to get out of the house and this is a way of making it happen.

Her employers like her. She looks like they expect a cleaner to look: that is, less successful than they are. What they see is a wiry woman with short, dyed-blonde hair, slightly off-kilter eyeliner and cheap clothes, usually incorporating something sparkly. She's an average cleaner but she's reliable and honest, and that's worth a few dusty corners.

Every Monday, Polla cleans Wendy Burford's house. Wendy lives in Balmain. It's far from Parramatta but Polla makes a day of it, taking a train and then a ferry and walking up the hill to the house.

Polla likes Wendy. ('Call me Wendy,' she said.) Wendy always has time for a chat. She wants to know how Polla's daughter's going, talks about her son Riley, who can't seem to hold down a job. Polla's seen photos of him and to be honest, he looks like a loser.

Wendy's divorced, a lawyer, works from home. None of her clients is Australian. They're nearly all men, Middle Eastern or African. Wendy explains they're refugees or asylum seekers and her job is to get the government to let them stay here. It's a hard road, says Wendy, the government is uncompromising. Polla feels sorry for the asylum seekers. She knows how tough this country can be if you aren't Anglo; when she and Dragos came, he drove taxis all night, had to learn the language, fast.

One Monday, on the Parramatta ferry, a man approaches her. He's about her age, solid, with greying hair and a black moustache. He's seen her before, he says, at Ms Wendy Burford's house. Would she mind if he sat next to her? His name is Jabar Saddiqi. He is Afghani. Polla's seen him too, liked the look of him. She introduces herself and together they chuckle at their poor English. She tells Jabar about Dragos and Jabar tells her he is alone in the world, he has nobody. His wife and son were killed in the war between America and the Taliban. He looks away, over the river. That's in the past, he sighs, what he needs now is residency. He paid an agent thousands of dollars to arrange it, then the agent disappeared and he's been left with nothing. Wendy is helping him get residency and he will pay her back when he can. Until he gets residency he cannot work.

Then he leans in, whispers. He thinks he can trust her. Can she keep a secret? To earn enough for food, he stacks shelves in a shop in Blacktown, cash in hand. In Kabul, he was an engineer. Polla says they have something in common. She was studying engineering too, though she never finished her course.

After his appointment with Wendy, Jabar finds Polla. 'I go now,' he says. 'I must come again next Monday. Maybe I come by ferry or maybe by bus but in any case, I see you, we talk some more.'

Next Monday, Polla looks out for Jabar but he isn't on the ferry. She's disappointed. Perhaps they'll meet later.

When she gets to Wendy's house the front door is open and that's strange because normally she rings the bell or uses the key Wendy gave her. When she goes in, everything's silent. The sort of silence that means something's wrong.

Wendy's in her office, on her back on the carpet next to her small round meeting table. There's an overturned chair. She's dead – Polla can see that right away. Her head is a mess of hair and blood. Jabar is standing next to her, staring, still as a statue. He's holding a glass ball, a paperweight, and that too is streaked with blood.

Before Polla has time to understand what's happened, there's a rush and a noise and four cops burst in. They're bulked up with bulletproof vests and they hold guns. There are three men and one woman and the woman grabs Polla and the men tackle Jabar to the ground. Behind them, a young man screams, *Get him get him get him!*

In a jumble of instants Polla and Jabar are handcuffed and pushed into police cars, one for each. Sirens screaming, the cars take off to Leichhardt Police Station. Polla is manhandled out and she turns to see Jabar, blood streaming down a cheek, being pulled and pushed behind her. He does not resist.

The policewoman sits Polla down at a table in a small room, leaves. She waits, alone, half an hour, an hour. Finally, a man comes in, the policewoman behind him. The man is not in uniform. He wears grey pants and a striped shirt, striped tie. He is shortish but tough. Has that beige look some Australians have, colourless hair cut close to the skull, colourless eyes. It makes him dangerous.

He and the policewoman sit opposite Polla.

'DO YOU NEED AN INTERPRETER?' he shouts.

Polla shakes her head. She understands just fine, it's speaking the words she has problems with.

The man pulls out a cigarette but doesn't smoke it. He leans back and rolls it between his fingers. Gives her a long, ugly look. 'So, Mrs...' he consults his notes, 'Albescu. What've you got to say for yourself?'

'I am cleaner. I come by ferry every Monday. Today I get there, I find Wendy...' Her voice falters. What more is there to say?

'What time did the ferry arrive?'

'Just before ten o'clock. The same as always.' Polla straightens her back. In her life, in Romania, she's had to deal with this kind of man before. 'You know my name. So what is your name?'

He frowns. He doesn't like her standing up to him. He says, slowly and sarcastically, '*Detective Inspector* Robertson. Now. What is your relationship with Mr Saddiqi?'

She hesitates. 'I see him on ferry and at the house.'

'That so?' his eyebrows go up. 'He's a friend of yours? See much of him, do you?'

'Only on ferry and in Wendy's house. I feel he is good man.'

Robertson changes tack, tells her to go through the morning. She describes coming across the body. He asks her about Saddiqi, over and over again. Then he and the policewoman leave her alone for two more hours. The policewoman comes back, briefly, escorts her to the bathroom.

Robertson returns. She needs to make a statement, then she can go. They've checked her out, checked the ferry timetable, phoned a couple of her employers. (A week later, one of those employers sacks her. 'You can't be too careful,' he says.)

'Where is Mr Saddiqi?' asks Polla.

'Mr Saddiqi's helping us with our enquiries.' Robertson grins with shark teeth. He indicates the policewoman. 'We'll be in touch. My colleague will take your statement.'

It's late afternoon by the time Polla gets home. She phones Ana, her daughter, who rushes over to see how she is. 'Omigod,' shrieks Ana, 'You're lucky to be alive! He could be a terrorist for all we know.'

The TV channels agree. The news that night is full of the murder. Robertson's there, standing behind the Police Commissioner, who says they have a suspect in custody. While they're keeping an open mind – the motive could be robbery – they aren't ruling out terrorism. It's their way of telling the public this wasn't an Australian, not "one of them". The Commissioner says his thoughts are with Ms Burford's son, Riley, who discovered her body and called the police.

Polla can't sleep. She can't understand what happened. How did Riley Burford find the body and leave Jabar Saddiqi there? It doesn't make sense. She can't get Jabar out of her mind. When she closes her eyes, it isn't Wendy Burford she sees, but Jabar being pulled from the police car, his bloody face.

The next day Polla keeps the radio on while she cleans. Jabar Saddiqi is named as a person of interest in the Wendy Burford murder. The government takes the opportunity to announce increased funding for Border Force.

Polla's last job is in Glebe, a short walk to Leichhardt Police Station. At the station, she asks to see Jabar Saddiqi. 'The terrorist?' says the constable on reception. 'He's been taken to the remand centre. Silverwater.'

She doesn't know where that is. 'How can I visit him?'

The constable's not unsympathetic. 'You have to phone and book. Two visits a week. You family?'

Jabar said he had nobody. 'Almost,' she says.

Later that day, Polla meets her friends Jozefa and Luba for a meal at the club. Luba points to a family at another table, two youngsters, a father with a full black beard and the mother in a headscarf. In Romanian, she says, 'They're everywhere. You can't trust them with anything.'

Polla slams down her tray. 'Not long ago they said the same thing about us.'

'What's wrong with you? You never know when they're going to come with a knife or a bomb. Good thing they stopped the boats.'

Polla spends another night worrying about Jabar. Why? She's only ever spoken to him once, and maybe he did kill Wendy Burford. But in the morning she phones in sick and takes the train and ferry to Balmain.

Already the house looks abandoned. Polla lets herself in with her cleaning key. Inside, it's shadowy, cool. Truth is, she doesn't know why she's here, or what she's looking for. She goes into Wendy's office. Everything's in its place. The overturned chair has been restored to the little meeting table. Against the wall, Wendy's desk looks organised and neat.

Wendy's laptop's on the desk, still plugged in. It's a silver MacBook Air with the top up. Polla skirts the stain on the carpet, sits in Wendy's office chair, pulls the laptop towards her. The screensaver, a desert landscape, appears. It needs a password.

Polla smiles. She knows the password. That's the thing about cleaners, people forget they're there. She heard Wendy on the phone one time, telling Apple customer service she'd locked herself out of her machine. She told them her password was her postcode.

Polla keys in 2041. The screensaver disappears and is replaced by the desktop. Inside the desktop is another screen, headed *Untitled Movie*. It's frozen on an image of this room, the office. The timeline at the bottom of the screen says *automatic cut-off* and there's a window asking if she wants to save it. Polla saves it and presses replay.

Wendy's face appears on screen. She says, 'Monday, 23rd of September. Meeting with Riley.' She's not smiling. She positions the laptop so it's camera is facing the room, so it captures the meeting table. She moves from her desk to the table and in a few minutes, a face Polla recognises appears at the door. 'Hi, Mum,' he says.

'You're late, Riley,' says Wendy. 'We don't have much time. I have a ten o'clock appointment.'

The argument is fierce and bitter. Riley wants money. Wendy says no, she's sticking by her decision: no more help till he goes to rehab. Riley says he doesn't need rehab. He accuses Wendy of hating him, of ruining his life, his father's life. He grows agitated, marches here and there, so Wendy has to swivel to see him.

She asks if he's on drugs right now. Riley says no. Wendy gets up, faces him, makes him stand still. She puts her hands on his shoulders, speaks slowly. She's scared, she says, scared he's going to harm someone, or worse, himself. He needs to go to rehab. If he won't go by himself then she'll make him. She's gathering evidence of his irrationality and if necessary she'll use it to have him sectioned. He'll be forced into care, and they'll get him off drugs. She doesn't like doing it, but it's for his own good. One day he'll thank her for it.

Riley springs away from her, comes up against the desk. The camera shows his back, and Wendy's serious face. The next thing Polla sees is Riley's hand swooping down, holding something that looks like a paperweight, smashing it into Wendy's head. Wendy falls back, crashing into a chair. Riley freezes – for a second Polla thinks it's the screen.

At that moment Jabar enters the room, saying, 'The door was open...' and stops still. He looks at Riley. Riley throws the paperweight towards him, an underarm bowling motion, and Jabar puts out his hand and catches it, a reflex. Riley runs. A minute later there she is, Polla herself, and everything that follows.

Polla lifts her hand towards the screen and finds it's shaking. She takes a deep breath, opens the top desk drawer.

She's still sitting in the office chair when she hears someone at the front door. There's just enough time to close the laptop and stand up and then Riley appears, framed in the doorway.

'Who the hell are you?'

Polla puts on her strongest Romanian accent. 'I cleaner. No clean Monday so come today.'

'What?'

'I clean!' Polla waves her arms. 'Every week I clean.'

She can't help glancing at the computer. Riley sees the look, darts around her, snatches it from the desk. 'Get out of here. Now!'

'You pay me?' asks Polla. 'Miss Wendy owe me money.'

'Get out!'

Polla goes, clutching the flash drive she found in the desk drawer. Her heart is beating so hard she thinks she might die.

She doesn't go straight to the police. She takes a taxi to Officeworks, then another to Leichhardt where she insists on handing the drive to Detective Inspector Robertson in person, making sure he understands she's got more than one copy.

She doesn't hear anything for a whole day. She guesses this is to give Robertson time to cover his back, to do the things he should have done in the first place. When the news does hit the media, however, it's a good spin. How all Australians, no matter their ethnicity, can expect impartial, fair, equitable and just treatment.

Polla phones Silverwater to make a time to see Jabar, only to be told he's been released – from prison, that is. Now he's in the Immigration Detention Centre, at Villawood.

It's harder to get into Villawood than Silverwater. She has to email, fill in forms, be accepted. It's three days before she can pack up some fruit and a tin of her special biscuits and get on a train.

Villawood's a walled compound in a concrete desert. After the first checkpoint, a surly guard confiscates Polla's food. She has to give up her bag, her phone. Finally she's led down a concrete path and through another checkpoint to a small, Perspex-enclosed space with booths like a diner. In one of them, waiting for her, is Jabar.

He rises when he sees her, opens his arms like it's the most natural thing in the world. She's completely enveloped in the hug. They break apart. Then suddenly it's awkward and they separate further, sit down opposite each other. Jabar looks bone-tired. There's a fresh scar over his left eye.

'What is happening?' Polla asks.

Jabar sighs monumentally. 'I am 501.'

Polla waits for an explanation.

Jabar puts his elbows on the table, recites. 'A 501 is someone who will not be granted a visa because they do not pass the character test.'

'What is this character test?'

'Because they are criminal. Or maybe they are *national threat*.' He recites the words.

'But you are not criminal.'

'It is enough I was there, in the house. It is their excuse. I do not have visa and they will deport me back to Syria.' He looks at the sky, through the Perspex wall. States a fact. 'In Syria, they will kill me.'

'We must find someone to help.'

'Who?'

She shakes her head. The one person who might know is dead. Then she has an idea. She grins at Jabar.

'If you marry Australian citizen, Jabar, they can't kick you out so easy. They listen to what you say. You get help, later you become citizen yourself. You know that?'

Jabar takes time to consider, smiles back. 'Polla, you mean I should marry you?'

Polla shrugs. 'Why not? I am Australian citizen."

He keeps his gaze on her. His eyes crinkle at the corners and for the first time she realises how beautiful they are, how liquid and brown.

'In my country,' he says, teasing, 'it is custom for man to ask woman to marry him.'

'So?' Her heart is racing.

'Polla, will you marry me?'

'Yes, Jabar,' she says. 'I marry you.'

They both burst out laughing. 'This is crazy,' Jabar says.

'Why? I come back with lawyer and with papers and everything will be OK.'

There is a long, quiet moment. 'You are a good friend,' he says.

She reaches out her hand. He takes it. They hang on for dear life.

THE CASE OF THE
MYSTERY TEXTER

I WAS INVITED TO SELWYN AND EDNA'S DINNER PARTY, THEIR FIRST since getting married. There were five of us: the newlyweds; Bella, Selwyn's grandmother; Charlie Mostyn, and me. The food, courtesy of Bella, was delicious, but the dinner wasn't a success. Selwyn and Edna only had eyes for each other, forever kissing or touching hands, shoulders, heads. It stifled conversation. You could forgive them anything, though, they were so happy. And Bella revelled in it, radiating what she called *nachas*, a Yiddish word meaning to garner pleasure from family success.

We were in Edna's old house. Selwyn had recently turned 40 and Edna wasn't far behind, and this was a first marriage for both of them. Selwyn had been living with grandmother Bella, so it made sense for him to be the one to move. They'd hired a decorator and the result was pretty luxurious, if a little stiff for my taste.

Selwyn proposed a toast. 'To Mavis,' he said, 'who brought us together. Without her I wouldn't have found my little *chick-chick-chickadee*.' And he leaned over and nibbled Edna's earlobe.

Charlie Mostyn rolled his eyes. Charlie was Edna's friend and his being there was a set-up, a blind date for me. He was tall, blond and just my type, and neither she nor Selwyn realised we already knew each other. We'd hooked up in London the year before and, after a brief, intense and extremely painful affair, managed to keep out of each other's orbits. Tonight, we avoided awkwardness by pretending to be strangers, but every now and then, when the happy couple were too lovey-dovey, either Charlie or I would make a face. He kept my glass filled, too.

He was interested in Selwyn's toast. 'So how did Mavis bring the two of you together?'

'Well,' said Edna, sipping sparkling water, 'It's a good story. A mystery, really. As you know, Selwyn and I are partners at Neustein Garfunkel. I must admit, I fancied him – *oh yesss, I did, I fancied youuu* – but resigned myself to the fact that he was never going to ask me out–'

'And I,' said Selwyn, placing a plump hand on Edna's shoulder, 'on my side, had my mind on work. But then I started to get these texts, telling me how, well, attractive I was, and how the sender would like to get to know me better. They were anonymous, and I didn't recognise the number. Very strange! So I asked Mavis here if she could work out who sent them. Because she's a linguist,' he explained, for Charlie's benefit. 'She analyses language and such. Very useful to a legal firm, as a matter of fact.' Charlie tried to look as if this was news to him. 'Well, Mavis said the texts were probably from Edna–'

'And so he asked me out,' said Edna, 'and–'

'And here we are,' said Selwyn, stroking her shoulder.

'So what's the mystery?' asked Charlie.

'I didn't send the texts!' squealed Edna. 'We don't know who did. Perhaps it was my guardian angel. Because–'

'Because we're *made* for each other!' concluded Selwyn. *'Aren't we, my poochie-woochie-pie?'*

'So you got it wrong?' asked Charlie, cocking an eyebrow. Was he taking pleasure in my mistake?

I contemplated my plate. I couldn't tell him what really happened.

I love Selwyn like a brother. I've known him since his parents died, when, as a bewildered eight-year-old, he came to Bella, who lived next door to me. Theirs was the quintessential migrant story: during the war, Bella escaped from Poland with her son, Bennie, and made her way to Sydney where she worked three jobs to give him an education. Bennie excelled, married, and Selwyn was the result. Then the accident. Bella enveloped her orphan grandson in love – a love she extended to me. Growing up, Selwyn and I spent as much time in her house as we did in mine.

We must have made an odd pair, the abrasive tomboy and the anxious scholar, but we were similar in ways that counted, in our only-child status and lack of social ease. He had my back, even after I left home. It was Selwyn who saw me through my divorce and it was his idea that Neustein Garfunkel place a linguist on retainer. He had to fight for it but after a couple of wins, I became a fixture.

So I was in my office when he burst through the door, brandishing his phone. 'Mavis,' he puffed, 'I need your help. Someone's stalking me.'

I looked up, astonished. Selwyn's not the type to inspire obsession. Don't get me wrong, he's perfectly adequate; but if you were casting a movie, you'd be inclined to make him the stalker, not the stalkee. He must have noticed my surprise, because he repeated, 'Stalking. Or sexual harassment. Perhaps someone's sexually harassing me?'

'That's a serious accusation,' I said. 'What do you mean? And who?'

'That's just it. I don't know who.' He wheezed slightly, feeling for his inhaler. 'Someone's been sending me texts. At first I thought...can you help me work out who it is?'

'Sit,' I said. 'Show me. Hand over your phone.'

The texts came in daily, one a day. They read:

>0467883410: Hello big boy. I watched you in the office today. U look handsome. LOL

>Selwyn: I think you may have texted me by mistake.

>0467883410: No mistake, Selwyn. When I see u my heart quickly beats. I like to get to know u better. LOL

>Selwyn: Who are you? I tried to call the number but there was no answer?

>0467883410: You make me crazy, Selwyn. How can we get 2gether? You are such a clever boy. LOL

>Selwyn: Who is this? There's no answer from this number

>0467883410: You do not no how handsome you are. A lovely piece of meat. LOL

'See? This is getting beyond a joke,' said Selwyn. 'Should I keep responding? What should I do?' He slumped into the visitors' chair.

'Well,' I said, 'we need to decide if this is harassment or not. If it is harassment, it's a crime, and we'll approach things differently. So my first question is, how do you feel about these texts?'

Selwyn removed his glasses and polished them on his tie. 'I'm a bit excited,' he admitted, blinking. 'Someone thinks I'm handsome.'

'Someone at work,' I added, 'if they noticed you in the office.'

'Oh, yes, of course!' His eyes glazed as he considered the prospects. 'The new receptionist, you think? The blonde one? Or...'

'It's not necessarily a woman,' I pointed out.

He replaced his glasses. 'Just my luck.' he muttered. 'Should I let them know I'm straight?'

'Let's assume for the moment it's a she. Let's also work out who sent the texts before we go down the harassment road. Agreed?'

He nodded. The field wasn't large. Legal firms aren't bastions of gender equality and Neustein Garfunkel was no exception. Apart from me, they employed only seven women: a receptionist, three secretaries, a paralegal and two female lawyers.

'We can rule out the receptionist, the secretaries and the paralegal.'

'What makes you say that?' Selwyn looked vaguely disappointed. The new receptionist was quite the flirt.

'They're all under 30. All of them know LOL stands for *laughing out loud*, not *lots of love*. It's an obvious mistake. Either the sender did it on purpose, in which case the texts are pretty creepy, or it's someone really unused to texting, most probably someone older. Also, there are no gifs or emojis – in fact, there aren't any visuals at all. That's really unusual these days, especially in texts of this kind. There are other reasons as well, and I can't be 100 per cent sure, but it's a pretty solid guess.'

'That leaves Julia or Edna,' said Selwyn, blushing slightly. 'Gosh.'

I knew what he was thinking. Julia Benson and Edna Epstein were the two female lawyers, junior partners both. Edna was what Bella calls *zaftig*, full-figured and bosomy. She was also smart, and a great lawyer. She was quiet though, and shy, in need of a hefty shot of self-confidence. Edna was the firm's workhorse, shouldering without complaint more than her share of the burden.

Julia was something else. Julia was light-haired and light-eyed, sexy in a louche, sulky sort of way. She wasn't impervious to the stir she caused in the office as she slunk her way through upheaval after upheaval. The male lawyers loved her. The secretaries, who had to pick up the pieces, loathed her. You could see, just by looking at him, Selwyn was quietly praying the mystery texter would turn out to be Julia.

'Oh,' he said. 'I just realised. If it is Julia, it can't be sexual harassment. Because it's not sexual harassment if the approach is welcomed, or consensual, or the harasser stops when asked.' He smiled from ear to ear. 'So. Where do we go from here?'

'First, I'll transcribe the texts. Then you have to get me a sample of Julia's writing, and Edna's too. Something not too formal, if you can manage it. I need to compare the writing with the texts.'

'I asked them to give their opinions on the Murray case. I've got both their memos. I'll bring them to you now?'

'No can do,' I said. 'Got a lunch date. See you this afternoon.'

In truth, I was playing for time. I didn't need the writing samples because I already knew the texter's identity and once Selwyn left, I called for an Uber, ending up at a door I knew as well as my own. Bella answered as she always does, keeping the latch on until she saw who it was. Then she threw her arms around me and cuddled me close. After which she pushed me away, for inspection.

'My darling, how wonderful to see you! But so thin, look at you, you don't eat. You're wasting away. Come, come. I've got scraps, we'll have lunch.'

I knew from long experience what Bella's "scraps" meant, and also the futility of resistance. So I watched her as she piled dish after dish on the table. Lately, she seemed to have grown smaller, frailer. Her grooming was faltering too, her hair as defiantly yellow as ever but her pants and top tired and wrinkled. Finally she sat, with a relieved sigh.

'*Nu*, eat!' she ordered. I opened my mouth to talk and she raised her hand in a stop sign. 'That can wait. Tell me, my darling, how's your love life? Anyone special?'

After the inquisition, relaxing over kugel and coffee, I took the transcribed texts from my handbag and laid them in front of her. 'Tell me about these,' I said, tapping the page.

Bella looked crafty. 'What's to say?'

'They're from you?'

'Sure. Of course they're from me. Who else?'

'Bella! What were you thinking? If Selwyn decided someone was harassing him, we could have had a full-scale investigation on our hands.'

'Pfft! He loves the attention. I bet he's like a little boy on his birthday. Am I right?' She grinned. 'Yes, I am. I know my Selwyn.'

'What I can't understand, Bella, is why you sent them.'

'Oh, please.' Bella tossed her head. 'This is a 40-year-old man, still living with his grandmother. It's not natural. Also, I'm tired of doing his washing and cooking and ironing. He's cluttering up the place and he – he needs to make his own life. That's why I sent them, to give him a kick up the *tochas*.'

'With all due respect, that's nonsense. There's nothing you love more than looking after Selwyn. You've dedicated your life to him, and not just because he needed you. You needed him, too. And now you tell me you've had enough? I don't buy it. If you were so keen to get rid of him, why didn't you talk to him first?'

After a few minutes' stare-off, Bella's eyes slid away. She sighed, heavily. 'My darling. You want to know why I sent them? I'll tell you. I'm nearly 90, a very old woman. I haven't got much longer – no, don't interrupt, I'm happy to go. Listen to me. I lost my parents, my family, even my sweet, sweet husband, in the Holocaust. I got out with my baby and made a new life here, and then they took him as well, my only son.' Bella pushed her lips together, fighting for control. 'That's gone, finished. Selwyn's all I have in the world, and...' she leaned forward to make the point, 'and I'm all he has, too. Unless he finds someone, when I go, he'll be all by himself. I don't want him to be alone. I can't stand the thought of it.'

She came closer, took my face in her hands. 'And you, Mavis, you're like a daughter to me. Unless you find someone to love I'll have to leave you alone, too.' There were tears in her eyes. Then she broke the spell, slapping my cheek lightly. 'Besides, I want to hold a grandchild before they bury me. Is that too much to ask? You and Selwyn both, you need to get a move on. You ask me why I didn't talk to him? Because who listens to an old woman?'

She wiped her eyes with a napkin. 'Tell me, sweetheart, how did you know it was me? I did such a good job. I bought a phone, specially, and Hymie at the seniors centre taught me how to use it. I copied the way those messages work. I even put *u* instead of *you*, and here, look, *no* instead of *know*.'

'You weren't consistent,' I replied, 'and you didn't get things right.' I explained about *LOL*. 'But it wasn't the texts themselves that made me think of you. It was other things, things that told me the writer has English as a second language. For example, look here: *I watched you in the office today*. A native English speaker would be inclined to say *I saw you in the office today*. That could mean someone who hasn't quite got the difference right, between "watch" and "see". And here, *My heart quickly beats*, where most people would say *My heart beats quickly*. You've mixed up the word order, as many Eastern Europeans do, because it's not as strict in your language. On the other hand, you spelled out words English speakers would have contracted, like *you are*, for *you're*, and *do not*, for *don't*. That formality, too, indicates a foreign speaker.

'But Bella, the absolute giveaway was when you called Selwyn *a lovely piece of meat*. I've never heard anyone say that, certainly not anyone young. I haven't done statistical comparisons but I'm willing to bet it's a phrase that hasn't been used for generations.'

'Stop, stop! You win.' Bella held up her hands in surrender. 'Smartypants. Anyway, what does it matter? It did the trick. Now Selwyn will ask Edna Epstein out and–'

'No, Bella, he won't. Just the opposite. He's hoping the texts came from Julia Benson.'

'Julia Benson? That skinny piece of sideways? She's...she'll eat my Selwyn alive. No, worse, she'll laugh at him and then he won't ask anyone out again, never mind Edna. Oh, no, that's terrible! Mavis, you've got to do something. I made a mess, I'm sorry, please can you fix it?' She grabbed the front of my jacket. 'Don't tell Selwyn I sent the texts. He'll be humiliated. He'll say I'm an interfering old fool, and he'll never forgive me.'

'Shh,' I said, 'Shh, now. Of course I'll fix it. Don't worry.'

I stayed with her till she calmed down, wondering how I was going to put things right.

Back at work, I was nowhere nearer a solution. On my desk, front and centre, lay the two reports, one from Julia and one from Edna, along with a covering brief. I began to read.

Half an hour later I took them to Selwyn's office.

'Any luck?' His face shone in anticipation.

I swallowed. My professionalism, as well as our friendship, was at stake. 'I think it's Edna.'

'Edna?' He sat back. 'Can you be sure it's not Julia?'

'Well, of course my verdict isn't definitive. I haven't had time to do a thorough analysis but, if you look at these memos, you'll see where I'm coming from. In your brief, you ask both Julia and Edna to assess points of weakness in the Murray Corporation, and to recommend responses. As I understand it, you're not asking for a formal legal document, just their thoughts. Take Julia's memo first. Linguistically, it's a mish-mash. Look at this, for example: *At this point in time there is a serious danger that the Murray Corporation will, going forward, be subject to the fallout created by previous blue-sky thinking.* Or this: *It is recommended that Neustein Garfunkel cascade memos about their responsive relative contingencies, to synchronise reciprocal projections.* I have absolutely no idea what she's talking about here, and I don't think she does either.'

Selwyn bit his lip. 'I do have trouble getting through her work, I admit.'

'I'm not surprised. She's a muddled thinker, or a devious one. A show-off, at the very least. Now, let's move to Edna's memo, which couldn't be more different. Her language is simple and direct, as for example, here: *The Murray Corporation has grown without establishing a solid administrative base, and in my opinion can no longer service its clients.* And she puts her recommendations in dot points, all with the same stem. She may even show a glimmer of humour, in recommendation 4: *that Neustein Garfunkel guarantee payment before starting work.*

'Selwyn,' I concluded, 'this memo is a work of art. This mind is clear, bright and open, as are the texts, and that is why I think Edna sent them. In any case, who would you rather spend time with? Julia's sludge, or Edna's diamonds?'

I hoped like hell Selwyn wouldn't notice the total lack of logic. And it worked. He fingered Edna's memo. 'It's true, she is smart,' he ventured. 'And she does have a nice smile.'

'Exactly.'

'You think I should ask her out for coffee?'

'Go for broke, Selwyn. Ask her to dinner.'

And that was that.

So you see, when Charlie fixed me with his blue stare, all I could do was look rueful and shrug. The secret was Bella's, and I knew she would share it in her own time – probably at the birth of their firstborn which, given Edna's insistence on sparkling water, looked like being sooner rather than later.

The dinner ended early. I drove Bella home, settled her in, and returned to my car. As I fastened the seatbelt my phone pinged. A text, from a number I didn't recognise. It read:

> You looked very lovely tonight. I miss you. Care for a nightcap?

No *LOL*. I checked the word order, and pressed reply.

THE BYBLOS CODE

THE BODY IN THE LIBRARY WAS DISCOVERED BY TWO STUDENTS who, desperate to be alone, had made their way to a remote corner of the stacks. What they found there was Dr Theodore Croucher, Chief Librarian. He was in the end carrel, slumped forward as if asleep. The students were turning away when one of them noticed blood on his collar.

My shift hadn't started yet so I wasn't there when they found him. Ludmilla Madden, Dr Croucher's deputy, phoned me. Ludmilla was a spiteful, angular woman given to beads and bangles. She wore her dresses long and sack-like and her hair geisha-style, complete with hairpins. 'We've called the police,' she said. 'They'll be here any minute. They'll want to talk to you. I told them you and Theo were...close.'

I didn't reply. Ludmilla was right, but it wasn't like that. Dr Croucher was – had been – my mentor. I'd encountered him in my first year and he'd seen beyond the glasses and fringe and singled me out. He'd spent time with me, encouraged me, and it was his enthusiasm which led me to this career. He'd even given me a part-time job while I completed my PhD. He was at least 30 years older than me but we were united in our love of libraries and their worlds of information and discovery. And now he was dead. I couldn't believe it.

By the time I arrived, it was afternoon and two hard-faced detectives were waiting for me. I saw them take in my beige pants and sensible shoes and pigeonhole me as the perfect librarian. Which, after all, I am.

The questions began. Did I know anyone who might want to kill Dr Croucher? I shook my head. Everyone respected Dr Croucher. Professional, courteous, correct to a fault, his world revolved around the library. No, he'd never mentioned a family. Dr Croucher kept his private life private.

The detectives ran out of questions. I could see they were stumped. They handed me business cards, told me to phone if I thought of anything. I said I would, then asked, 'How did Dr Croucher die?'

They looked at each other, shrugged. 'He was stabbed in the neck with a long, thin object. We'll know more when we hear from forensics.'

I wandered down to the staff area in a daze, the reality of Dr Croucher's death starting to hit home. I didn't think I could focus on work, and I certainly couldn't face the cluster of colleagues gossiping at the coffee machine. Might as well clear some paperwork, I told myself. I started with my pigeonhole. We rarely get mail these days, but I like to be thorough. One envelope only, white, good quality. On the front, in cursive script, *For Juniper Jones*. For me, in Dr Croucher's handwriting.

I took it to my desk and slid the flap open with a finger. Inside were two sheets of good quality paper, handwritten, the lines uneven as if the writer had hurried. I looked at the first page.

Dear Ms Jones,
If you are reading this, it means I am dead. Please advise the people on the attached list of this fact and warn them they are in danger. Many apologies for the inconvenience, but it is a matter of the utmost importance.
I place this burden on you because I have chosen you for Byblos.
Please do not refer the matter to the police.
Yours sincerely,
Theodore Blythe Croucher.

The first sentence of the letter was so shocking that for a while, I couldn't take it in. When I eventually did, all I had were questions. If Dr Croucher knew, or at least suspected, he was going to die, why hadn't he told anyone? What did he mean, *danger*? And what, or who, was Byblos?

No answer from beyond the grave or anywhere else. I turned to the second page. It bore a list of six names and next to each, the name of a library and phone numbers, landline and mobile. Each person was in a different country, and the spread was amazing.

Ms Immi Kornhonen, the Oodi, Helsinki Central Library.

Mr Lester van Buren, South Omaha Public Library.

Dr Sahil Dewan, Deshbandu Government District Library, Darjeeling.

Dr Olivier Moreau, the Sorbonne University Library, Paris.

Dr Tobias Marlowe, the Bodleian, Oxford.

Mr Adam Armstrong, Central City Library, Auckland.

I tried to make sense of the list. There was an obvious library link, so perhaps these people had met Dr Croucher at a conference. How could they be in danger? I stared at the page for a few minutes, then shook myself slightly. Dr Croucher wanted me to warn them, and so I would. I checked my watch, then googled time zones. 4pm in Sydney made it 10am in Helsinki.

I lifted the landline and dialled.

The phone was answered on the second ring by a man with impeccable, formal English. I explained I was calling from Australia and asked to speak to Ms Kornhonen. There was a long silence. Then he said, 'I regret to tell you, Madam, Ms Kornhonen passed away last week.'

'Oh,' I stammered, trying to think of what to say. I blurted, 'Wh-what did she die of?' and, belatedly, 'I'm sorry to hear that.'

'She died quite suddenly, of natural causes. She was over 70, and long retired. Her work here was as Emeritus Librarian, as you are probably aware.'

'Of course,' I lied.

He asked, 'Is there anyone else here who might help you?'

'No, thank you,' I said, and we ended the call.

Natural causes? A coincidence, or something more sinister? Only one way to find out. Afternoon in Omaha, so I tried Mr van Buren. A woman's voice, this time, older. 'Oh *no*, dear, all the way from Australia? You haven't heard the news? Our poor Mr van Buren. Were you a particular friend? His wife–'

I tried to edge my way into the torrent of words. 'Are you saying Mr van Buren's dead?'

'Yes, dear, our Mr van Buren, just yesterday, so sad, and in the prime of his life. *Such* a beautiful man, and the pillar of–'

'How did he die?' I could hear the hoarseness in my voice.

'He was k... He died in a car accident. His brakes...' She began to sniff. I hung up without saying goodbye.

I began to google the names on the list. Dr Dewan of Darjeeling, shot dead in a random attack, like van Buren only yesterday. Dr Moreau of the Sorbonne, missing, and anyone with information must contact the Gendarmerie Nationale. Dr Marlowe of the Bodleian, found dead in the Duke Humfrey Library. Possible heart attack. This one in today's newsfeed, because of the famous location.

Never mind Dr Marlowe's heart; my own was pounding hard. I moved to the last name, Adam Armstrong. Apart from a bio and a photo of a youngish, dark-haired man, nothing on Google. Auckland wasn't so far away. It was night-time there now, but Dr Croucher had supplied a mobile number. The phone was answered on the first ring.

'Adam Armstrong.' A deep, pleasant voice.

'You're alive!'

'Who is this?'

'You don't know me. Juniper Jones, City University Library. I took a deep breath. 'Mr Armstrong, I think you're in danger.'

'Slow down. I'm not following.'

'Do you know Dr Theodore Croucher? He's dead. Someone killed him. Stabbed him in the neck. And a whole lot of other people are dead as well, and all in the last day or so.' I sounded like a crazy woman, so I added, 'Dr Croucher left me a letter with your name in it.'

Armstrong spoke slowly. 'So they got him.'

'What do you mean? They? Who are–?'

'Listen to me, Juniper Jones.' Armstrong broke in. 'If I leave now I'll make the last plane out. I'll explain when I see you, but what you've discovered puts you in danger too. Where are you calling from?'

'The library.'

'OK. Go home. I'll meet you there. What's the address?'

His voice was so urgent, I didn't hesitate. 'Number 42 Hordern Street, Newtown. It's a small terrace house.'

'My plane gets in around ten your time. I'll be there as soon as I can.'

I stowed the letter in my backpack and headed for home.

Patience isn't my strong suit and the time passed slowly. I fed Gutenberg, the rescue cat, put on *The Koln Concert* and listened to it while I drank a glass of Pinot Gris and made myself a cheese omelette. Then I washed up. Eight-thirty and still an hour and a half to go. I opened my book, *Gaudy Night* by Dorothy Sayers. Mystery and romance combined. Sigh.

It was no good; I couldn't concentrate. I kept looking at my watch. Ten o'clock, and then, by millimetres, eleven. Perhaps Adam Armstrong had missed the plane? I tried his mobile number. It went to voicemail. Half an hour later, I tried again. It was way beyond my bedtime now and the least he could have done was to keep me informed. 'Listen, Mr Armstrong,' I said to his voicemail, 'it's late. I'm going to bed.'

At long last, a knock on the door. I ran to open it but it wasn't Armstrong. It was two dark shapes, big men in black. One of them grabbed me and half-lifted, half-dragged me to a waiting car, a black sedan with open doors. He threw me on the back seat and piled in after me. I heard my front door slam – I remember thinking they'd locked me out – and the second man reappeared. He ran to the driver's side. I had a sense of the car taking off, but by then the first man had stuck a needle in my neck and the world receded.

I woke in bright sunlight, to roses. Not real roses, but overblown chintz blooms on a bedspread. I was lying on the bed on my side, my head on a pillow, and I could see a wet patch where I'd drooled while I was unconscious. I rolled onto my back, making the mattress squeal, and tried to sit up. The room started to spin and I lay back. I must have fallen asleep again because I was woken by someone shaking me. I opened my eyes. A dark-haired man was bending over me.

'Juniper Jones? I'm Adam Armstrong.'

The clouds were receding. 'What happened to you? Did you miss your plane? What time is it?'

He looked at his watch. 'You've been out for nearly 12 hours. It's eleven o'clock.'

Twelve hours! No wonder I felt groggy. I propped myself against the bedhead and took in my surroundings. We were in a bedroom, old-fashioned and clean but strangely impersonal. A hotel, perhaps, or bed and breakfast? Armstrong had retreated to an armchair, where he sat with arms folded, legs crossed at the knee. He wore a blue shirt and cream moleskins and R M Williams boots, and even in my dazed state I saw he was attractive. I felt my face redden, straightened my blouse.

'Where are we?'

He didn't answer. I fought a rising panic. I had to get out. I saw two doors. I tried to stand, fell back. 'Don't bother,' Armstrong said. 'The white one leads to an ensuite. The wooden one's locked.'

I looked at the windows. Behind the net curtains I could see bars and beyond them a concrete wall. We were in a city.

A carafe of water covered by an overturned glass stood on the bedside table beside me. I poured and drank. 'Mr Armstrong' I said, trying to keep my voice from trembling, 'please tell me what's going on.'

Armstrong uncrossed his legs, recrossed them. 'My name's Adam.'

'Adam. Why are we here? Who took us?'

A short silence. 'How much did Theo Croucher tell you?'

'He didn't tell me anything. He just left me the letter.'

'The letter listing the people he thought were in danger, and choosing you for Byblos?'

My heart contracted. When I'd phoned Adam I'd told him Croucher was dead. I'd told him he was in danger. But I hadn't mentioned Byblos. The only way he could know about Byblos was from the letter and the letter was in my backpack, or had been. I'd told him my address: he must have arranged my kidnapping, broken in to my home and stolen the letter while I lay unconscious. I was stuck in a room with a criminal. What had he planned for me next? I opened my mouth to scream, or cry – I didn't know what – then shut it again. Histrionics weren't going to help. Instead, voice shaky, I asked, 'What's Byblos?'

'You really don't know?'

All my anger and fear, everything that had happened since yesterday, burst up and out like a geyser. 'Of course I don't know!' I wailed. 'How could I? I only got the letter yesterday. And you! You had me kidnapped. Drugged. For all I know you're planning to... to...' Wildly, I looked around for a weapon, grabbed the carafe and lifted it. Water sprayed across the bed.

He was fast. He caught my wrist before I could throw, removed the carafe, sat on the bed next to me. Quietly, he said, 'Juniper, calm down. I don't want to kill you. On the contrary, I thought you might want to kill me. But I believe you when you say you don't know about Byblos, so at least we can leave this horrible room.' He stood up, took his phone from his pocket, pressed a button, and said, 'All good. We're on our way.' Then he replaced the phone and produced a key. 'Up you get.'

I folded my arms. 'I'm not going anywhere with you, you...rotten crook.' And then, with great delight, I heard myself add, 'Fuck *off!*'

Adam Armstrong smiled. He had a nice smile, dammit. He gripped my arm and lifted me up. I struggled and kicked, but he was bigger and stronger than me and besides, he had the key. I gave up. I let him unlock the door and, still gripping my arm, walk me down a long, carpeted passage to an old-fashioned cage lift, where the door folds back upon itself. He pressed G. From the lights, I saw we'd been on the second floor.

The lift opened onto a large room dotted with couches and armchairs, the same era as in the bedroom above. No people, so perhaps a private club. I guessed we were in central Sydney, in one of the pre-war buildings you get around Castlereagh Street.

Adam frogmarched me through the room and down another passage until we came to a set of double doors. He knocked softly, then leaned in to me and whispered, 'Listen, Juniper Jones, I know I haven't given you any cause to trust me so far. But things aren't what they seem.' Before he could continue, a voice from inside the room said, 'Come.' Adam released my arm, opened the doors and ushered me inside.

The room was windowless and lit by four green-shaded chandeliers. They shone on a long oval table, polished and bare except for a few bottles of water and a videoconferencing machine. Sitting at the table and facing us were two men and a woman. The woman was Ludmilla Madden, Dr Croucher's deputy and the bane of my life. I should have known.

Finally Adam released me. I looked back at the double doors, now shut. Ludmilla snorted. 'Don't even think about it,' she said. 'Juniper. Sit.'

I sat. Adam sat next to me. I edged as far away from him as I could.

'Well done, Mr Armstrong,' said one of the men. He was elderly, bowed, with rheumy eyes and a few white hairs plastered on a mottled skull. He wore a suit jacket over a plaid waistcoat, and a yellow bowtie.

'Thank you, Professor White,' Adam said, inclining his head.

The other man was younger, in his 50s, plump and pale. His hair, thin and plastered to one side, was light brown. His fingernails, long and filed into ovals, made little clicking sounds as he drummed them on the table. 'Well?' he said, 'What does she know?'

'Nothing,' said Adam. 'Croucher left her the letter, that's all.'

Ludmilla clicked her tongue. 'Stupid,' she said. 'But she's heard about Byblos now and that's enough to have her...dispatched.'

The old man sighed. 'Unfortunately, yes.'

'Dispatched?' I squeaked. 'I haven't...' Adam didn't look at me, but I felt his hand on my thigh, warning me to stop.

'There's another way,' he said. 'We make her a member.'

The three people across the table looked at him. Eventually the pale man said, 'What do you mean? You–'

Ludmilla interrupted. 'You know the Code. It specifically states that any stranger who stumbles across Byblos or–'

Adam cut her off in turn. 'The Code also states that membership be held at five per region. Theodore Croucher's death leaves a vacancy.'

'Oh *please*,' scoffed Ludmilla. 'She's not yet 30. Junior. And look at her. As much initiative as wet bread. I can think of better prospects and besides, new members must be nominated by current ones. She has to go.'

'She's fully qualified and about to complete a doctorate on library practice. From what I hear, she's dedicated. Besides,' Adam pulled the letter from his back pocket, unfolded it and read aloud, '*I have chosen you for Byblos*.' He looked up. 'We have it in writing. Theo Croucher chose Ms Jones himself.'

The old man, Professor White, reached for the letter. 'Show me.' He glanced at it. 'Yes, this is Theo's handwriting. It seems indisputable. He has chosen Ms Jones and we will admit her as a member forthwith.

I'd had enough. '*Admit me to what?* You're all talking in riddles and I refuse to join anything I know nothing about.' I folded my arms.

'Very well.' Addressing the others, Professor White said, 'As chair of the Oceania Chapter, it is my duty to explain. Please leave us.'

Ludmilla and the pale man exchanged a look, both reluctant to move, but old, trembly Professor White emanated a sense of power that made them comply. Adam was already holding the door open. He ushered them out and, joining them, closed the door behind him. I felt a pang as he left, then remembered how badly he'd treated me.

Professor White must have read my mind. 'First of all, Ms Jones, I would like to apologise for the ordeal we put you through. When I explain, you will understand.'

'What is Byblos?' I asked.

White gave a phlegmy chuckle. 'Ah, well. Byblos. From the Ancient Greek Βύβλος which, as I'm sure you already know, is the name of a town in Lebanon, one of the most ancient towns in the world. Byblos the town gave its name to papyrus and thence to books. It is connected to the earliest written records.

'Excuse me, but what's your point?' I knew all this, and the last thing I needed was mansplaining.

'My point, young lady, is that as soon as we humans began creating written records, we began curating them.'

'You mean librarians?'

'Exactly. Librarians have existed as long as writing has and what people fail to recognise is the power librarians can wield. I would go so far as to say librarians are the most powerful people in society.' White looked at me, saw scepticism, chuckled again. It developed into a rheumy cough.

When he'd recovered, he said, 'Consider, Ms Jones, consider. Information, and the communication of information, is the lifeblood of the human race. Librarians control information. To be more precise; librarians have it in their power to control information. The question is: what to do about it?'

'What do you mean *do about it*?'

'Well, those who control information can decide what to send out and what to...keep back.'

'You mean censorship?'

'That, yes, but in its widest form. Say you had information which, if disseminated, could lead to war. Would you allow its publication?'

'No...yes, I'd have to.'

'Even if it led to thousands of deaths?'

'Librarians don't own knowledge, Professor White,' I said. 'We just curate it.'

'We just curate it,' he said, repeating my words. 'Curation in itself involves choice, doesn't it?'

'I suppose so.'

'From the beginning, Juniper,' a small smile as he said my name, 'there have been two factions in the world of librarians. One faction believes our job is to store, recover and disseminate all the information we receive. The other faction believes librarians have a duty to select what information may or may not be revealed.'

'So if I belonged to that faction,' I said, drawn in despite myself, 'I'd keep back information that could start a war.'

'Or,' White said, 'if you were so inclined, you could release that information. You could start that war.' He let his words sink in. 'You could sell that information, or you could use it to benefit a third party; a government, say, or a corporation. The war in the Ukraine, for example, or Vietnam, or going further back, the Crimea, or,' he waved a dismissive hand, 'any number of conflicts caused in this way. Conversely, of course, you could release information for good, as for example in the moon landing, or the development of antibiotics.' He trailed off.

I nodded slowly. I was beginning to see his point. 'But how does this relate to Byblos?' I thought of something else. 'And what about Dr Croucher's murder, and the deaths of the other people on the list?'

White took in a breath. 'From the earliest times, those involved with libraries realised the responsibilities of their calling. They formed a society to share and transport information and called themselves Byblos, to honour the written word. However, their enemies, those who realised the possibilities inherent in controlling information, rose against them. These enemies were prepared to do anything to achieve their ends, even kill for it.'

He placed his hands on the table, fingers spread, and leaned towards me. 'You've heard of Hypatia, the famous 5th century librarian? She was killed by an angry mob. History calls them fanatics. We know better. And there are more, right through the ages: Catherine of Dinan, the 12th century abbess. Rabbi Pinkus of Lublin. Fan Qin of China. William Torrent, Abraham McCafferty. All murdered in the name of evil.' Suddenly he stopped, fell back. He looked spent and so old I could see the skull beneath the skin.

He continued. 'Byblos became a secret society, working against those who would corrupt our calling. And even though our members are chosen with care, from time to time they defect and seek to destroy us. Imagine the power those people would have if Byblos did not exist!' He shook his head sadly. 'Theo Croucher suspected some of our members had gone rogue, but he didn't know where and he didn't know who. We set up a group to investigate.'

'The people who were murdered,' I said.

'Exactly.' White nodded. 'And that is why we treated you as we did. Adam is the only survivor of that group and we didn't know if your phone call was a trap or not. He had to see the letter. Again, apologies.'

'So the rogue members haven't been caught? And they might still be after Adam, in case he knows who they are?'

White thought about it. 'Yes.'

Suddenly, and without conscious thought, things fell into place. I blinked with the shock of it. 'I know who killed Dr Croucher,' I said, 'and unless I stop them they'll kill Adam too.' I leaped up. 'Wait here,' I told White. As if he had the strength to run after me.

I flung open the doors. No sign of anyone. Without stopping I headed for the stairs, for the only place I knew, the bedroom on the second floor. The door was shut, but I could hear voices. Trying to quiet my breath, I slowly pushed the handle down and peered in. Adam sat in the armchair, facing me. Facing him and with their backs to me were Ludmilla and the pale man. Ludmilla held a gun. Neither of them noticed me, but Adam's eyes veered over and back again. His expression didn't change.

'So if you won't join us, I'm afraid...' Ludmilla said. She raised the gun.

I threw myself forward and tackled her. The shot went wide and the gun flew out of her hand. At the same time, Adam propelled himself up and out of the chair and without much resistance overpowered the pale man.

'How did you know Ludmilla killed Theo?'

Professor White, Adam and I were back in the conference room of what I now knew to be the Byblos club, aka the Presbyterian Ladies Club. It was late afternoon and White had been contacting his international counterparts. Ludmilla had proven intractable, but Bradley Le Seuer, the pale man, had given up his co-conspirators without hesitation. Wheels were turning, and soon the rebel cell would be eradicated.

'How did I know? Well, the police said Dr Croucher was stabbed with a long thin object. I suddenly thought of Ludmilla and how she wears those Japanese hairpins and it all came together. Dr Croucher wouldn't have gone to the stacks for just anyone. He must have known his attacker and his attacker must have known the library. And I know Ludmilla. She's ruthless. What will happen to her now? Will you hand her over to the police?'

Professor White and Adam exchanged glances. Adam said, 'If Juniper is to join Byblos, she must know.'

White sighed deeply. 'Oh, my dear,' he said, 'it pains me to say this, but according to our Code the penalty for treason is death.'

'So Byblos is just as bad as its enemies?'

Adam said, 'No. We're on the side of right, and to operate effectively, it's imperative Byblos remain a secret. Besides, once Ludmilla knew her cover was blown, she would be capable of anything.'

White waved a hand dismissively. 'The matter is being dealt with now. More to the point, Juniper, we have to arrange for your inauguration.'

They were kidding themselves, and it was on the tip of my tongue to tell them I wanted nothing to do with them or with Byblos. Then I considered the consequences. If I refused, they'd have to kill me. Byblos or death? Hmm. I thought how pleasant work would be without Ludmilla. I thought about Adam, and the warmth of him sitting next to me. I thought about being a librarian.

'Bring it on,' I told them.

POLICE STORY

Her first day, and she was late. Not her fault, just the bloody Sydney traffic. By the time Jazz Kovacs found parking and pounded up the stairs, Inspector Hawke had started speaking. As Jazz slunk to the back of the room, he noticed her, shook his head. Hawke was in charge of the team and they'd got off to a bad start. At their introductory meeting, he greeted Jazz with a penetrating look and the drawled comment, 'On the short side to be so ambitious, aren't you?'

He was right. Jazz was short, and she was ambitious. Top marks at college, dedication on the beat, now one of two constables seconded to Homicide. On probation: only one of the two would be made permanent, and Jazz wanted it, hard. She'd heard all the jokes before, from the male cops: blonde jokes, girl jokes, size jokes. She refused to be intimidated so she stared straight ahead, answered, 'Yes, *sir.*'

Meanwhile, Hawke was emphasising the need for results. Two killings now, no sign of progress. The media were scaring people; the Minister was hounding the Commissioner and pressure, as they knew, always flowed downhill. He got a weak laugh at that. At least the publicity had led to more resources, he said, namely Constables Jasmine Kovacs and Brydon Lee. For their benefit, he reviewed the cases.

The first, three weeks ago, was Angela Mulvaney. A primary school teacher, Angela lived alone. She was conscientious, and when she didn't appear at school her head teacher drove to Glebe to see if she was all right. She wasn't. She was on her bed, strangled, bound hand and foot. Dressed for going out, but her top torn open and her breasts dotted with cigarette burns. A horrible death. No sign of a break-in. Nothing out of the ordinary, except a hungry cat. Prints and DNA, but none that matched any records.

Angela was divorced, gregarious, loved a drink. She was a regular at The Distant Drummer. She hadn't been there the night she was killed, though, and none of her friends could help. No steady boyfriend but she dated, even belonging to a few online sites. The theory was she'd met someone and brought them home, and things had gone badly wrong. Between the boyfriends and the pub and the online emails, the list of possible suspects was daunting.

Then, three days ago, Zeinab Haddad. Zeinab was an events manager at the Sheraton and, like Angela, single. Like her, Zeinab was found on her bed, killed in exactly the same way, including the burns, a detail not released to the press. Zeinab was by all accounts a loner. She and Angela had nothing in common except, according to Zeinab's computer, an interest in online dating.

Hawke summed up. 'These women were both in their 40s, single, and professionally competent. They both belonged to online dating sites. So, apart from following up the people in their lives, we have to identify the men who corresponded with them online, contact them, and eliminate them, one by one.'

Someone in the front row raised a hand. 'Constable Lee?' said Hawke. 'Go ahead.'

Lee stood, spoke loudly. 'I'm assuming you followed up on the first victim's dating emails?'

'Good question. Yes, we did. But given the second victim also used online sites, we'll have to revisit them. You and Constable Kovacs will make this your priority.'

Jazz felt a ripple of resentment. Why couldn't she have thought of a question like that? If she didn't shine, there'd be no possibility of her becoming a permanent member of the Homicide Squad.

'Anything else? No?' said Hawke. 'Right. I can't emphasise enough how critical this is. The killer's struck twice, and we have to stop him before he strikes again.'

Jazz and Brydon Lee were squeezed side by side into a corner of the open plan office. Lee dropped into his chair, rolled it close.

'Lee,' he said, 'Brydon.' He scanned her up and down. 'Well, now, I got lucky.' Gave her the benefit of his smile.

'Kovacs,' Jazz replied, nodding curtly. Lee shrugged. She stole a glance. Fit, with close-cropped black hair, Brydon Lee looked like a man going places. *Of course*, she thought bitterly, *he'll be the one. Hawke will choose a man, not me.*

Lee said, 'We'll start with the websites.'

God, he was irritating! How dare he tell her what to do. No good antagonising him, she reminded herself, they had to work together. 'Exactly what I was thinking,' she replied, hoping her voice sounded reasonable. He pulled his chair closer and they went to work.

Angela Mulvaney had spread herself around. She belonged to five sites. In contrast, Zeinab had joined just one, Kismet. But she'd been a member for a while and the Kismet file on her computer showed emails to or from 50 men. Problem was, Kismet wasn't on Angela's list.

Lee sat back. His phone pinged. He looked at the screen, grimaced. 'Girlfriend trouble,' he explained, turning his back and hunching over it. While Lee texted, Jazz read the murdered women's profiles. What did it matter that Angela liked to play the piano, or that Zeinab wanted to travel the world? Neither of them would fulfil their dreams now. She sighed. Then she googled the Kismet site. 'How does it work?' asked Lee, putting his phone away.

'You can browse all the profiles. But if you want to respond, or post a profile, you have to join, and pay. It's a monthly fee.'

A hundred and twenty women, all living in Sydney and aged 40-45, were looking for love on Kismet. 'Try the men,' said Lee.

There were ninety men in the 40-50 age group. 'And this is one of the smaller sites,' said Jazz. 'We'd be better off concentrating on the victims' emails.'

That didn't help. Angela, they found, had been in contact with 80 men. There were 50 on Zeinab's list. 'Jesus,' said Lee. 'This'll take forever. We'll have to interview them all.'

Jazz spoke slowly, almost to herself. 'Perhaps we're going about this the wrong way. People lie on the internet all the time. There's no guarantee the men in these emails used their own names, or even supplied their own photos. But there's only one killer. To find out who he is, we'd have to contact every single man mentioned in the dating emails, and trace the real ones behind the names. It could take weeks.'

'No shit, Sherlock. That's what I just said.'

She ignored him. 'Let's assume the killer is one of these men. If so, he must have written to both these women. Wouldn't it be smarter to look for similarities in the emails themselves, to see if we can pick him that way? At College, we did a seminar on how language can identify people. We could ask an expert to help.'

Lee linked his fingers behind his head. Arched backwards, in a stretch. 'Oh, I dunno,' he said. 'Sounds like a long shot.'

'Kovacs! Lee!' Hawke called from his office door.

'So,' he said, 'you two got a plan? Or did you spend the morning chatting each other up?'

Before Jazz could speak, Lee butted in. 'Actually, I have. Instead of wasting time hunting down and interviewing the people mentioned in those emails, I suggest we concentrate on the language in the emails themselves, and try to find similarities that point to one writer.'

It took Jazz a couple of beats to realise Lee was taking credit for her idea. When she did, she was shaken by a wave of fury so strong it took all her self-discipline not to move. She felt her cheeks flame, sensed Hawke eying her.

'Hmm,' he said, scratching his long neck, 'could work. I'll contact our linguistics consultant, Professor Chalmers.'

They returned to their desks, Lee avoiding Jazz's eyes. He sat down, she went up to him, got in his face. 'Listen, you wanker,' she said, 'what you did back there, that was the slimiest, most unprofessional thing I've ever seen—'

'Ooo,' he said, 'I'm scaaaared. Why don't you run and tell daddy? Maybe he'll give you the job then.'

She stood back. Telling Hawke what had happened would make her look like a whining schoolgirl. And it wouldn't help catch the killer. *Get a grip*, she told herself. *You're not here for your own benefit. Concentrate on getting justice for these women.*

'Just so you know,' she said, 'I'm on to you.'

Professor Chalmers, an older woman in arty glasses, arrived surprisingly fast. Hawke must have told her it was urgent. He greeted her like an old friend, took her to an interview room and left her to it.

Two hours later, Chalmers called them in. She distributed sheets of paper. 'That was fairly simple,' she said. 'Compare the two emails I've printed for you. The first is from Lewis Collins, to Angela Mulvaney:'

From: Lewis Collins (lewis.collins99@gmail.com)
To: Angela Mulvaney (angie@fastnet.com.au)
Hey Angela.

I am responding to your profile on the Hoopoe dating site. I was nervous about joining the site. I did not expect the number of replies that arrived. Apparently a lot of ladies are looking for a 40-year old farmer. Even though I did not post a photo.

I was interested in you because of your photo. It says in your profile you are playful. So many ladies today are serious and feminist. That is not for me. I am old-fashioned that way.

As my profile says, I am single. I grew up in the Hunter Valley and that is where I live. I like to read and I listen to most kinds of music.

That is all there is to tell about me. I am interested in hearing about you. I enclose a photo so you can see what I look like. I hope this does not make you loose interest in me.

cheers
Lewis

The photo attached to the email showed a middle-aged man standing on a pier, holding a fishing rod and brandishing a large fish. He was ordinary, greying, squinting into the sun.

'The second email,' said Professor Chalmers, 'is from someone calling himself Calvin Long, and it's to Zeinab Haddad:'

From: Calvin Long (callong99@gmail.com)
To: Zeinab Haddad (Zhaddad@sheraton.com)
Hey Zeinab.

Thanks for writing back. I was waiting for your email. My wife died not so long ago and it was hard to loose her. I hope that does not make me sound desperate.

I am glad you enjoy your job. It is important to like your work. I think event management would be stressful. I prefer to be in the back room.

Do you like to cook? I am learning to cook for myself. Perhaps one day you can show me how.

That is all for now. I am looking forward to your email. I will include a photo next time.

cheers

Calvin

Chalmers put her elbows on the table, clasped her hands and went into lecture mode. 'These emails contain linguistic similarities which point to them being written by the same person. For example, both start with the salutation "Hey". That in itself isn't noteworthy; much more interesting is the fact that both salutations end with a full stop. I haven't seen that construction before, and once I noticed it I simply looked for emails that used it. There are, however, other similarities as well. Both these emails misspell "lose" as "loose". Both are notable for the shortness of their sentences. Neither of the writers use contractions like "it's" for "it is", or "doesn't" for "does not". Both use the informal "cheers", spelled with a lower case "c", as a valediction, a sign-off. And – something not strictly linguistic – both these writers use Gmail addresses with the number "99". By themselves, these features are small, but taken together they point to the emails being written by the same person.'

Jazz was excited. 'That's great! At least we've got something to go on.'

'One thing,' Chalmers said, 'a niggle, but it bothers me. The salutations and valedictions – that is, the greetings and closes – on the emails are informal, but the text is quite formal, even stilted. At a guess, I'd say the writer tried to convey a personality other than his own.' She sat back. 'I hope I've been able to help.'

After that, it was easy. The names were false, but the dating agencies, Hoopoe and Kismet, used their software to trace the single credit card that paid for membership. It belonged to Victor Morgenson, 56 Lady Davidson Drive, Lane Cove. According to his Facebook page, Morgenson was an accountant, recently widowed and with one son. He enjoyed fishing, gardening and reading histories of World War II. Jazz was surprised at the banality of his life. *What did you expect?* she asked herself. *An alcoholic, tattooed hermit?*

It was evening by the time two cars, Hawke in one and Jazz and Lee in the other, drew up outside a double storey house in a bland, suburban street.

At the door, Hawke stopped. 'Ready? Got your weapons? Whoever did this isn't afraid to kill.' Jazz nodded. Her Glock was snug in its underarm holster, hidden by her jacket. 'Good.' Hawke said. He knocked, badge open and out.

'Can I help you?' The man wore trousers and a white shirt tight over a solid paunch, his brown tie loosened at the neck. He was the man in the photo, the fisherman.

'Victor Morgenson?' Hawke was intimidating, and Morgenson took a step back.

'Yes? What's this about?' He seemed genuinely puzzled. Then he put a hand to his chest. 'Is it David?' Something's happened to my son?'

'No, this isn't about David,' said Hawke.

'Come in,' said Morgenson.

They stood in a sparse, dusty living room, religious paintings on the walls. Morgenson saw them looking. 'My late wife. She was a devout woman.'

'Victor Morgenson,' said Hawke, 'we have reason to believe you can help with our enquiries into two recent murders, of Angela Mulvaney and Zeinab Haddad.'

'I read about those in the papers.' Morgenson frowned.

'You made contact with these women through dating sites.'

Morgenson looked as if he'd been struck by lightning. He blinked, then shook his head. 'Murders? Online...' He sat down, suddenly, on a beige leather couch. 'I don't know what you're talking about.'

'Mr Morgenson, where were you on the nights of Thursday, February 10 and Thursday, March 3?'

Morgenson raised his head. 'I don't know. I – I suppose I was here? I don't go out much.'

'Mr Morgenson, I must ask you to accompany me for questioning. You are not under arrest at this time, but you may contact a lawyer if you wish. Also, we have a warrant to search these premises. Lee, Kovacs, get going. Bring any computers back to HQ.'

Morgenson had to be helped up. Jazz watched from the front window as Hawke half marched, half supported him to the car.

Lee's phone rang. 'Girlfriend,' he said, 'better take it. I'll be round the back.'

Jazz shrugged him off, went exploring.

Downstairs, there was a kitchen, a laundry with a door leading to a garage, and a study. It felt warmer, more lived-in, than the rest of the place. Shelves held books, mostly about war. On the desk, a framed family photograph comprising a younger Morgenson, a grim woman and a large, awkward teenager, probably David, the son. Next to the photo sat a monitor, bright and blinking. Jazz pulled up a faded office chair. If she could find proof and bring it back to Hawke, then they could wrap this case up and she'd regain lost ground.

She opened the Sent file. Nothing about dating or dating sites. Plenty of emails though, most to do with a company called Secure Accounting, about fishing, newsletters for gardening and World War II sites. Jazz opened one.

Dear Hugh,

Thank you for inviting me to speak at our next meeting. I'm delighted to accept. I'm not sure what you want, but I could start with an overview of General Patton's speeches and how they relate to his strategy. Let me know if that suits, and I'll get on with it.

Regards
Vic

And another

Dear Jim,

If you want to claim for the use of your car, you'll have to keep a log showing mileage, where you went, dates etc for at least six weeks straight. You can buy log-books at any stationer. Contact me if you need more info. Hope Jenny has recovered!

Regards
Vic

What did Chalmers call them? Salutations and valedictions. The salutations and valedictions were different from those in the dating emails. And so was the language: it was looser, chattier, more personal. But perhaps Morgenson had donned a linguistic mask, to go with the fake names. If so, why send his real photo? It didn't make sense. She couldn't see any other email accounts. Perhaps he had a second computer hidden somewhere.

Jazz left the study. To her right, a staircase. She paused at the bottom. Perhaps she should wait for Lee. There was no sign of him, so she kept going. Upstairs she found a master bedroom with an unmade bed, a bathroom, a spare room filled with boxes, and a closed door. She opened it. This must be the son's bedroom. It smelled stale and yeasty, of cigarettes and sweat. Otherwise, it looked innocuous: a framed poster of *The Avengers;* a bed with a beige doona, a chest of drawers with clothes tumbling from them, a small table with a laptop on it.

Jazz lifted the lid. The laptop woke from sleep mode, asked for a password. She looked around for clues. Tried the usual, then all the Marvel names she could think of. No luck. Damn. She'd have to take it in after all, get IT to crack it. She lifted the laptop, turned it sideways. Underneath, she saw a sticker. It was from a computer repair shop, and it read: NerdNation. Job #46599. P/w Greenshadow99.

It worked. The screen lit up to show a night sky. Jazz opened the emails. The first read

Hey Mr Kapur.
The Saturday shift is fine. I will be there at 8.30 instead of 7.30. I will work the extra time so as not to loose any pay.
cheers
David

Jazz stared at the screen, processing what she saw. Not Victor after all, but David, his son. Why would a young man write to women in their 40s, lure them to their deaths? She shook herself. Leave the whys for later. Right now she had to find Lee, phone Hawke. She reached for her phone.

'What the *fuck* do you think you're doing?'

At the door, the David from the photograph. This one older, taller, heavier. Jazz stood up, stepped forward. 'Jasmine Kovacs, Homicide.' She reached for her badge. 'David Mortenson, I am arresting you...'

David Mortenson raised his arm high and backhanded her across the face. She went flying, landed on the floor, her head striking the bed as she went down. A moment of darkness and then he was on her, grabbing a fistful of blouse and jerking her upright. He slapped her again, spoke in a soft hiss.

'You think you can come in here and take over from her? Think you can run my life?'

Jazz tried to clear her head. She put up a hand, felt blood. 'Who do you mean? Take over from who?'

He closed in, spraying spittle in her face. 'Don't pretend you don't know, you piece of shit!' He threw her on the bed, put a knee on her chest, his full weight behind it. Stared unblinking at her while he undid his belt, wrapped the ends around his fists, drew them apart.

'You pretty ones pretend to be so nice, but underneath... Say your prayers, bitch, and say them fast.' He snapped the leather belt. 'Come on, your prayers. I'm waiting.'

Think! Jazz told herself. *Just think!* 'Oh, hello,' she said, conversationally, looking past David. 'I've been expecting you.'

An ancient trick, but it worked. Instinctively, David glanced back, easing off a fraction. Just enough for Jazz to get her gun. She shoved it into his neck, undid the safety catch.

'Get off me. Now. Or I shoot.'

David was past reason. He bellowed, came back hard and strong. Jazz aimed down and left, shot him in the shoulder. He fell back, screaming.

'What the hell's going on here? Who's shooting?' Finally, the cavalry, in the form of a panicked Lee, arrived.

It was a long, long night. Hawke appeared, and others. Among them ambulances, to carry Jazz and David Mortenson to their respective hospitals. David was raving about his mother. Jazz was suddenly very nauseous. They stitched her head, diagnosed concussion, made her stay at least another day.

In the afternoon, she had a visitor. It was Hawke, folding his lanky body into the visitor's chair.

'How goes it?' he asked.

'Fine,' she said, though she didn't feel it. 'I can go home tomorrow.'

'Thought you'd like to know,' he said, 'we found emails on David

Mortenson's computer, addressed to a new victim. He'd made arrangements to see her next week.'

They both sat quiet, thinking about what that meant.

After a while, Hawke said, 'You did good. Hope you keep it up.'

'What?'

'Think I was born yesterday? I saw your face when Lee told me about the linguistic thing. Also, of course, he had to explain where he was while you were being attacked.'

'Oh.' She hadn't thought of that.

Hawke grinned, not a pretty sight. He rose to go. 'You've got the rest of the week off. Doctor's orders. See you Monday morning, Kovacs.'

Jazz grinned back. 'Monday it is, boss.'

'Don't be late.'

NOT FOR SISSIES

THE POLICE TAKE THEIR TIME AND WHEN THEY DO COME, I CAN tell by their body language they've classified me as a nuisance. There are two of them, constables, and I've met both before. A blocky woman, hard-faced; and a younger, freckled man who defers to her even though they're the same rank.

'Yes, Ms Fortright?' The woman, whose badge identifies her as J Drakos, has her notebook out and ready. She speaks in a weary voice, letting me know she thinks I'm wasting their time.

'It's him again,' I say. 'He–'

'Speak up, please.'

I try again, louder. I need to sound confident. I have rights, don't I? 'It's the man upstairs,' I tell them. 'The one who's been giving me trouble.'

'Yes, we know,' Drakos, impatient, interrupts again. 'What is it this time?'

'He woke me during the night. He was outside my bedroom window, whispering, threatening to kill me.'

'You sure of that?'

I feel a flicker of anger, a tightening at the top of my skull. 'Of course I'm sure. Why would I make it up?'

Drakos gives me a disbelieving look, as if to say *How would I know why you're making it up?*

What is it about growing old that makes people despise you? I used to have a place in the world, a job; I used to attract admiring looks and the attention of waiters and the respect of people I met, and there was a time when Drakos would have jumped to help me. Now I'm grey, tentative, diminished, and they won't give me the time of day.

The male constable, Robertson, is more inclined to sympathy. Perhaps I remind him of his grandmother. He says, 'What were his exact words? Did you record any of it?'

'N...no, I didn't think of that. I was too frightened.'

'Well, next time, record what he says and then we can take it up with him.' Drakos puts her notebook back in her pocket. 'You got a smartphone? Know how to work it?'

I swallow my bile. I need their help, after all. So I just nod. 'Yes, I know how to record on my phone. But can't you do something now? He's making my life a misery.'

Drakos shrugs. 'We've spoken to him before. He denies he's approached you in any way. Unless we have some evidence, there isn't a lot we can do. We'll note your complaint.'

'Can't you...can't you keep a watch on him or something?'

Her radio bursts into life. All I can hear is *"in progress, Burns Road"* She lifts the handset to answer and starts walking to her car, all in the same movement. 'On our way.'

Constable Robertson looks sheepish. 'We have to go.' He doesn't wait for my reply.

I watch them drive off. I close and lock the door. I check the lock.

I live in the lower half of a Victorian-era house which has been converted into two flats, an upstairs and a downstairs, with separate entrances for each. The building has seen better days but it's charming and it's cheap. Also, it's near a park, I have a small garden, and I'm allowed to keep Zorro, my cat.

I've been here over 35 years, watching tenants in the top half come and go. The last, Mary Marinos, became a dear friend. Older than I am, she took herself off to assisted living, claimed it was better to be an immigrant than a refugee. I'll miss her.

A week after Mary goes, Trevor Rollins arrives. He's a tall man, shaven-headed and steroid-fit, with tattoos on his arms and neck. I get a shock the first time I see him – he looks like my worst nightmare – but I try not to judge. I introduce myself, tell him to ask me if there's anything he needs to know. After that, when we encounter each other we exchange nods, smiles. Like me, he lives alone, no visitors I know of. I run into him early mornings as he leaves for work and I set off on my walk.

I was right about Trevor being a nightmare. He hasn't been here long when trouble starts. Old buildings like ours aren't well insulated and I can hear him through the floorboards. There are bangs and crashes and music, very loud – the sort of *doof doof* music that makes your teeth ache – until late. A couple of times I smell alcohol on him when we pass in the mornings.

The noise gets louder and lasts longer and eventually I'm forced to knock on his door and ask him to keep it down. I'm apologetic and so is he and for a few weeks things are quiet. Then it ramps up again. This time I complain to the estate agent and silence returns. The next time I see Trevor Rollins I smile as though nothing's happened. He smiles back. I breathe a sigh of relief, realising I've been tense, worried about how he'll respond. I'm a couple of steps beyond him when he says, 'Hey.'

I turn. He's wearing a high-viz vest, orange. He tilts his head to one side. There's a tattoo on his neck, a bird in flight. He lifts his right hand, forms it into a gun, and points the barrel – his first two fingers – at me, jerking his thumb and making a soft *pow* with his lips as if shooting. He lifts the fingers to his lips and blows on them like a cowboy. He smiles broadly, showing gapped teeth, says, 'Have a good day.'

It's early morning. There's no-one around. I find myself trembling and have to sit on a nearby wall to recover. What should I do about this? Who can help me? I ring the estate agent, who tells me I'm overreacting. It's bluff, she claims, and besides, I should be careful of being labelled a busybody or a nuisance.

I don't want you to think she's right, that I am a busybody or a nuisance. I'm not a lonely old lady who calls the police for company. I have a full life, gardening and reading and music. I take courses at the local community college, keep up to date with the world. But I reflect on what the agent says and don't report the incident. It unsettles me, though. During the day, when Trevor's at work, I relax, but at night I hold myself tight, straining to hear what's going on above my head. I sleep badly.

A week later, as I begin to unwind, I find a dead rainbow lorikeet in my letterbox. Pins have been forced into its eyes. I take it to the local police station and explain about Trevor. They say they have no evidence he's the one who killed the bird, but they'll have a word in any case.

That's a mistake. The police visit seems to inflame Trevor and things get worse. Faeces are smeared on my doorstep. My herb patch is trampled, my wheelie bins overturned. I call the police each time, show them photographs. Sympathetic to begin with, they become increasingly impatient, always singing the same tune: *we'll talk to him, but without evidence our hands are tied.*

Then the night visits start. I'm woken by scratching at my window and I think it's a possum but when I part the curtains I see Trevor, waving his fingers. By the time the police arrive he's back in his flat, answering the door sleepily, telling them I'm crazy.

And now the death threat. Constable Robertson was right, I should have recorded it, but I don't know what Trevor's going to do next and when he does do something I'm too terrified to think rationally. He's turned me into a nervous wreck. I lock my doors and keep my windows shut.

One morning, a week or so after the death threat, I let Zorro out. He's allowed in the garden. He doesn't come when I call him at lunchtime and mid-afternoon I go looking. I find him splayed on the lawn, his throat cut, his belly slashed all the way open. I sink to my knees. When I go to get a box to put Zorro in, I look up to see Trevor at his window, smoking and watching. He gives me a sketchy salute.

I bury Zorro, tears running down my cheeks, cover him with earth and go back inside.

This has to stop.

I dry my eyes. I gather up Zorro's bed, his food bowls and toys, and stow them out of sight. Then I sit at the kitchen table. I'm not hungry. Instead, I open a bottle of Shiraz. A couple of glasses steady me enough to review my options. I have two choices, I reckon, to cave or to fight back. Caving means conceding defeat, either staying and living in fear or moving out completely.

The idea of fighting back is daunting. I'm old, I admit it; too old and weak to withstand Trevor.

My mother comes to mind. She suffered from arthritis and I remember how, as she painfully levered herself out of a chair or struggled to put on a skirt, she'd shake her head slowly and say, 'Old age is not for sissies.'

No. Growing old takes guts. Caving is not an option.

Trevor wants trouble? I'll give him trouble.

Next day I scrabble through drawers, looking for the spare key the last tenant, my friend Mary Marinos, gave me in case of emergency. With luck they won't have changed the locks. Yes, there it is, a Yale key on a red plastic tag.

Trevor's at work. I walk up the stairs to his part of the building and try the key. The lock gives, the door opens. I close it behind me and walk from room to room. For the first time in months, I'm in control.

The flat smells of stale smoke and alcohol. There's a whiff of Trevor too, a deeper, feral note. I thought his place would be a mess but it isn't. It's tidy but there's dust everywhere. It's like being in a cheap motel.

The living room has a faded grey couch, a fold-up chair, a glass coffee table. The table holds an ashtray, emptied but not cleaned, a pile of bills and a laptop, charging. The kitchen, too, is neat, and the bathroom cabinet's almost bare – toothpaste, toothbrush, shaving stuff. There's a row of pill boxes: aspirin, anti-inflammatories, cold and flu medicine, sleeping tablets. I consider planting something to make Trevor ill, but dismiss the idea. I don't want him home during the day, so I can't do anything that affects his job.

The other two rooms are a bedroom and a spare room. I take the spare room first. There's a yoga mat on the floor and around it a selection of weights which explain some of the overhead crashes. The built-in wardrobe is empty, unused, the shelves dusty.

Next, the bedroom. The single bed is unmade and in here the feral smell is stronger. The wardrobe holds a small selection of casual clothes, a leather jacket, one suit. The bedside cabinet reveals an assortment of papers, a muddle of electronic bits and pieces, an opened box of condoms.

Nothing else of interest. I return to the living room.

The laptop needs a password. I try *1234, Password,* all the common variations. No luck. Most people keep a record of their password and I pray Trevor hasn't stored it on his phone. I go looking, reckoning it will be close. It's on a post-it note stuck under the laptop, *Fuckwit2424.* How appropriate. I key it in, watch the screen open, and settle on the sofa, into the same indentations Trevor's made. I get to work.

I start by exploring his texts, the ones I can access remotely via his laptop app. They tell me he doesn't have many friends and no family that I can see. But he's corresponding with a woman called Janine. She lives in Canberra and he's chatting her up, proposing a visit. I can't text because he'd notice it at once so I move to his email. Good. He's talking to her that way as well. On his behalf I send her an email explaining in graphic detail what he'd like to do to her when they catch up. Then I delete the email.

Janine replies, telling Trevor she never wants to hear from him again.

Every morning now, after my walk and after breakfast, I visit Trevor's flat. I don't stay long because I don't want him to sense anyone's been there. You know what I mean, don't you, the way people make the air in a room feel different? I don't look out of his windows, use his bathroom, drink from his taps, or touch anything I don't have to.

I just invade his life the same way he's invaded mine.

For someone his age, Trevor doesn't use social media much. Facebook seems to be his only outlet and it's a rich seam. He spends a lot of time here, posting bodybuilding images, hanging on the coattails of Q-anon, trying to attract the attention of groups I've not heard of. I flex my fingers, start posting on his behalf, working more broadly.

A couple of days later I see Trevor on his way back from work. His face is bloody and he has a black eye. Perhaps some of his Facebook friends have disliked his posts.

I need to push things along. The noise from above is still loud so I complain to the agent, demanding she tell Trevor to quieten down. Sure enough, a couple of nights later, there's tapping at my window and his face appears. 'It won't be long, bitch,' he says, 'I'm coming for you. You'll be as dead as your fuckin' kitty. Soon. Soon!' He blows me a kiss, grins at the sight of me cowering in my nightie.

This time I'm recording and when the police come – it's Drakos and Robertson again – I play it back to them.

'What will you do?' I ask. 'Will you arrest him?'

Now that she knows I'm not a crackpot, Drakos unbends. 'We can't. Sorry. We'd have to catch him in the act to arrest him. We will caution him, though.'

'That'll make things worse. Every time he hears from you he takes it out on me.'

Drakos sighs, lifts her hands and lets them drop by her side. 'It's frustrating for us as well. So, do you want to press charges?'

'Yes, I say,' 'Go ahead. Caution him.'

The timing's good. Everything's pretty much in place.

Three days later, I take a coin and scratch it all the way along the side of Trevor's car. That should do it. I lock myself in my flat, waiting for retribution. My locks aren't strong enough, though, because the next night I wake to find Trevor leaning over my bed. For a moment I think I'm dreaming, then I feel his breath. He puts his hands on either side of my head, bends his face forward till it's right up against mine. I can't move. I clench my guts to stop my bowels loosening.

He says, 'Scared now? Gonna call the cops now? Suddenly he straightens, swings round, swaggers off. At the door he turns back. 'You're dead meat, cunt. You just don't know it yet.'

My heart is beating so hard I think it's going to burst. I force my body up, slam and lock my bedroom door and dial 000. 'Please come! He's broken in and threatened me. I don't know how long the lock will hold. I'm scared, please come now!'

Of course, by the time they do come Trevor's back in his flat, denying everything. I don't recognise either of the responders and have to explain the situation from the beginning. 'Don't you have reports?' I ask them. 'Don't you people share information?' Obviously not, but pointing it out gets them offside and they lose the desire to cooperate. They give each other a glance I've come to recognise.

'There's no sign of a break-in. Did he take anything?'

'I don't think so. He was just after me. He forced the kitchen window. I closed it again.'

They check the window and fiddle with the latch, which is old. 'Hard to tell,' one of them says, shrugging his shoulders. They straighten, gather themselves to leave.

I realise something. Trevor could have killed me tonight. He's come too close and I can't risk another visit, can't stretch things out any longer. Time for the endgame.

'Wait,' I say, my voice quavering, 'I thought... I just thought, given the paedophilia complaint?'

They turn. 'What paedophilia complaint?'

I falter. 'The woman up the road. She said her daughter saw Trevor Rollins taking pictures of the kids in the park, and... She said she'd phoned Crime Stoppers. She didn't give her name.'

'How did she know it was him?'

'She knows who he is. And she saw the tattoo on his neck, a bird.'

They flick eyes at each other, move down the driveway, have a small confab.

'Stay here,' they say, and make their way upstairs. I stand on my front step, waiting. I can hear what happens and it's not pretty. It isn't long before they reappear. The stairs to Trevor's level are narrow and they have to descend in single file. First comes a policeman, then Trevor, handcuffed. The other policeman follows, a laptop under his arm.

Trevor seems docile. Then he spots me and I can't stop myself, I make a gun with my fingers and shoot him with it, the same imaginary gun he used on me.

He goes berserk. He kicks out at the first policeman, knocking him down the stairs. Jerks an elbow into the one behind, who collapses with an *oof,* scrabbles at the rail and loses his grip on Trevor but manages to hold on to the laptop. Trevor leaps down to me, lunging for my throat. He swipes at me with manacled hands, knocks me flat, kicks; but the cops recover fast and pull him off. They lay into him, both of them, and shove him into the car. Then an ambulance comes and paramedics and more cops and by the time they leave, the sky's grown light.

It's all over the news. *Man caught with child porn; member of international child exploitation ring; hardened policemen sickened by child cruelty clips...* it goes on and on. Trevor's face stares at me from every media outlet. He looks like a rabbit caught in the headlights. Despite the evidence, he continues to deny any knowledge of the material. As if. They've added resisting arrest and aggravated assault to the charges, but the child porn by itself will put him in jail for a long, long time. And knowing what they do to kiddie fiddlers in there gives me a quiet glow.

Mostly it was straightforward, nothing I hadn't learned at community college. All I had to do was to trawl the net until I found a group Trevor could join, sign in on his behalf, specify what I wanted, pay with his credit card – the details handily on automatic fill – download the clips and place them in a secure file. Then bury the file, but not so deep it couldn't be found. I gambled on having a few days before he noticed the transactions.

The difficult part was getting hold of child porn magazines to put in his spare room wardrobe. But you can get anything online these days.

J Drakos and A Robertson drop by. The estate agent's there too, organising the cleaning of Trevor's flat. She says Forensics left it a shambles.

Drakos and Robertson apologise for not taking me more seriously. They want to know if I'm OK, if I've fully recovered. I think they want to find out whether I'll sue, but I assure them as far as I'm concerned, the matter is over.

As they leave, Robertson asks if he can use the bathroom. When he comes back he says, still trying to make good, 'I saw the set-up in your study. That's some equipment you've got there. You're quite the tech-head.'

'Ach.' I wave away the compliment. 'I do courses. I stay in touch.'

Drakos, still trying to make good, can't help condescending. 'That's excellent. Well done. Must be hard to keep on top of things at your age.'

'Yes,' I reply. 'Getting old is not for sissies.'

ABOUT THE AUTHOR

Natalie Conyer is the author of *Present Tense*, first in the Schalk Lourens series, originally published by Clan Destine Press in 2020. It won the Ned Kelly Award for the Best Debut Crime Novel of 2020, was shortlisted for the Davitt Awards, and was nominated as one of 2020's best reads by *The Australian*. The second book in the series, *Shadow City* (Echo), was released in September 2024.

Natalie's short stories have won several awards in the annual Sisters in Crime Australia Scarlet Stiletto competition. They've also been featured in other anthologies, including *Dark Deeds Down Under 2*; *The Only One in the World*; and *Murder You Wrote*.

Natalie, who lives in Sydney, is a swimmer, a TV addict, a world-class procrastinator, and a crime fiction tragic who loves the genre so much she did a doctorate on it.

https://natalieconyer.com

ACKNOWLEDGEMENTS

Thank you, first of all and again, to Sisters in Crime Australia. I started writing these stories for the Scarlet Stiletto competition and though I've never managed to crack the shoe, my competition wins gave me the confidence to keep going.

Thank you also to Lindy Cameron of Clan Destine Press, my generous publisher, and Narrelle Harris, my wise and diplomatic editor.

Thanks to early reader Alexia Bannikoff. And of course to members of the Best Writers Group: Yvonne Edgren, Erin Gough, Isabelle Li, Jane Gibian, Alison Martin, Peter Boyle and Liz Allen.

Thanks especially to my brother Arnie, chief critic and cynic; and finally to Henry, my excellent feline supervisor.

NATALIE'S PRIZE-WINNING STORIES

The following stories in Natalie's collection won category prizes or special commendations in the annual Scarlet Stiletto Crime & Mystery Short Story Competition run by Sisters in Crime Australia:

Alys – 2022 Art and Crime Prize

Not for Sissies – 2020 Special Commendation

The Séance – 2019 History with Mystery Prize

Manny – 2019 Cross-Genre Prize

The Black Curse – 2018 Special Commendation

In Memoriam – 2017 Body in the Library 2nd prize

Police Story – 2017 Special Commendation

Public Service – 2016 Special Commendation

New Start – 2015 3rd Prize and Romantic Suspense Prize

Sydney Love Story – 2015 Special Commendation

The Book Club – 2014 Body in the Library Prize

www.ingramcontent.com/pod-product-compliance
Lightning Source LLC
Chambersburg PA
CBHW032117020726
47494CB00007BA/2121